EMMANUEL PAIGE

THE BLACK HOUND

AND OTHER STORIES

Copyright © 2019 by Emmanuel Paige

Stark Raven Press

ISBN 978-1-952798-16-0

Thou call'dst me dog before thou hadst a cause;
But, since I am a dog, beware my fangs . . .

—William Shakespeare, "The Merchant of Venice"

Contents

The Black Hound

Robert Flint pounded his fists on the bar, demanding another drink. He lost his balance and almost fell off his barstool. The bartender, a short and balding man with a toothpick in his mouth, shook his head in a gesture of disapproval as he picked up Robert's empty glass and wiped down the bar.

"Give me another drink," Robert said. "What's a guy got to do to get some service around here?"

The bartender shook his head, looking critically at Robert, who had the appearance of an unshaven, middle-aged man who was obviously drunk, and said, "Sorry, buddy. I think you've had enough. Maybe you should go home, huh?"

"Like hell," Robert said. "I want another drink! Just one more for the road."

Robert fumbled with a pack of cigarettes, put one in his mouth, lit it, and exhaled slowly. He turned and looked at the lady sitting next to him. Her features were plain, her complexion pale. Her blonde hair was like dried straw; she was wearing a red dress. She looked back blankly.

"Can you believe this guy?" Robert said. "He doesn't want to give me another drink."

"Maybe that's because you've had too much already," she said. She wrinkled her nose in disgust and looked away.

Robert looked back at the bartender, pulled his wallet from his pocket and took out a crisp twenty-dollar bill and placed it on the counter, pointing at Alexander Hamilton. He said, "This might help you change your mind. What say you just reach over there and pour me a double of that Johnny Walker, and you keep the change?"

"Sure. Why not?" the bartender said. "What's one more gonna hurt, right?" He plucked the bill off the bar and looked at it to make sure it was not counterfeit, then put it in his shirt pocket. He produced a bottle of Johnny Walker and refilled Robert's shot glass.

"Now that's what I'm talking about," Robert said, putting the shot glass to his lips. He tipped his head back and downed the drink in one gulp, grimacing from the burn of the liquor in his throat.

"I think it's time for you to go now," the bartender said. "I'm not serving you anything else."

"Okay, fine," Robert said, wiping his lips on his sleeve. "Whatever you say, friend. Just trying to have a good time. That's all." He got up from his stool and almost fell over when he lost his balance, swayed, and recovered, and then righted himself. He smashed his cigarette out in an ashtray on the bar and then put on his overcoat, staggering out through the door without looking back.

Outside in the night windblown rain beat down on the town of Grand Junction. Robert stood under the protection of the overhanging roof. He lifted his collar and buttoned up his coat. He noticed a black dog tied to one of the columns that support the roof. He reached down to pet the dog, but it snarled and growled, snapping viciously at his hand.

"Jesus H. Christ," he said. "What's your problem? Stupid mutt." Robert leaned back and started singing to the dog, "You ain't nothing but a hound dog. Crying all the time." He smiled and ran his fingers through his hair, pleased with his imitation of Elvis Presley. For a moment he was tempted to kick the dog but changed his mind. He didn't feel like getting bitten, so he thought better of it. He turned and staggered down the sidewalk to a blue Chrysler sedan that was parked against the curb.

The rain was splashing against his face as he fumbled drunkenly with his keys. He opened the door and jumped into the driver's seat, shut the door, and started the engine. He pulled the car away from the curb and cruised down the street, running a stop sign and nearly crashing into another oncoming vehicle; the driver of the other vehicle honked the horn angrily.

"Learn how to drive asshole," Robert said, shaking his fist.

Robert drove the car down the road and pulled up in front of a small convenience store. He got out and pumped gas into his car, spilling it everywhere. He went into the store and bought a six pack of beer and cigarettes, arguing with the clerk over the price of the items which were supposed to be on sale, but were not, and he was charged the regular price. He gave up and paid the clerk in full.

Back in the car, he cracked open a beer and chugged it down, tossing the empty can into the backseat. He burped and started the engine, then put the car into gear and drove back through town. He drove past the bar he had just left moments before. He noticed that the black hound was gone now. He turned on the radio and cracked another beer, taking a long drink and then singing along with the music. He turned onto a secluded road and stepped on the accelerator.

He could hardly see through the windshield as the rain beat down on the street in silver streams. The windshield wipers were whipping back and forth with a drumming sound. The headlights cut white cones of light through the rainy night.

Suddenly, someone dashed out into the road. Robert saw the person in his headlights and stomped frantically on the brake. He recognized who it was . . . it was the blonde-haired lady in the red dress he had seen at the bar. She had the black hound, that was tied to the pole in front of the bar, with her. The dog was on a leash. She was holding an umbrella in her other hand. Robert made eye contact with the lady in the red dress, frozen in shock, as he collided with her and the black hound, running them down with his car. The woman flipped over the top of the car; the umbrella flew from her hand. The dog went directly under the car with a thump and a bump. The tires screamed in agony as the car came to a sudden stop. Robert jumped out and dashed over to the woman who was lying deathly still in a crimson pool of blood on the side of the road. He rolled her over and saw blood oozing from her mouth. Her eyes were crossed and glazed.

"Oh my god," Robert said in disbelief. "Oh my god. Oh, my fucking god."

He looked around for the dog, but it was nowhere to be found. He looked over his shoulder to see if anyone had witnessed the incident and was satisfied that no one was around. The coast was clear. There was only one thing to do, he thought: get the hell out of there, and quickly. He jumped back in the car, stomped on the gas, the tires peeling out on the wet pavement. Robert drove down the road and away from the scene of the crime at a high rate of speed. He couldn't believe this was happening. He would tell no one about this.

Robert pulled the blue sedan down a secluded driveway, and stopped in front of a clean, well-lit, house with a double garage. The porch light turned on automatically. He pushed a remote garage door opener on his visor and one of the doors opened. He drove the car into the garage and pulled up next to a red Ford Mustang parked in the opposite bay. The garage door closed.

Inside the garage, Robert got out and surveyed the damage to the Chrysler; it was spattered with raindrops and the engine ticked and hissed as moisture touched hot metal under the hood. There was a dent on the fender and hood, and he could see some blood on the cracked windshield. That would need to be fixed, he thought, and he would need a story to explain why the car was damaged. He would think of something, but for now he found a rag and quickly wiped up the blood, tossing it into a trash can when he was finished. He tried to go into the house through the connecting garage door that led into the house, but it was locked—it was never locked and that only meant trouble. His wife, Cynthia, was surely angry at him for coming home late. He knew he was in trouble. He exited the garage, turning the light off behind him. As he crossed the front yard, he could see Cynthia peering out through the living room window. She shook her head and then closed the curtains.

Robert opened the front door and stood in the doorway with a blank look on his face. Inside the living room, Cynthia, pretty and petite, was sitting on the couch in her nightgown. She was watching an infomercial on TV that was selling some magical detergent product that was guaranteed to remove even the toughest stains or your money back. She didn't make eye contact with Robert; she continued to watch the TV set.

Cynthia said, "You've been drinking again, haven't you?"

"Don't start on me, Cynthia," Robert said. "I'm not in the mood."

"I don't know what I ever saw in you," she said. "You drink too much. I can't stand you sometimes. You know that?"

"Aw, leave me alone," Robert said. "I had a rough day. Can't a guy stop and have a few beers after a hard day's work?"

"That's a joke," Cynthia said. "You don't drink a few beers, Robert. For you it's twelve, or twenty. You can't ever get enough. You're an alcoholic."

"Yeah, okay . . . whatever you say, dear," Robert said. "I'm hungry and tired. Is this discussion over?"

Cynthia remained silent. She crossed her arms and looked away from Robert.

"You have to stop. If you don't get some help . . . I'm going to leave you," she said, still looking away.

"Huh?" Robert said. He was obviously not prepared for this conversation.

"I love you, Robert," she said. "I love you with all of my heart . . . but if you keep on doing this . . . I'm going to have to leave you. Understand?"

"Yes, dear," Robert said. "I understand. I'm just really having a bad day. Can we talk about this later?"

"Nothing is going to change," Cynthia said, glaring at him. "I'm going to bed. There is some dinner in the oven for you. I made it over four hours ago, but it's still warm. Help yourself."

"Okay," Robert said. "Thank you, honey."

She didn't respond. She turned off the lamp and then went upstairs and left him standing there in the darkness of the living room by himself.

He went to the liquor cabinet, poured a double shot of bourbon with a shaky hand and drank it down in one swallow. He poured another, drank it and then went directly to bed without eating the dinner in the oven—he just turned the oven off and left the food inside to cool. He had lost his appetite.

• • •

The next morning Cynthia was hanging clothes out to dry on a clothesline in the backyard. She was humming a melody. The sun was shining brightly, and birds were flying overhead and singing in the trees.

She heard a whining and whimpering sound coming from under the porch and stopped to listen more closely. She approached the porch, cautiously, picking up a shovel from the flower garden to use as a weapon and slowly bent down to look under the porch. The noise stopped. She couldn't see anything in the darkness under the porch.

She walked to the garage, went inside, and reappeared with a flashlight.

Underneath the porch she was surprised to find a black dog, wet and shivering, cowering in the far corner. It looked frightened and it tried to hide behind the posts and beams beneath the porch.

"Oh, you poor thing," Cynthia said. "Come here . . . come out of there." She kept calling to the dog in a calm, soothing voice until it slowly came out to her. It was cautious and licked here hand, hesitating until it was convinced that she meant it no harm and that she could be trusted. She took it inside the house immediately, on impulse, feeling compassion and sympathy for the poor-looking creature.

Inside the kitchen, Cynthia fed the dog some of the food that Robert left in the oven overnight. The Salisbury steaks were still good enough for a dog to eat. She put a bowl of water down on the floor and then got a towel and rubbed the dog down, drying its wet fur while it drank, spilling water everywhere.

She went into the living room and coaxed the dog to come along with her. She put a blanket down in front of the heater and motioned the dog to lay down. It ambled over to the blanket and laid down and wagged its tail. She stroked the dog's fur and it groaned and sighed with satisfaction.

• • •

That night, Cynthia was doing dishes when she saw Robert drive up in the red Ford Mustang. She watched through the window as he drove into the garage and the door closed behind him. He exited the garage and walked toward the house.

She dried her hands on a dishtowel and went into the living room to meet Robert at the door.

Robert came in and the first thing he noticed was the dog lounging contentedly in front of the heater. His eyes bulged and he looked as though he was about to have a heart attack. He stared uneasily at the dog, a look of puzzlement on his face.

"What in the hell?" Robert said. "What is this? Are you out of your mind? You know I don't like dogs. Get that thing the hell out of here."

"He was under the porch this morning," Cynthia said. "He was all wet and cold. I just couldn't stand to see him suffering like that. He's a good dog. Really."

"I don't care what his story is," Robert said. "That mangy mutt has got to go."

"He's not hurting anything," Cynthia said. "He's just cold and scared. He needs help. I figure he can stay here for the night, and we can decide what to do with him in morning."

"I guess I'm going to have to take it to the pound," Robert said. He glanced at the dog again, meeting its piercing golden-brown eyes for a moment and then looked quickly away, frowning in disgust.

Robert was enduring a severe hangover and needed some hair of the dog to cure his aching head. Just one drink to calm his nerves, he thought. Something was bothering him, but he couldn't put his finger on it, exactly. Due to the heavy drinking he had done the night before he had suffered a blackout and he couldn't remember any of the details leading up to hitting the lady in the red dress with his car. However, he had an inclination that something terrible had occurred.

Abruptly, he had a flashback to the scene from the night before at the bar. He remembered: *standing under the protection of the overhanging roof as rain poured down from the night sky; raising his collar and buttoning up his coat against the wind and rain; the black hound tied to one of the columns that support the roof; reaching down to pet the dog as it snarled and growled, snapping viciously at his hand; the lady in the red dress as she dashed out into the road holding the black hound on a leash; stomping frantically on the brakes*—he snapped back from the memory with a violent jerk. His eyes were wide with terror and disbelief as he looked at the dog sitting in his kitchen, astonished as he realized what had transpired the night before, speculating on the possibilities.

"It can't be," he said. "It's impossible."

"What?" Cynthia said. "What are you talking about?

"Huh?" Robert said, confused. He had a distant look in his eyes. "Oh, it's nothing. It's nothing. I was just thinking out loud." His heart skipped a beat and then he said, "That dog has to go—now!"

The dog growled and showed its teeth in response to Robert's statement.

"Can't we at least keep him until we find out who he belongs to?" Cynthia pleaded.

"Absolutely not," Robert said, slamming his briefcase down on the coffee table. "No way. I don't like dogs. You know that."

He kicked off his shoes, peeled off his overcoat, hung it on the coat rack, and then loosened his tie.

"I bet the neighbors will keep him," Cynthia said. "They have a big farm. They like animals. I'll call them in the morning. And if they don't want him, then we can find someone who does. Just one day, that's all I'm asking."

"What's this 'we' crap?" Robert said. "I don't want anything to do with it. You're biting off more than you can chew—mark my words. You'll be sorry you ever messed with that mutt. He might have rabies—and I'm sure he's got bugs. Look at him. He's as dirty as a shithouse rat."

"Please," Cynthia said. "He's a nice dog. He deserves a good home. I think he's hurt, too. It looks like he got into a fight, or something. He was limping when I found him this morning."

Robert cringed as he looked at the dog. The dog looked back at him, bowing its head in a submissive posture, reminding Robert, oddly, of a coiled snake that is about to strike. It wagged its tail, drumming a beat on the floor.

"Okay. Fine. I guess you're not going to take 'no' for an answer," Robert said, against his better judgment. "But just for one night. That's it. Period. Just keep him out of my sight. If he isn't gone by tomorrow night, I'm taking him to the pound and they can give him the gas for all I care."

Cynthia danced up and down happily. She kissed Robert on the cheek.

"Thank you, honey," she said. "I'll find him a good home. Everything will be just fine. You'll see."

Robert rolled his eyes and shook his head in defeat. He said, "I hope so, for his sake. You know what they do at the pound. It's nothing nice."

He couldn't stop thinking about the night before; what had *really* happened? It was lingering there just out of his recollection. He had hit something . . . *or somebody . . . the lady in the red dress . . .* and the scariest part was that he couldn't quite remember everything. He knew that there was damage to his blue sedan, but he couldn't remember exactly how it happened. He had a good idea

what the truth *was,* but he didn't want to speculate on the finer details. It was easier to just ignore it and try to forget what happened.

Robert went to the living room and sat down in his reclining
chair. He picked up the remote control and turned on the television and changed the channel to the evening news. The reporter on
the screen shuffled some papers and then a news clip was shown.
The voice-over was from a female reporter at the scene. She said, "
*. . . police are still looking for the driver of a black sedan that struck
a woman dead on the night of August twenty-eighth . . . authorities
have little to go on other than a single eye witness that claims to
have seen a black sedan that was traveling at a high rate of speed
down Arlington Boulevard last night . . .*"

Robert watched in shock as the clip showed paramedics rolling
a body covered in a sheet on a gurney toward an ambulance. Bright
blue and red lights flashed on the screen as the body was placed
in the ambulance. He dropped the remote control because his hand
was shaking violently; he reached down, picked it up and quickly changed the channel. A movie was playing on the next channel,
Clint Eastwood was pointing a gun at a frightened man, cocking the
hammer back, world famous smirk on his face.

"Can you believe that?" Cynthia said, entering the living room.
"Somebody hit that poor woman and then ran from the scene, leaving her for dead."

Robert cringed, grinding his teeth. He said, "That kind of stuff
happens all of the time. You hear about it every day."

"Yeah, but not around here," Cynthia said. "What is this world
coming too?"

"Is supper ready?" Robert said, changing the subject.

"There is a TV dinner in the oven," Cynthia said. "I'm going to
take him for a walk."

"Fine," Robert said. He suddenly felt the urge to have a drink.
"Go on with your precious dog. Get it the hell out of my sight, why
don't you."

She put on her shoes and coat and walked to the door. The dog
eagerly jumped around in circles as she opened the door and called
him out onto the porch.

Robert watched them as they ambled down the driveway in the
direction of the sunset until they were out of sight. He jumped up
from his chair and went directly to the liquor cabinet, took out a

bottle of whiskey and poured a generous amount into a glass, spilling some of the alcohol on the counter. He tipped the glass back
and guzzled down the content, grimacing at the bite and burn of the
liquor.

"It can't be," he said. "That can't be the same dog. Impossible.
Oh, God, what have I done?"

He poured another drink and then went back to his recliner. He
watched the second half of *The Good, The Bad, and The Ugly* and
fell into a deep sleep where he had terrible nightmares the whole
night through.

• • •

Cynthia and the dog returned to find Robert sleeping in his chair.
She covered him with a blanket, turned off the TV and then went to
the bedroom. She brought the dog with her and put down a blanket
on the floor. The dog laid down on the blanket. She got into bed and
turned out the light.

• • •

The next morning, Robert was out in the backyard splitting and
stacking firewood.

Cynthia woke up and yawned and stretched. She could see Robert outside through the window. She got out of bed and went to the
window, opened it and stuck her head out, breathing in the fresh
morning air.

Robert saw her but said nothing. He put another piece of wood
on the chopping block and split it in two with a single whack.

"Good morning," Cynthia said, smiling at him. "It's a beautiful
morning, isn't it?"

Robert glared back at her and split another piece of wood, swinging the ax violently. He still said nothing.

"What's the matter, hon?" she asked, sensing that he was in a
foul mood.

"What's the matter?" Robert said, angrily. "I'll tell you what's
the matter. That dog chewed up my shoes. Not only that, but he
chewed up the newspaper too. If I get my hands on that little bastard,
I'm going to ring its neck."

Cynthia left the window and looked around the room and saw that the dog was gone. She poked her head back out the window.

"Where is he?" Cynthia asked.

"I don't know," Robert said, chopping another piece of wood, "and I don't care. I chased him off this morning. If he comes back, I've got a good mind to put this ax through his head."

"You're such an asshole," Cynthia said. "You know that? A real, genuine asshole . . . *and* an insensitive jerk."

"Oh, okay," Robert said. "I see how it is. I should be happy that he chewed on my new shoes and shredded my newspaper. How do you like that? Okay. Fine. But I'll tell you one thing: from now on it's either me, or that dog. Understand? There isn't enough room for both of us around here."

He stuck the ax into the chopping block and stomped across the yard toward the garage. He went inside and slammed the door shut behind him. He turned on the light and went past the Chrysler and Ford Mustang to where he kept his John Deere riding lawn mower. As he was checking the fuel level in the mower, he heard a deep throaty growl coming from behind one of the cars. He was surprised and startled. He picked up a hammer from the workbench and slowly, stealthily, crept in the direction of the growl.

"Is that you, doggy?" he said. "Here boy. Come on out. I've got something for you."

Without warning, the dog sprang from behind the Chrysler, snarling and snapping, all slavering teeth and jowls, as it leaped toward Robert. He swung the hammer wildly and as hard as he could, missing the dog and hitting the Chrysler; sparks shot out from the impact of the hammer on the trunk, paint chips hitting him in the face. He swung wildly again and broke the rear windshield. The dog snapped its jaws savagely, caught only air, and then struck again and made a purchase on Robert's leg, locking on and sinking its teeth into his thigh. Robert brought the hammer down solidly on the dog's head. The dog let out a yelp as the pain registered. It let go and lunged for Robert's face, biting his cheek, and peeling back the flesh. Robert fell backward and the dog continued to attack, snapping, and biting and—luckily for Robert—catching mostly air and shreds of clothing between its teeth. Robert staggered to the door, fumbled with the doorknob, and managed to open it, falling out into the sunlight. He staggered to his feet and made a run for it. The dog chased after him growling like a rabid wolf. Robert was still clutching the hammer, and he turned and swung blindly, smacking the dog in the ribs. The dog's attack was stifled as it took the blow full force in mid-air, letting out a cry of pain as it fell to the ground, rolled over, and took off in a mad dash across the yard and disappeared into the bushes.

Robert's adrenaline was flowing, and his temper was smoldering. He was short of breath and running in a panic and he lost his footing on the damp grass and slipped, landing on his back, and hitting his head. The wind was knocked out of him; he couldn't breathe. His vision was blurred. He lay there for a moment until he caught his breath and then stood up and went into the house.

There was a shotgun mounted over the fireplace mantle. He took it down and pumped it, making sure it was loaded. He was bleeding from several puncture wounds and lacerations on his hands, legs, and face. His pants were torn and bloody. He looked like a deranged lunatic.

"What are you doing?" Cynthia asked frantically. "You're not going to—"

"That's right," Robert wheezed. He had a maniacal grin on his face as he went toward the front door. "I'm going to shoot that dog. It just attacked me in the garage. So, I'm going to put him out of his misery. Don't even try to stop me." He stormed out through the front door with Cynthia right behind him.

Robert stopped for a moment on the back porch. Cynthia was following so closely that she ran hard into his back when he stopped.

"Robert. Wait," she said. "You don't have to do that. Please don't."

"Oh yes I do," he said. "That dog is as good as dead."

"Please don't shoot him," Cynthia pleaded. She stopped, realizing that her efforts were in vain.

The sun was rising high into the sky. Robert covered his eyes from the brightness of the sun and scanned the surrounding landscape for the dog. He tromped across the yard toward the bushes where he last saw the dog, his finger resting on the trigger of the shotgun, ready to squeeze it at a moment's notice. He combed through the bushes, tossing sticks and rocks into the brambles attempting to scare the dog out in the open.

It worked.

The dog came out of hiding and ran away down the driveway.

Robert took aim and pulled the trigger. Smoke and sparks blasted from the shotgun with a deafening report. It was a near miss; the dog was already out of range. The shotgun blast, did however, add momentum to its hasty retreat. Robert chased after the dog, ejecting the spent shell, and loading another into the chamber. He searched thoroughly for the dog, but the trail went cold. The dog was gone.

Robert started back to the house defeated yet determined to get the dog later when, and if, it came back. He supposed that it would come around again. It was inevitable. As luck would have it, while he was walking back to the house, he saw the dog sneaking up the stairs and onto the front porch where Cynthia was holding the door open.

"What the fuck?" Robert said, picking up his pace. "Oh, that's it. Your ass is mine."

Robert crept up to the porch, stopped out of sight with his back to the wall to gain the element of surprise, and then dashed up the stairs and through the door. He saw the dog and took aim with the shotgun. The dog scrambled under a chair as Robert pulled the trigger. The shotgun blast exploded with a deafening roar in the enclosed confines of the porch. It was another miss. The dog ran between Robert's legs and stopped behind him, growling, and preparing for a retaliatory attack. Robert turned around and pulled the trigger again. He was in a frenzy. He pulled the trigger repeatedly, the shotgun blasts flashing brightly and booming loudly, tearing up chunks and splinters of wood on impact.

Cynthia was in the way and took a direct hit, the shotgun blast and the buckshot striking her directly in the chest, the impact sending her sprawling across the porch. She landed on the floor and lay deathly still in an expanding pool of blood. A single rivulet of blood trickled from her mouth. The dog squeezed through a hole that had been blown in the damaged door and disappeared.

Robert grew faint and nauseous, his mind lapsing into complete denial and bewilderment, as he looked down at his dead wife lying in a pool of blood. He dropped the shotgun and fell to his knees and embraced her limp body, stroking her hair and holding her close to himself.

"No, no, no," he said, stroking her face with his fingers. "Oh, no. Don't be dead. Please wake up, baby. Wake up. It's going to be all right. Everything is going to be all right. This is just a dream. Please,

God let this be a dream."

He began to weep and sob hysterically. He cried until his tears ran dry. He stayed there in that position for several hours, lapsing into a state of sleep and dreams, nightmares and illusions, time slipping away as Cynthia grew cold and stiff from death and rigor mortis.

• • •

The sun had set over the mountains and night was coming fast, and Robert was still holding his dead wife. He had a blank look on his face, his eyes empty and void. He had the empty stare of a man who has lost everything and is completely devastated and has yet to go through the grieving process.

After night fell, he got up and carried her outside and into the garage. He placed her down on the cold cement ground and then rolled her up in black plastic. He tied the plastic off with twine and then picked the packaged body up, grabbing a shovel on his way out as he left the garage.

He carried the body over to where Cynthia had planted a flower garden on the side of the house and set it down. He began digging a deep hole. After the hole was deep enough, he put the body down in the damp earth and buried it. He patted down the dirt and then stuck the shovel into the ground leaving it standing like a makeshift grave marker.

He lumbered wearily back toward the house and went inside. He took a bottle of Scotch from the liquor cabinet and drank straight from the bottle. He plopped down on the couch and drank himself into oblivion.

• • •

The next morning, Robert planted roses over Cynthia's grave. When he was finished, he went back into the house. He picked up the shotgun and went out onto the front porch. He sat down in a chair and put the shotgun on his lap. He leaned over and took a beer from a Styrofoam cooler, opened the bottle with a twist of the cap and took a long drink. Waiting and watching could be thirsty work. He was watching the driveway for the dog to come back. He would be ready when it came back. It would come back; he knew that much.

• • •

A year later, Robert was still sitting on the porch. He had a full beard and he had lost weight, only a shell of the man he used to be. He was still waiting and watching. He only left when it became necessary. He quit his job and completely disassociated himself from the outside world. He didn't answer the phone and was short and to the point with any curious visitors that came to his house. He had a story he had made up to explain the disappearance of his wife. His story was that Cynthia had left him for another man and that he hadn't seen her since. He didn't concern himself too much with their curious looks or inquisitions; it was none of their business, and they could just be damned. He merely told them to go away and leave him alone; he had more important things to worry about than fussing over such trivial banter and gossip.

As for the dog, he knew that someday it would return; it was his nemesis, or fate, or karma—a curse and reprisal from some unearthly realm for all of the evil things he had ever done—and he had accepted this fate and was determined to take the dog to straight to Hell, even if it meant going with it. And finally, one day, across the yard that had gone to seed, and past the thriving lush rose bushes, Robert saw the black hound. It was trotting casually along the driveway, sniffing here and there. It stopped and looked toward the house. It saw Robert sitting on the porch; it sniffed the air and then looked away as if it was not too concerned about much of anything. It was carefree in a way that only a dog can be. It looked back at Robert.

They made direct eye contact.

Robert jumped up onto his feet, clutching the shotgun in his hands. He watched the dog, patiently, making no quick movements. He didn't want to scare it away—that struck him as funny because he knew the dog would never go away.

"You came back," Robert said. "I knew you would. It's time to finish this once and for all."

Robert left the confines of the porch that had been his only domain for the past year and, slowly, went through the door; it slammed shut behind him. He stopped and stood in the grass, watching the dog as it slowly approached.

The dog dashed over to the flower garden and started digging around the rose bushes. Dirt flew up into the air in chunks and clods.

Robert walked slowly toward the dog, raising the shotgun to his shoulder, and taking aim. He would make quick work of this mutt, finally. The dog kept digging, ignoring Robert, deeper and deeper into the ground. Robert felt a bead of sweat run down his face and into his eye. He wiped it away with his sleeve and then aimed the shotgun again. His finger was tightening on the trigger.

Suddenly, out of the corner of his eye, Robert saw a police cruiser turning off the main road and onto his driveway.

The dog continued to dig.

Robert eased his finger off the trigger and lowered the shotgun.

The police cruiser pulled up and two officers, one heavyset and the other tall and lanky, got out.

"Hey there," the heavyset officer said. "What's with the heavy artillery?"

"Why don't you put down that gun, sir," the lanky officer said, reaching for his service revolver.

"I'm going to shoot that damn dog," Robert said.

The officers looked at each other, at the dog, and then back at Robert with synchronized motions.

"Why?" the heavyset officer asked.

"Because it's a pest," Robert said. "It keeps tearing up my flowers and shitting in my yard. Just to name a few things." He was only slightly aware that he had concocted an elaborate lie—and it all seemed like the truth to him now.

The dog continued to dig. Robert ran toward it and tried to shoo it away, but the dog continued to dig.

"See what I mean," Robert said. "It's a hound from Hell, and I aim to put it out of its misery."

"Sure, sure," the heavyset officer said. "That's really all dogs are good for . . . eating, digging, and shitting. Right? What can you do? But I don't think shooting him is going to solve the problem."

"Oh, I think it will," Robert said.

The lanky officer unsnapped his holster and drew his service revolver, stepping back in a shooter's stance, saying, "Sir, I'm only going to ask you one more time to put down the gun."

"Calm down, now," the heavyset officer said. "Everybody just relax. This ain't the O.K. Corral or the Wild West. Why don't you both put away your weapons? We don't need to make this into a situation, do we?"

The tension lightened, but nobody put away their guns, yet.

"Is it your dog?" the lanky officer asked. "You can't just shoot a dog whenever you get the notion to do so."

"Yes," Robert said, considering, "as a matter of fact, it *is* my dog. I own it. So, I can shoot it if I want to. It was actually my wife's dog . . . but she's gone now. I guess that makes it mine."

The officers looked at each other with mutual uncertainty and then back at Robert.

"I see," said the heavyset officer. "And where is your wife?"

"I haven't seen her in over a year," Robert said, slipping easily into the lie without even a hint of deception in his voice or demeanor. "She ran off with some hotshot lawyer from the city. I guess they had been having an affair for quite some time. I was just too blind to see it until it was too late."

"Then I imagine that you know there is a missing person report that has been filed on her, huh?" the lanky officer said.

"Actually, no," Robert said, "I didn't know that."

"Seems some of her kinfolks upstate are worried about her." the heavyset officer said, putting his hands on his hips. "They can't seem to locate her. She just up and disappeared. They think you might know something about it, maybe . . . ."

"I don't know where she is," Robert said, adamantly. "And that's all I know. She left me for another man. What can I say?"

"Not much, I suppose," the heavyset officer said. "I guess a woman can get a notion to do what she wants to do . . . and nobody can stop her even if they try. It happens all the time. There really is a fine line between love and hate."

"Yep," Robert said. "Don't know what got into her. I don't care anymore, either."

"I don't suppose you would mind if we had a look around, would you?" the lanky officer asked.

"Of course not. Be my guest," Robert said.

"On second thought, why don't you give us that gun," the heavyset officer said. "I'd feel a little more comfortable that way. It's safer for everybody."

"Okay," Robert said. "I guess so."

He gave the gun to the lanky officer—who grabbed it quickly and secured it in the trunk of the cruiser. "You can come and get that at the station," he said, slamming the trunk. "We'll just hold on to it for the time being."

"Fine," Robert said. "You're the boss."

The heavyset officer said, "Boy, howdy. Look at that dog go. He sure is a digger, isn't he?"

The dog was still digging, deeper and deeper into the dirt beneath the rose bushes. Robert picked up a rock and threw it at the dog. It flinched and jumped out of the way, the rock narrowly missing its head, and then it went right back to digging. Robert ran over and grabbed the shovel that was sticking in the ground and swung it wildly at the dog; this was enough to discourage the dog from digging; it ran off with tail tucked between its legs and disappeared behind the house.

"That dumb ass dog just won't stop," Robert said. "Now you see what I am up against. That is why I had the gun."

The officers were unimpressed. They just looked at Robert with blank faces.

Robert took them inside the house and gave them a grand tour; they strolled through the house looking around casually. He took them out into the garage and the officers looked around with mild interest. The lanky officer took out his notepad and wrote down the license plate numbers on each of the cars. After a less than thorough search, the officers seemed satisfied; they left the garage and headed back in the direction of their patrol car.

They stopped by the flower garden and admired the lush rose bushes; there was a large muddy hole at the base of the largest bush where the dog had been digging.

"What do you think of those roses?" Robert asked. "Aren't they beautiful. I planted them last year and they are already growing like weeds."

"Very nice," the lanky officer said. "They are beautiful."

"They are truly magnificent," the heavyset officer said, feigning interest. "Anyway, I guess we're done here, and we'll just be on our way. You give us a call if the missus happens to show up around here or gets in touch with you. Okay?"

"Sure. I'll do that," Robert said. "Would you like some of these roses to take home to your wives?"

"No thank you," the lanky officer said. "I'm flattered by your offer . . . but we aren't allowed to accept gifts."

"Suit yourselves," Robert said. "Just look at how beautiful these roses are. They are very sturdy plants. These are the best roses in the county. They have very strong roots and stalks."

"Uh, yeah. If you say so," the heavyset officer said. "I don't know much about flowers. My wife has the green thumb. Me . . . I can't even grow a green lawn in the rainy season."

They proceeded toward the police cruiser. The lanky officer turned around and looked back just in time to see the black hound run out from under the porch and start digging again.

"What in the hell?" he said.

"What?" Robert said. "What's the matter?" He turned and saw the dog and felt his heart do a drum roll in his chest. He ran toward the dog knowing that it was too late.

The lanky officer ran after him, over to the flower garden, and stopped with a look of bewilderment and shock on his face. The dog was wrestling with something . . . pulling, tugging, and finally dragging the black plastic that contained Cynthia's body up from the dirt; one of her bony, decaying arms protruded from the plastic like a dead tree limb.

Robert fell to his knees and cried out like a madman, grabbing handfuls of his hair, and ripping it out by the roots. "It's her," he confessed. "I killed her and buried her under those rose bushes. I didn't mean to do it. It was an accident. I loved her. You have got to believe me. I loved her. That damn dog made me do it. I loved her."

Hilljacks

"This is it. It's still here," Nick Stone said, looking to where an overgrown trail wound through the tall grass and undergrowth into the woods. "It's been a while since I've been out here . . . but the trail is still here. I knew it would be. You guys are going to love this." He stepped carefully over the sagging rusty barbed wire fence where a rotted post had fallen over, stopped, and waited for the others to follow. He shifted his fishing pole between his hands and strained to adjust his knapsack. Dean, who was struggling to carry a Coleman cooler full of iced beer, and a fishing pole, followed, but Karen stood fast, hesitating. She was clutching her fishing pole and a tackle box as she assessed the trail leading into the woods. Her knapsack was weighing heavily on her back.

"Are you sure this is okay?" she said. "What about that?" She pointed at a weathered sign nailed to a nearby tree:

NO TRESPASSING
violators will be shot!

"It's okay," Nick said. "That sign has been there forever. I used to come out here with my dad when I was a kid. Nobody ever said anything. The guy who owns the property doesn't care."

"It looks okay to me," Dean said. "What's the worst that can happen?"

She sighed and stepped carefully over the barbed wire, ignoring her better judgment. "I don't know, but I've got a funny feeling I'm going to find out. They put those signs up for a reason, you know?"

"Yeah. To keep people away from the best fishing hole around," Nick said. He disappeared around a corner into the undergrowth, crashing through brambles and bushes. "Last one there is a rotten egg," he said, voice echoing through the trees.

They trudged through the trees and bushes, the overhead canopy blocking out most of the midday sun, except for occasional sun-beams that pierced through leaves here and there dappling the forest floor in spots of illumination.

Somewhere in the distance there was the sound of gunfire.

"What was that?" Dean asked.

"Bird hunters," Nick said. "They are after quail, or grouse, or maybe squirrels."

"They have guns?" Karen said. "I think this is a bad idea—being out here like this."

"They are a long way away," Nick said. "Don't worry. They are only shooting at birds in the air . . . we are safe. Now let's go. We're almost there."

The tree line ended abruptly, and the forest opened into a clear-ing where wild grass shivered and shimmered in a gentle breeze. It was a vast green pasture where cattle had once grazed. There was an abandoned truck, nothing more than a rusted hulk in the field like the skull of a dinosaur.

"The lake is just over there," Nick said. "Beyond those trees." He pointed across the clearing to where a tree line skirted along the grassy meadow, beneath rolling hills and distant mountains; puffy white cumulus clouds floated overhead like cotton. Nick breathed in deeply. "Smells like it might rain. Let's get going."

They crossed the meadow, passing the rusted truck. As they neared the other side of the grassy clearing, they heard more gun-shots; several shots rang out in rapid succession, echoing from the hills. Nick thought he counted eight shots.

"They must be getting some birds. Luck is with them," Nick said. "Maybe we'll get lucky and catch some fish, too."

The trail led into the trees on the other side of the meadow and they could now see glimpses of the lake down the hill through the tree trunks, the sun reflecting off the water like glittering diamonds.

Nick was growing anxious. He picked up the pace through the woods and soon they were descending a steep trail that wound to the left and right and then they were standing at the edge of Timber Lake.

A fish jumped out on the lake with a splash.

"This is it," Nick said, already setting up his fishing rod and bait.

"It's beautiful," Karen said. She sat down on the Coleman cooler Dean had been carrying. "It's just so peaceful out here." She opened her knapsack and took out a red and black checkered wool blanket.

Dean lit a cigarette, inhaled deeply, and coughed out smoke.

"Thought you were going to quit smoking," Karen said. "Those things will kill you."

"I know," Dean said, smashing the cigarette under his boot heal. "But you only live once . . . if one thing doesn't kill you, something else probably will."

"You're such a pessimist," Karen said.

"You know me. It's my nature," Dean said.

Nick was ready to fish, moving along the lake, casting his line out into the water.

"Help me with this blanket so we can sit down and be comfortable," Karen said, motioning to Dean.

"Okay," Dean said.

They unfolded the blanket and spread it out on the ground. Karen sat down and rummaged through the cooler.

"Do you want a beer?" she asked.

"Sure," Dean said. "I'd love one."

She handed him a beer. She turned to offer a beer to Nick, but he had wandered away and was out of sight.

"Are you ready to fish?" Dean asked.

"You go ahead," Karen said. "I just want to sit here and enjoy the scenery."

"Let me at least rig your fishing pole up for you, so that you can sit and fish," Dean said.

"Okay. That would be nice," she said.

Dean set up her fishing pole and cast it out into the water. He had placed a bobber on the line so that she could watch it. He handed her the fishing pole, then leaned down and gave her a kiss.

"I love you," he said.

"Love you too," she said.

Dean prepared his own fishing rod and went to join Nick, who was now quite a distance away. He was standing on a fallen tree that reached out into the lake.

"Catch anything yet?" Dean asked.

"A little one," Nick said, reeling in his line. He cast back out into the water; there were several seconds of hang time in midair before the hook, line and sinker plunked into the water.

"Nice cast," Dean said, casting out his own line.

"There are some big fish in here," Nick said. "They don't seem to be biting today, though."

Suddenly there came a fierce tug on his fishing rod. He jerked the rod upward to set the hook. The fish splashed on the surface of the water. Nick reeled in the fish, pulled it out of the water and removed the hook from its mouth. The fish was a largemouth bass.

"Nice fish," Dean said.

"It's a beauty," Nick said. "Going to let it go, though."

"You're not going to keep it?"

"Nope. I'm just in it for the sport," Nick said, releasing the fish back into the lake.

After a while the fishing got better and they both caught several nice fish in rapid succession. Dean decided that he wanted to go back and check on Karen. He didn't like leaving her alone, out of sight for so long. Nick followed behind him.

Karen was still sitting on the blanket. She saw them coming toward her and smiled.

"You guys catch anything?" she asked.

"Yes, we did," Dean said. "Mostly Nick did the catching, though. I caught all the little ones."

"I haven't caught a thing yet," Karen said.

"You need to check your bait," Nick said. "Always put fresh bait on when in doubt."

"Of course," Karen said. "I'm sure you are right about that."

She reeled in the line, lifted the hook out of the water, and, sure enough, the bait was gone. The silver hook glinted in the sunlight.

"See," Nick said. "I told you."

Dean grabbed the line and replaced the bate for Karen.

"Thank you, kind sir," Karen said.

"Don't mention it, my lady," Dean said. "There you go. Now cast it back out there."

Karen stood up, leaning back with the fishing pole, and then cast the line out into the lake.

"Nice one," Dean said.

Nick took a beer from the cooler, cracked it open, and had a long drink. He burped, wiped his lips, and sighed contentedly.

Out on the lake in the distance there came the sputtering sound of an outboard engine. Around the corner, at the nearest point, a small boat appeared and approached them over the water, drawing to within a stone's throw. There was a wiry looking man hunkered down in the boat, peering at them from beneath the brim of a greasy baseball cap as he steered the rudder. He had a nose like a hawk and beard stubble that looked as rough as sandpaper.

"Hello," Nick said, waving and smiling cheerfully.

The man in the boat did not reply. He glared back at them with a hateful stare. He spit tobacco juice into the water, twisted the throttle on the outboard engine, and cruised away until he was out of sight. The sound of the boat diminished and then stopped.

"What a creep," Karen said.

"Who was that?" Dean asked.

"Don't know," Nick said. "But he sure looked like an asshole."

"Maybe we should get out of here," Karen said. "That was probably the owner of this property."

"I don't think we have anything to worry about," Nick said. "That guy is probably just out fishing, too."

Dean looked at his watch, rubbed his chin, and then lit a cigarette. He said, "Maybe we should get going. It is getting late. It will be dark soon."

"We just got here," Nick said.

"I'm with getting out of here, too," Karen said. "That guy gave me the creeps. He looked . . . mean."

"Fine," Nick said, defeated. "We'll go. But at least let me get a couple more casts in before do."

Nick cast his line out into the water. He was stalling. He did not want to leave yet, so he was taking his time. Dean and Karen, on the other hand, quickly gathered everything together and were ready to go immediately. They waited, anxiously, for Nick to reel in his line.

"Let's go," Karen said. She turned and climbed up the winding trail that led away from the lake.

Dean and Nick followed.

They reached the top of the hill and followed the trail out into the grassy meadow. As they crossed the clearing, a 1990s model Chevy Suburban truck raced along a primitive road toward them. It was cream colored and rusty, covered with mud, a whip antenna on the back bumper, and a spotlight mounted on the roof. The truck bounced and skidded across the grass, slamming into potholes, swerving, and zigzagging crazily as if the driver were insanely drunk, accelerating as it approached at a high rate of speed.

Karen, Dean, and Nick stopped, frozen in their tracks like animals in bright headlights at night, watching, unbelieving, and unable to move out of harm's way, as the Suburban bore down on them like an angry grizzly bear.

"Lookout!" Nick shouted.

They jumped out of the way just as the Suburban skidded to a halt, narrowly missing them. The doors flew open and three men and a dog jumped out, each wielding a shotgun. One of them was the wiry man with the greasy hat who had been in the boat earlier, and he spat dark tobacco juice on the ground. Another man, the size of a gorilla, was holding a nylon leash attached to a big dog, a snarling and slavering, angry rottweiler that was tugging and pulling at the leash so hard that it was wheezing as the collar cut off its air supply. The driver—and apparently the leader of the group—was an elderly man, short in stature, but as sure-footed and cocky as a bantam rooster.

"Get down on the ground," the driver screamed at the top of his lungs.

"What's the prob—" Nick started to say.

"Shut the hell up, asshole," the driver screamed, "and get the fuck down on the ground, now."

"—lem? What did we do?" Nick finished.

"You're trespassing. That's what you done," the driver said. He pumped his shotgun for emphasis and fired a warning shot into the air.

Nick was furious. "You can't do this—"

"Shut the fuck up!" the driver said. "Get down on the ground, or I'm gonna mash your face. You hear me? I'm going to mash your fuckin' face to a pulp, asshole. Now get down."

Dean and Karen both got face down on the ground immediately. They were frightened and didn't want to test the old man with the shotgun. Nick got down, hesitatingly, on the ground, never taking his eyes off the old man.

"Oh my god," Karen cried. "This can't be happening."

"Hush," Dean said. "Just do whatever they say. When the police get here this whole thing will get sorted out."

"What you think we ought to do with them, Pa?" the big ape-like man with the dog said.

"I say we shoot 'em right now," the other man with the greasy hat said.

"Now just hold on," Pa said. "Give me a minute to think."

"We weren't hurting anything," Nick said. "I used to come fishing out here with my dad back when I was a kid . . . nobody seemed to care then, so I just thought—"

Pa whacked Nick on the head with the barrel of the shotgun; the gunmetal made a hollow *thunk* on his skull.

"Shut your pie-hole, mister," Pa said. "I didn't say you could talk. And I don't give a shit about what you did back in the day. That was a long time ago when someone else owned this here property. I own it now; and I don't go for no trespassers on my private property. Didn't you read the signs posted all over the place?"

"Yes, but . . ." Nick said. "I didn't think—"

Pa whacked him on the head with the shotgun again.

"See, now?" Pa said. "There you go jaw jackin' again when I didn't say you could talk. Now, what did the signs say? Anyone. . . ?"

He looked back and forth at everyone.

Nobody said anything; they were all too scared to speak. The guy holding the dog began to hee-haw with glee, finding humor in the interrogation.

Pa put the barrel of the shotgun up to Nick's forehead and pulled the hammer back and said, "I'm gonna blow your fuckin' head off, mister. You're toying with me now. First you won't shut up—now I ask you a question and you won't answer. I don't like smart-ass city slickers like you, anyway. Maybe I ought to just pull this here trigger and splatter your brains for ya. What about that?"

"Do it Pa," the man with the greasy hat said, happy with the current turn of events. "Blow his damned head off." He made a yuk-yuk-yuk sound and then spit tobacco in the grass.

"Shut up Clarence," Pa said. He looked back at Dean. "Now, what did that sign say?"

"No trespassing," Nick said. "But look, we can work this out. I have money if that's what you want—"

"I don't want your money," Pa said. "You think I need your money. That's a hoot. What I want to know is what the sign said and why you didn't pay attention to it. The signs were clearly posted in plain sight."

Dean spoke up first: "'No Trespassing. Violators will be shot.' That's what the the sign said."

"Ta-de-fuckin-da," Pa said, looking over at the ape-like man with the dog. "Jethro, give that man a cigar."

Jethro guffawed, then said, "I ain't got no cigar, Pa."

"Put a cork in it, Jethro," Pa said. "It's a figure of speech. Anyway, that is correct. The sign said no trespassing and violators will be shot. And what do you suppose that means? Hmm? Do you need me to spell it out for you?"

"We don't want any trouble, sir," Dean said. "It won't happen again. We just wanted to do some fish—"

"Shut your mouth," Clarence said, pointing his shotgun at Dean. "Pa didn't say you could talk, either."

Karen was crying hysterically, sobbing, and shaking, a bubble of snot forming at her left nostril.

"Shut the hell up, lady," Jethro said. "Nobody wants to hear all that blubberin'."

Nick was angry and had seen enough. This was intolerable. He didn't care what happened, he would not sit idly by and let these three backwoods bullies treat his friends and himself in such a manner. He said, "Listen, you assholes! You can't treat us like this. I know you have seen the movie *Deliverance* and you are acting like you stepped right out of that movie. But this is the real world, not a movie, and you can't be so fucking stupid as to think that you can get away with harming innocent people—"

"Innocent?" Pa chimed. "Boy, you just signed your death warrant. I don't appreciate being talked to like that. Not to mention, you broke the law. Trespassing is illegal. See what I'm saying?"

"I don't care what you think," Nick said. "I'm going to get up and walk away and you are going to let me and my friends go. Understand?" He got up and nobody stopped him. He looked down at his friends and said, "You guys can get up and follow me, too. These backwoods hilljacks aren't going to do anything to you. I'm going to call the cops on my cell phone right now." He took his cell phone from his pocket and dialed 9-1-1, waiting for the call to connect. He looked at the men with a smirk on his face, as if he had won after all.

Pa was getting angry; his face, nose and ears turned bright red; his finger twitched on the trigger of the shotgun. Jethro and Clarence were aghast, looking as if they had just been shocked by an electric fence; they couldn't believe that Nick had just spoken to Pa in such a manner.

"Hilljack?" Pa said. "What the hell you call me?"

"You heard me," Nick said, scared but ready to call the man's bluff. "You're a fucking hilljack. Worse than a hillbilly, or a redneck. You're a backwoods white-trash Podunk asshole. That's what you are."

Pa's lips puckered into an O and his eyes squinted as his jaw muscles clenched tightly, his teeth grinding together audibly.

Dean and Karen were both relieved to see Nick making the phone call; however, they were now more frightened than ever with the dialogue that was passing between the two men.

Pa raised the shotgun and pointed it at Nick's head. He took aim, squinting with one eye, his tongue sticking out of the corner of his mouth.

Nick looked down the barrel of the shotgun with disbelief; he didn't think the old man had the testicular fortitude to pull the trigger. It would only be a matter of time before the cops were out here and this would all be over.

"Call me that one more time and watch what happens," Pa said.

Everyone was silent, watching, waiting, the tension so thick it was suffocating like a fetid fog.

"You're a fucking hilljack. Fuck you," Nick said, holding up the cell phone as if to say *I win*.

The operator's voice could be heard on the phone: "Hello, nine-one-one, what is your emergency?"

Pa looked as though he had decided that murder was a bad idea and that he was going to lower the gun and then suddenly he pulled the trigger. The shotgun blast roared and echoed across the field. Nick's head exploded like an overripe pumpkin struck with an excessively large mallet. His body stayed standing for a moment, blood squirting in jets from his jugular veins, and then collapsed to the ground, the cell phone falling out of his hand and hitting the ground. Pa fired the shotgun again, hitting the cell phone on the ground and blowing it to pieces. The call was terminated.

Karen let out a high pitch scream as bits and pieces of Nick's skull and brains landed on her face.

Dean jumped to his feet and took off running across the field. He was in shock, fleeing as quickly as he could, running in a flight response to the terrible event that he had just witnessed. He saw the railroad tracks up ahead and he was pumping his legs in full strokes, survival his only goal, but he was not aware that he was running in the wrong direction. He thought he might get away, because now he was out of reach of the guns, and the men were too old or out of shape to give chase.

That was when Jethro let the dog off the leash and said, "Go get him, Rocky."

Rocky the dog kicked up clods of dirt as he took off after Dean; he growled and barked furiously as he closed the distance between predator and prey.

"You stay here and watch her," Pa said to Jethro. "Make sure she don't try nothin' funny."

Jethro nodded, saying, "Okay, Pa. I'll watch her."

"Clarence, you come with me," Pa said. "We ain't gonna let that son of a bitch get away."

They got into the Suburban and took off after Dean.

The dog was catching up to Dean.

Dean sensed that he was being chased and when he turned and looked over his shoulder he saw the dog closing in on him in a hurry; there was only one thing left to do; he reached into his pocket and pulled out his Buck knife. He opened the knife with a flick of the wrist. The blade glinted in the sun. He was still running as fast as he could, but Rocky the dog was coming in for the kill now, white foam forming at the corners of his mouth, tongue hanging out and flapping as he ran. He jumped up into the air and pounced on Dean, going for the throat.

Dean reacted quickly; he turned around and stabbed the knife into Rocky's chest, piercing the heart; the dog let out a yelp and then fell to the ground squirming in the throes of death. Dean was still running, in shock, holding on tightly to the bloody knife, as he looked back over his shoulder at the dog quivering in death. He heard the revving engine from the Suburban as it bore down on him like a lion on a wounded animal. He turned and started to run toward the railroad tracks. If he could just make it across the tracks, he would be safe, he thought.

Pa and Clarence were determined even more when they saw Dean kill Rocky with a knife. Pa stomped the gas pedal to the floor and gripped the steering wheel tight; Clarence leaned out the window and pointed his shotgun at Dean. He pulled the trigger and pumped the gun repeatedly, missing with every shot.

Dean heard the gunshots and that is when he stumbled and fell, hitting the ground and getting a mouthful of dirt and grass.

"We got him now, Pa," Clarence said, excitedly.

"Kill my dog, will ya?" Pa said. "I'm gonna fuck you up, now."

Dean was trying to get to his feet when the Suburban hit him like a meteorite. He went underneath the vehicle and came out from behind the vehicle like a battered bag of flesh and bones.

Pa slammed on the brakes and he and Clarence jumped out and ran back to where Dean was lying, moaning, and groaning, not dead yet, but close to it. Clarence ran up to Dean and kicked him repeatedly.

"You fuckin' piece of shit," Clarence said. "You killed my dog."

Pa ran up and, without hesitation, shot Dean in the head with the shotgun.

"Put you outta your misery, you son of a bitch," Pa said, spitting on Dean's corpse. He looked back at Clarence and said, "Go get a shovel. We need to dig some holes and bury the bodies."

Suddenly, from behind, there came a shout—it was Jethro—they could hear him clearly, screaming at the top of his lungs.

"She's gettin' away, Pa!" Jethro shouted. "She tricked me. She's gettin' away!"

Pa and Clarence looked back to see that the woman was running away, and Jethro was jumping up and down in excited confusion. He couldn't catch her if he tried.

"Come on," Pa said. "Let's go get her and finish this."

"Yeah," Clarence said. "Can I have some fun with her first?"

Pa smacked him on the head and said, "Get in the damn car, you idiot."

Jethro was running toward them, out of breath, not wanting to be left behind.

"Hurry up," Pa said, watching Jethro run. "You need to lose some weight, boy."

"I'm coming, Pa," Jethro said.

"She's going to get away," Clearance said.

Jethro finally caught up and he climbed into the Suburban and they took off in the direction of the fleeing woman.

• • •

Karen was running with all her might. She had seen the opportunity to get away, when Jethro was watching all the action between Dean and Rocky, and she had kicked Jethro squarely in the balls and took off running. She ran past the old rusted-out car they had passed earlier when they first arrived, and she knew that she was going in the right direction. If she could just make it to Nick's pickup, she might stand a chance. She knew that Nick kept a hunting rifle behind the seat and that was her only hope to save herself. She was almost to the railroad tracks now and they would not be able to follow her in the vehicle across the tracks; they would have to pursue her on foot, and she had a good lead on them already.

She could hear the Suburban revving up and she couldn't help turning around for a quick look. She saw that the Suburban had stopped to pick up Jethro and that they were aware that they couldn't catch her by following her so the vehicle spun around in a semi-circle and took off toward the direction where they could cross over to the main road. They were going to get on the pavement and beat her to the truck.

"Fuck that," she said, aloud. "I'm not going to be beaten by a bunch of hilljacks."

She ran even faster, ignoring the stitch of pain that was stabbing into her side. Gasping for air, she climbed over the sagging barbed wire fence at the end of the trail and stumbled, falling onto the railroad tracks, the course rocks and gravel tearing skin from the palms of her hands, knees, and elbows.

The sound of the Suburban was loud and not too far away. She would have to hurry. She pushed herself up onto her feet and took off running, now with a limp, and followed the tracks toward where the Ford Ranger pickup was parked. She could see it up ahead in the distance. It was not that far. She could make it. She was going to make it.

Within a minute or two she was at the edge of the clearing where

Nick had parked his pickup. She closed the distance quickly.

The hilljacks were approaching on the road; the engine of the Suburban was louder than ever.

Karen made it to the truck and pulled the door open.

The Suburban was less than the length of a football field away now and getting closer.

She pulled the bench seat in the Ford Ranger forward, saw the Winchester 30-30 rifle. She grabbed it and turned around, pulling the lever to be sure there was a bullet in the chamber.

The Suburban was coming at her fast. She raised the rifle to her shoulder, took aim at the driver's head and squeezed the trigger. The rifle kicked as flames and sparks spewed from the barrel, the report deafening as it echoed through the surrounding hills. The bullet pierced a hole in the windshield. She fired two more shots.

The Suburban swerved and careened out of control, heading straight toward her. She jumped out of the way just in time, as it smashed into the Ford Ranger pickup. Glass burst from the trucks in stinging shards, metal screeched and whined as it tore and folded, smoke and gas fumes filled the air.

The occupants of the vehicles appeared to be knocked unconscious, or dead, because they were not moving and remained perfectly still and silent.

Karen raised the gun to her shoulder and approached the wreck cautiously. She could hear someone moaning. There was a small tongue of flame licking at the side of the twisted metal, threatening to start a fire. She pulled the door open and was sickened by what she saw. Pa and Clarence were both dead, parts and pieces of their bodies mangled and smashed into chunks of bloody meat. Jethro was still alive, but his legs were snapped in compound fractures. He was reaching toward her and begging and pleading for her to help him.

"Please help me," he said. "I'm hurt. I don't want to die. Help me."

The flames were spreading. Soon the vehicles would catch fire and burst into an inferno.

Jethro had all the appearance of a scared child who was sincerely asking for help.

"Why should I help you?" she said. "I should shoot you and put you out of your misery."

"I'm sorry," Jethro said. "Please help me. I don't want to die. I don't want to die. I'm hurt."

Karen wanted to help him. She was confused. Her anger at what they had done to her friends was making her vengeful, but her sense of duty was making her want to help this injured man.

"I'm going to pull you out of there," she said. "But don't try anything stupid. I'll just leave you in there to burn . . ."

"Okay," Jethro said. "I promise. Just help me."

Karen reached in with one arm—still holding the rifle in her other hand—and grabbed Jethro by the shirt. She pulled hard, but he was a large man and she couldn't get him to budge.

Jethro showed his true intentions. He grabbed her by the hair and pulled her into the burning wreckage.

"I got you now, you bitch," he said. "I'm taking you with me, you fuckin cunt. You think you're better than me, don't you? Well now you're going to die with me."

Karen felt appalled by the fact that she had been duped; now she was trapped.

Jethro punched her repeatedly in the face in rapid succession.

Karen saw stars with each punch. She poked the gun barrel into one of Jethro's broken legs and ground the tip into the wound. He howled in agony at the excruciating pain and instantly let go; she jumped back and put the gun to his head and pulled the trigger. She managed to jump back out of the way just as flames caught the puddle of gas that had formed under the wreckage and erupted into a massive fireball. The heat wave hit her face and singed her eyebrows.

Karen fell to the ground and scrambled backward to get away from the blazing wreckage. She wanted to get away before there was an explosion. She made it to a safe distance and collapsed in the middle of the road, clutching the rifle and sobbing. She was overwhelmed with shock and her body shook as she cried.

The sun was beginning to set, and a car approached up ahead on the road; its headlights were on; it slowed down when it got close to the scene of the accident. The driver got out, a young man dressed in a suit jacket and penny loafers. He rushed over to Karen.

"Are you alright?" the young man asked. "What happened?"

"They are all dead," she said.

"Who—what happened?" the young man asked.

"They're all dead," she repeated. She began recounting the events that had transpired, but she was not making any sense and the young man couldn't understand exactly what she was trying to say.

He called the police on his cell phone.

• • •

After the police, firefighters, and an ambulance arrived, the paramedics put Karen onto a gurney and wheeled her toward the back of an ambulance.

"What in the world happened?" a police officer asked her.

"We were attacked," Karen said. "They were mad because we were trespassing. They didn't like us."

"That's no reason to start shooting everybody," the officer said. "It sounds like things got way out of control."

"They didn't leave me any choice," she said. "I was fighting for my life. They started it."

"I guess you had to do what you had to do," the officer said.

"Yes," she said. The morphine was kicking in and she was getting groggy. "Yes. I did what I had to do. I don't think I'm better than anyone. They were just mad at us . . . city slickers. They are all dead now . . . crazy hilljacks."

She passed out and the paramedics put her into the ambulance and rushed her away to the hospital.

A Fugitive's Hideout

It was raining on the verge of a terrible storm, the day that Cooper and I set out to rob the First National Bank located on the south end of Sandpoint, Idaho. Cooper pulled the black Dodge Charger into the parking lot behind the bank, and we quickly jumped out of the vehicle. We had guns and masks in the trunk, and we hastily donned our disguises. He was wearing a gorilla mask and I was wearing a Bozo the Clown mask. We went in through the front door and wasted no time as we dashed toward the bank tellers behind the counter.

"Everybody get down on the ground now!" Cooper shouted. He pumped the shotgun for emphasis. "Nobody move and nobody gets hurt."

I turned and saw a security guard going for his gun.

"I wouldn't do that if I were you," I said, pointing my Smith and Wesson .44 magnum at his head. "Don't try to be a hero. Get down on the ground . . . nice and easy."

The security guard thought better of any plans of being a hero he might have had and raised his hands in the air. He got down on his knees and said, "Okay. Just don't shoot anybody." He then laid down face-first on the ground, hands out to the side.

Cooper ran directly to the teller behind the counter and said, "Put all of the money in the bag." He placed a duffle bag on the counter and motioned with the gun. "Don't try anything cute, either."

She took the bag and filled it with money from the drawer. She handed it back to him.

"No," he said, shaking his head in disagreement. "Don't fuck with me, darling. I'm not in the mood to be fucked with today."

She took the bag back and went to the other drawers and removed the money, placing it into the bag. The rest of the customers and the teller were on the floor, and it was extremely quiet. It was so quiet you could have heard a mouse fart. The rain was picking up outside and it beat down on the plate glass on the front of the bank where gold leaf letters said, Parksville First National Trust. Somebody coughed and broke the silence.

"We need to go, Coop," I said. "We got to get the hell out of here."

"Now you've gone and done it."

"What did I do?"

"You gone and said my—" He looked around to see if anybody had noticed; everybody pretended not to hear but it was plain that they had. "Aw, never mind. Let's get the fuck out of here."

Right about then the security guard made a quick move for his gun and Cooper let him have it right in the chest with the shotgun. The shot blast was loud and echoed with flashing bright white light and a cloud of acrid smoke through the bank lobby.

"Damn it!" Cooper said. "You idiot! You went and made me have to shoot your dumb ass."

"Let's go," I said. "We got to get out of here right now."

We burst through the bank doors and out into the rainy daylight. The sound of sirens could be heard in the distance and that meant that the cops were on their way. We jumped into the Charger and Cooper hit the gas. The car shot across the parking lot and Cooper turned the steering wheel sharply, swinging around and turning down an alley past an old junkyard. There was a high rickety fence on both sides of the alley and the Charger roared loudly across the gravel, splashing through mud puddles.

"Fuck!" Cooper said, looking in the rearview mirror. "They're on to us."

"What?" I said. I turned and saw a solitary patrol car with lights flashing behind us. I could see the officer driving the car; he was wearing mirrored Aviator sunglasses.

"Get back there and take him out," Cooper said. He handed me the shotgun.

I climbed into the back seat and bashed out the rear windshield with the butt stalk of the gun. I fired at the patrol car and hit the windshield. The buckshot tore into the glass, causing the officer driving the patrol car to swerve wildly out of control. He regained control and stepped on the gas; the engine of the patrol car responded with a monstrous roar. He put his service revolver out the window and returned fire. The bullets hit the Charger with a metallic clanking sound: *thwack-thwack-thwack.* I fired several more shots back at him and he lost control again, only this time he crashed into a telephone pole and came to an abrupt and smoking halt. It looked like lady luck was on our side and that we were going to get away and then all the sudden the Charger engine died, and Cooper couldn't get it to start again.

"What the hell?" I said.

"He must have hit something when he shot at us that fucked up the car," Cooper said. "We got to make a run for it on foot."

We grabbed our guns—Cooper reclaimed the shotgun—and the duffle bag with the money in it and we took off on foot down the alley, through a loose board hole in the fence, past a bunch of old wrecked cars in the junkyard. A mongrel dog was chained up to a tree and it barked at us, snarling, mad, slavering jaws snapping, as it tugged at the end of the chain lunging at us.

Sirens wailed in the distance reminding us that the police were closing in on us, or were at least surrounding the bank, and they were hot on our trail in pursuit.

The dog wanted a piece of us.

We were at a dead end, and it was looking bleak.

That was when we noticed the freight train rolling slowly along the tracks across the junkyard.

"That's our way out," Cooper said. "Let's get on that train. It is our only hope to get away."

"Let's do it," I said.

We ran past the barking dog, just out of reach of his chain, ducked through the hole in the fence—the junkyard fence was in serious need of repair—and ran toward the cars of the train. It was gaining momentum and speed, so we needed to be quick. Cooper and I ran alongside the train; he threw the duffle bag and shotgun into an open door on a boxcar and jumped aboard. When he gained footing and stood up, he reached down to help me get on.

"Give me your hand," he said.

I was afraid I wasn't going to make it. The train was moving way too fast.

"I ain't going to make it," I said. "You go on without me."

"Hell with that," he said. "You can do it. Come on."

I ran with all my strength and might, stretching out my hand toward his until our fingertips touched. I almost tripped, stumbled, and then just as I was about to fall, he grabbed my hand and hoisted me up into the boxcar. I was greeted by a dusty, oily smell inside of the empty boxcar.

We looked back toward town and it looked as though we had made it away unnoticed. Cooper closed the boxcar door and we sat down to catch our breath. My heart was beating a thousand miles per hour and my lungs burned, there was a stabbing stitch in my side.

"I think we made it," Cooper said.

"What if someone seen us get on the train?" I asked.

We were still wearing our masks and Cooper pulled off the Gorilla mask. I took off my clown mask also.

"Hopefully nobody seen us," Cooper said. "We can only hope now." He reloaded the shotgun with some shells he had in his pocket. "If they did . . ." he pumped the shotgun ejecting a spent shell and chambering a fresh one. "We'll just have to take care of business. Won't we? I don't plan on going back to prison. They'll have to kill me."

"Sure. I guess so," I said. I checked my pistol and reloaded it.

"What are we going to do now?" I asked.

"We just stay on this train," he said. "We just have to compensate for this detour. We ride this train as far as we can and then find a place to get off. We get on down to Mexico and start our new lives down there, just like we planned. Sound good?"

"I guess so," I said, dumbfounded.

Cooper opened the duffle bag and we started counting the money, looking for any booby traps like die-pack bombs or tracking devices, and found that the money was free of traps and all the serial numbers were sequential. We counted all the money and there was a grand total of seven thousand dollars. Not a great amount by any means, but it was enough to help us out. We put the money away and then Cooper got up and risked opening the door a crack to look back from where we had come. We looked out and saw that we were now heading out into the wilderness. The White Falls River ran alongside the railroad tracks, the water rippling and roiling over rapids in some areas and shallows in others as it wound its way down from the mountains. Autumn was setting in and all the trees, aspen, birch, cottonwood, and alder were changing into their beautiful fall foliage colors. The river was aglow with reflections of different hues and shades of color ranging from gold, red, green to purple. The apple orchards were already stripped and cleaned of fruit from that year's harvest and there was a pleasant smell of wood smoke lingering in the air. Mountains loomed in the distance behind foothills covered with sporadic growths of pine trees.

We relaxed at that point because it appeared that we had pulled it off. We were free; we had gotten away with the bank heist; our plan was working. We were on our way to Mexico. It wasn't over yet, but we were out and, on the run, and they would not take us alive.

"You think we are in the clear?" I asked. "I'm still worried that they might have seen us get on this train."

"I think they would be stopping it by now if that were the case."

"I don't know," I said. "I got a funny feeling—"

"Quit your bellyaching," he said. "You worry too much."

"Alright, Coop," I said. "You're the boss."

"That reminds me . . . Why in the hell did you call out my name back there in the bank? That was just stupid. Now they will be able to figure out who we are."

"It was an accident," I said. "I only said 'Coop'—surely, they didn't notice that . . . or can't figure it out."

"You can bet your ass they will—but it don't matter anyway. We'll be long gone by the time they figure it all out."

We sat down and relaxed, smoking cigarettes and sitting in reflective silence. I was thinking back on how Cooper and I had met in prison. He was a good friend; he had saved me from getting stabbed over a poker debt; I was forever grateful to him for saving my life. I trusted him and I knew that he trusted me. He looked back at me blankly. I couldn't tell what he was thinking. He always had a good poker face. All I knew was that I had known him for almost ten years, and he was like a brother to me. I trusted him with my life, and even though we were fugitives from justice, bank robbers at large, there was still some sort of honor between us. It sounds bad, and it was—looking back on it now, I realize the wickedness of what we were doing—because it was terrible, but we felt justified in our actions, nonetheless.

The train ascended ever higher and higher into the Kootenai National Forrest and soon we were in the coolness of fresh mountain
air. The craggy peaks were beautiful, but it was getting cold, and
Cooper and I were forced to huddle together to stay warm.

"It's damn cold," I said, plumes of icy mist wafting from my
mouth.

"Only up here in the mountains," Cooper said. "We'll be on the
other side of the pass before long and out of this cold weather."
He looked out through the door, the wind blowing his hair back.
"There's a tunnel up ahead. We're going to be in the dark for a minute."

No sooner had he said this, the train entered the tunnel, and we
were plunged into darkness, the only light coming from Cooper's
cigarette. Every quarter of a mile, or so, a small arched top room
with a single incandescent bulb would loom ahead in the distance
and then whisk by in a flash, leaving a green glowing trace in my
eyes and then darkness again. Cooper puffed on his cigarette and
his face glowed orange; sinister plumes of red smoke rose above his
head. After he finished the cigarette, he flicked it through the door
where it hit the tunnel wall and burst into a shower of orange sparks,
quickly sucked away into the wake of the speeding train. The smell
of diesel fuel exhaust from the locomotives was thick and cloying
inside of the tunnel, and it made me wonder about suffocation. Was
it possible? I didn't want to think about it.

"There's the end of the tunnel coming up," Cooper said. He was
leaning out the door and looking ahead toward the front of the train.

"It's about time," I said. "This tunnel is giving me the creeps."

Cooper just looked at me and grunted his disapproval at my
statement.

After what seemed like an eternity in the darkness of the tunnel
we were launched into the brightness of daylight. We were now on
the opposite side of the mountains and it was raining. It was notice-
ably warmer on this side, but it was a lot wetter from the rain, so we
had another element of nature to contend with.

The train began to slow down and eventually came to a complete
stop.

"Why are they stopping?" I asked.

"How the hell should I know," Cooper replied. "They might be looking for us—" He jumped to his feet and grabbed the duffle bag and his shotgun. "We have to get off this train. Now! Let's go!"

"What?" I said, confused.

He jumped down from the boxcar and hit the gravel, his feet already running ahead of him. I wasted no time and jumped down right behind him. I followed him into the bushes and forest. We quickly made our way away from the train. The bushes and undergrowth were wet, and my clothing quickly dampened, along with the rain that was beating down on us. We ran for a long time with no idea where we were going, other than as far away from the train as fast as possible. Cooper stopped several times, listening intently.

"What?" I said. "What are you—"

"Shh," he said, finger to his lips. "Be quiet." He listened, looked around nervously. "Do you hear that?"

I didn't hear anything. "I don't—"

"It sounds like a helicopter," he said. "There . . . hear it?"

I listened again, but still heard nothing, other than the galloping of my heart in my chest.

"Quick," he said at last. "Let's get going."

We waded through high ferns and huckleberry bushes, devil's clubs, and Oregon grape like a couple of wet rats seeking shelter. The rain was coming down now in a steady torrent with drops the size of what seemed like golf balls—they pelted us like hail stones, stinging when they hit us on the face. This was beginning to seem hopeless. We continued through the dense woods for what seemed like hours.

"What the hell are we going to do now?" I asked. "We're lost in the fucking woods."

"Put a cork in it, would you," Cooper said. "We have to improvise. Nobody said it was going to be easy. How's the saying go: 'When the going gets tough, the tough get going' . . . right?"

"I guess . . . if you say so," I said.

We were standing at the edge of a hill and Cooper started descending the muddy slope. When we got to the bottom there was a clearing where several small creeks converged in a delta. We approached the clearing with caution and stopped at the edge to survey the surrounding area. There was a meadow with tall grass and assorted bushes and small trees growing there. Far across the meadow, to our surprise, was an old cottage or cabin, it was hard to tell from where we were standing.

"What do you make of that?" I asked.

"It looks like a cabin to me," he replied.

"Wonder if anybody is home?" I mused.

"It looks abandoned," Cooper said. "Only one way to find out."

He started toward the cabin, careful to stay within the cover of the trees and never stepping right out into the clearing where there was a meadow in case somebody did indeed live there.

"I don't like it," I said. "It gives me the creeps."

"Would you shut up," Cooper said.

"It's wrong. Something isn't right," I said. "It looks like someplace a crazy person—a serial killer or somebody might hideout in."

"Shh," Cooper said. "Quit all that jabbering."

We ducked down and crept carefully up to the rear of the cabin. It was an old, dilapidated dwelling that didn't look as though it had been inhabited for a long time—perhaps since the 1950s. It was constructed from cedar shingles, logs, tin, plywood, glass, and other miscellaneous items. It didn't fit any building plan that I had ever seen before. It reminded me of something John Dillinger might have claimed as a hideout, a place to lay low after a bank robbery, which was fitting considering what we had just done. It would make a good place for us to hide out.

Cooper approached the cabin stealthily like a cat stalking its prey. He sidled up to the cabin in a maneuver that reminded me of a SWAT team raid, peeked into the window, and then after further examination through the glass he ran around the side of the cabin and disappeared. I thought about following him, but I figured it would be a better idea to stay put. I didn't have to wait long before Cooper came back around the other side of the cabin—he had covered the entire perimeter—and motion for me to follow him.

"Get over here," he whispered.

"Is it safe?" I asked, in a hushed tone.

"Just come on, man."

"Okay."

I followed him to the front of the cabin. We stopped there for a moment. The front door was tightly secured by an old rusty padlock. Cooper kicked the door open; the lock broke away easily and the door flew inward. He ran inside, shotgun ready, and I followed close behind him, my weapon drawn and ready. We were greeted by the dank odor of dust, mildew, and age. It reminded me of the smell coming from a root cellar.

Inside of the cabin there was furniture: a wooden table and chairs, a 1960s vintage sofa, a coffee table, a brass lamp stand. All the decorum was outdated, and everything was covered with dust and mildew. What caught my eye was an upright piano against the farthest wall. It seemed oddly out of place. Why would anyone want such a large piano in such a remote place as this? I wondered. There was sheet music on the piano and stacked on a side table. Cooper saw the piano and went directly over to it.

"Look at this," he said. He struck the keys and the piano emitted a horrendous discordant musical cacophony.

"Don't do that," I said. "Leave that thing alone."

"I used to play the piano in school," he said. "I bet you didn't know that."

"No. I didn't."

He put both hands back on the shotgun and finished looking through the cabin. There was a storage room in the back, and beyond that was a bedroom. The bed was neatly made waiting for whomever lived there to climb into it for a restful night's sleep. There was a ladder leading up to a trapdoor in the ceiling. Cooper climbed up the ladder and pushed the trapdoor open. He poked the shotgun up through the hole and then climbed up into the attic.

"Nothing up here," he said. "Just some old boxes of junk. I think we'll be safe here for a while." He climbed back down the ladder.

"What if someone comes here while we are inside?" I asked.

"I pity them," was all he said. "It's going to get dark soon and we need to find some light. I don't suppose the electricity works." He said this as he tried a light switch. Nothing. There was an antique solid-state radio on the counter in the kitchen area. He turned the power switch on, but nothing happened. It was obvious by now that the cabin had no electricity. Cooper rummaged through a drawer and found a butcher's knife, silverware, skewers, and a flashlight—unfortunately, the batteries had died long ago so he put it back in the drawer. After further searching, we found some old Ohio Blue Tip matches, candles, and an oil lamp. The matches were so old that they fizzled and popped when struck, but eventually we were able to get on to ignite and we quickly lit a few candles and the oil lamp.

We made ourselves at home the best we could considering the

circumstances. Cooper, and I, kept a vigilant watch outside to be prepared for any visitors. It seemed safe then, at first, until I found the box of antique books and manuscripts in the back room.

While I was digging around through the meager supplies and items in the cabin—I was hungry and was looking for something to eat, of which there appeared to be nothing. I found an old cardboard box with strange books and manuscripts within. Most of the books were written in a foreign language that I didn't understand, and there were strange drawings and diagrams of what looked to be mythical beings, some of them extremely hideous and grotesque, completely indescribable, and others more recognizable as demons and what appeared to be Satan or a devil. I recognized the words: Satan and Lucifer, even in the foreign script. What was stranger still was the other books which contained musical scores.

"Look at this," I said, handing the books to Cooper.

"What is it?" he asked. He looked at the books, only mildly interested. "Looks like some Satanic bullshit to me. I've got no use for all of that. This music looks interesting, though."

"You can read that . . . music?" I asked, bemused.

"A little bit," he said. "I told you that I used to play—took music lessons back when I was a schoolboy. This is some weird shit, for sure." He stood up and took the sheet music over to the piano.

"What are you doing?" I asked.

He sat down, placed the music on the piano, cracked his knuckles for dramatic effect, and then raised his fingers above the ebony and ivory keys. For a brief instant he looked like a mad composer about to give a maniacal musical recital, and then he struck the keys with his fingers, reading the music from the mysterious and aged manuscripts. The sound that emanated from the old piano was indescribably wretched, chills ran up and down my spine as he played the chords and scales on the piano. It sounded to me like sinister music from a scary horror movie.

"Okay," I said. "That's enough of that." I grabbed him and tried to stop him from playing that terrible music.

He would have continued playing as I struggled with him to stop, had it not been for a sudden noise coming from outside of the cabin. It was an ear-piercing shriek of a banshee, the wale of something injured, followed by an unruly thrashing and crashing through the woods. The sound was much like what I imagined a grizzly bear would make as it crashed through the brush during a full-scale attack on some unsuspecting prey.

"What the hell was that?" Cooper said. He grabbed his shotgun from where he had set it against the wall.

"I don't know," I said, terrified. "And I'm not really sure I want to find out, either."

Cooper went to the door, opened it, and peered outside. He pointed the shotgun in front of him. It was now twilight outside, and an eerie fog had settled in making it hard to see anything at all.

"Can't see a damn thing out there in that fog," he said. "It sounded big—whatever it was—making all that noise."

"What do you think it was?" I asked.

"Some kind of animal, maybe," he said. "How the hell should I know? I don't have all the answers to everything."

Cooper shut the door and locked it from the inside. It wasn't much of a lock, so he braced the door with one of the wooden chairs, wedging it beneath the doorknob.

"If it comes in here," he said, "it is going to get one nasty surprise when I stick this shotgun up its ass."

"What are we going to do now?" I asked. "I mean are we going to stay here overnight or what?"

"We'll hold up here until tomorrow," he said. "I need time to think about what to do. So . . . yeah. We stay here tonight."

"What are we going to eat?" I asked.

"There ain't nothing here . . . so I guess we'll just have to rough it for tonight."

"I'm going to look through this cabin again," I said. "There has to be something we can eat."

"Be my guest," Cooper said. "I don't think you're going to find anything though."

I started looking everywhere I thought someone would, or could, hide food in a cabin such as this. I found a box in the storage room that was underneath some other boxes and to my surprise there was a cardboard box full of military C rations. I picked up the box and carried it back out into the main room. I saw that Cooper was seated at the piano again, but he wasn't playing it. He was intently reading one of the books with the strange writing in it that I had found earlier.

"I found some food," I said.

"Okay. Whatever," he replied. He was too interested in the books to look at what I had in my hands. He hummed an ominous melody that sounded like the music he had played on the piano earlier.

"What are you doing?" I asked.

"Just looking at the music in this book," he said. "This is all so strange."

"Well, anyway. I found some food," I said, trying to get his attention. "They are military C-rations. But I don't know how old they are, obviously."

Cooper started talking about something to do with the music of the spheres and how it could open gates to other dimensions where there were celestial beings that inhabited the inner regions, but I wasn't interested because I was hungry and could hear my stomach growling. I reached down into the box and took out a can of food. That is when Cooper began to play the piano again. The music was even worse this time; it was sinister and had an evil quality; the notes and chords were extremely unpleasant to the ear.

"Quit that," I said. "Have you lost your mind?"

He didn't respond.

"Stop that shit," I said. "That sounds terrible. And what if somebody hears it? You could attract attention, you know?"

He continued to play, growing increasingly animated with each stroke of the keys.

Suddenly there came a terrible noise again from outside, the same as before, only more intense this time. It sounded like there were more of them, whatever they were, gathering outside. I could only imagine what it was out there lurking in the shadows. Outside the window the fog had increased and was thicker, white, so thick that visibility was impossible. I peered into the foggy darkness and thought I saw something sneak past the window. It looked like a large man, but I couldn't be sure. Whatever it was, I knew it was not good.

Cooper continued to play the infernal music on the piano, and I knew that I had to stop him, immediately, or there would be terrible repercussions. I had to stop him at that instant, but it wouldn't be easy. He was enthralled by the music he was playing.

"Cooper, stop!" I said. "Stop playing that piano, man."

I grabbed him by the shoulders and attempted to pull him away from the piano, but it was as if his feet had grown roots or as if he were a stone pillar and I could not get him to budge. He possessed an uncanny strength and solidity that turned him, for all practical purposes, into an immovable object like a giant stone or hickory stump. He swung his arms around wildly and pushed me away, never missing a beat on the piano, the sinister music growing louder and louder, a demented crescendo. I grabbed him by the shoulder and tried again to pull him away, but he stayed steady and firmly seated at the piano.

"Cooper! Stop now!" I screamed in his ear. "You're freaking me out!"

He didn't respond and kept on playing the piano, an insane musician enthralled by his passion, entranced by the strange music written on the pages before him. He was sweating profusely, and his eyes bulged from the sockets. His lips were puckered into an O shape and his eyebrows were raised, his face becoming fiendish. It was as if he was possessed, and I believe that was exactly the case. His pupils glowed a fiery red color and his breath was hot and smelled of sulfur.

"Oh no," I said. "This is bad. You have to stop right now, Cooper."

I tried one last time to pull him away—suddenly outside there was a terrible shrieking like ten demons from Hell and then an insane laughter that reminded me of an experience I had once while under the influence of LSD back in my youth. I could hear a rushing wind blowing outside and then a horrible sound, low and sure, of some cosmic musical notes that seemed to be accompanying Cooper and the piano. The music was so loud now that it shook my very bones. Strange lights swirled about in the fog outside the window like a tie-died neon glimmering light show from a hallucination. I grabbed Cooper's shoulders and pulled back hard, but he resisted me with little effort, his strength of inhuman proportions. One of my hands slid across his sweaty face, and it was cold and clammy, his bulging eyes repulsive beneath my fingers. I tried to tackle him, but he wriggled loose and, in the struggle, a wayward arm swung around and knocked the kerosene lamp down onto the floor. It shattered into flaming shards of glass and one giant tongue of flame that spread quickly across the floor and engulfed the piano and Cooper, even while he still slammed his fingers down on the piano keys. I tried to stamp out the fire with my foot, quickly realized that it was of no use. I searched for something to extinguish the flames with but found nothing. The fire engulfed Cooper and the piano, spreading, and yet he continued to play the piano.

Abruptly, the ground shook as if an earthquake had struck and all the windows in the cabin imploded in a shower of stinging shards of glass. I was knocked to the ground. The fog from outside poured into the cabin and mixed with the smoke from the fire. A wind blew into the room and caused the gaseous vapors and flames to flutter, around and around, creating a maelstrom of smoke and smog and flames. I could almost see demons dancing in the flames, writhing and swaying to the demented music. I climbed to my feet and made one last attempt to rescue Cooper from the demonic inferno. It was too late. I could see his flesh blistering and melting away from the bone, his skull protruding and grinning as his face fell away like molten plastic. He played on and on in his trance, burning, possessed, bony fingers clacking away at the piano keys like an insane writer typing on an old IBM typewriter.

The entire cabin was going up in flames now and I knew then that I was going to be forced to abandon Cooper because he didn't acknowledge that I was there. His eyes were aglow like red hot coals, and he hissed an evil hiss like a serpent. I ran for the door, crashed through it, and fell on the ground outside, gasping for fresh air.

When I caught my breath, I climbed to my feet and took a quick look around, trying to decide which way to run. That was when I saw multiple sets of eyes looking at me from the darkness; there were literally dozens of pairs of red glowing eyes peering back at me. What kind of beings were looking at me I could not discern, but I could see their fiery eyes hovering in the darkness. I was encircled by them. I fled in a panic and ran headlong into the woods. I tripped and fell, crawling on my hands and knees, surrounded by the ever-present watching eyes and the music coming from the burning cabin behind me. I looked up into the night sky and nearly fainted from fear and shock. I felt my heart leap into my throat. I was looking into space at stars and planets that I had never seen before or could recognize. The cosmos was spiraling before my very eyes and seeming to turn ever inward, twisting, and flowing away into infinity like water being sucked down a drainpipe in a sink. It was like a black hole, and it was swallowing everything. I ran headlong through the bushes and trees; a branch struck my eyes causing me to see bright sparks as I ran blindly into the darkness. I could hear the beasts with the red glowing eyes following closely behind me; I could hear the music still playing in the distance; I could hear the black-hole-sucking-spiral-from-outer-space as it consumed all of existence. I was going insane, my grasp of reality slipping away.

After running for what seemed like an eternity, I ran across a deserted highway. There were no vehicles in sight. My feet slapped loudly on the smooth pavement. The red glowing eyes were still following me. I could feel their hatred, and I could hear savage growling and snapping of jaws and gnashing of teeth.

I started to scream like a madman as I ran down the highway believing that at any moment, I was going to meet a terrible end, that I could be torn to pieces and consumed alive by whatever lurked in the darkness. I imagined they would leave only my bloody corpse on the highway. Meanwhile, overhead the spiraling night sky spun around faster and faster, and I felt as though I would be sucked up into outer space into the black hole. Suddenly I was blinded by bright light. I fell to my knees screaming, flailing, and kicking, clawing, and scratching at my own eyes, unable to comprehend what was transpiring around me.

The bright light was the headlights and spotlight from an Idaho State Patrol car. It was the police and I was somewhat relieved, but I was unable to control myself and I resisted the officer as he tried to apprehend me. I was quickly subdued and handcuffed. They thought I was on drugs and that I had gone crazy because I was making no sense, whatsoever. They took me to jail and I was somewhat relieved, at first.

• • •

Looking back on it now, I can remember most of this experience very clearly, yet other parts of the entire event seem so unreal, perhaps existing only in my imagination. I know that it all took place, regardless of what they tell me. I was there and I wasn't on drugs, and I know what I saw. This really happened: the day of the bank robbery I wound up in a fugitive's hideout in the mountains where there was some evil presence summoned forth by the music written in those old manuscript books. Cooper had managed to conjure up an ancient demonic force through some sort of porthole to another dimension when he played that malevolent music on the piano in the cabin. I don't know if it had anything to do with the occult or ancient evil forces from the Bible. I can't say for sure, but I do know that I saw the old books and manuscripts and heard the terrible music and everything I say is true. It really happened, but no one here believes me. The shrink and everyone else here all think I am crazy. What did happen for sure is that I lost a friend that night. I can still see him playing the piano even as he burned to death, trapped, and entranced by the hellish music he was playing.

They told me I was crazy and that I had killed Cooper and burned down the cabin to hide the murder. They told me I was responsible for the murder of a security guard at the First National Bank. I wound up being blamed for everything, and they said I was truly insane, so they didn't sentence me to death—I wish they had, and I begged them to do it in court, but alas, I am still alive. I was sentenced to spend the rest of my life in prison—which would not be so bad if it weren't for the music I hear in my head at night.

Sometimes it isn't just in my head, though, and I can hear the subtle notes of music through the thick glass in my prison cell; sometimes I can hear somebody, or something, humming the melody from just down the hall, mocking me, the sound echoing off of the prison walls. I don't know who it is, but I have my suspicions; I think the Devil walks the halls of this prison at his leisure. This is really his domain, after all; he dwells here; his disciples dwell here; prison is the gateway to hell, in my opinion. Then there are the red glowing eyes outside in the darkness; I can see them at night outside my window, and sometimes they are very close, looking in on me, waiting . . . waiting for me . . . why I don't know, other than just to let me know that they are there, and they are patiently waiting for me to finally come to them. I wake up screaming at night, reliving the nightmare over and over again. The other prisoners tell me to shut up when I wake up screaming.

I have a solution, however: I have a small, thin blade I removed from the disposable razors they hand out for us to shave with, and I have it hidden under my mattress; it will be quick, I hope. They gave me a notebook of paper and a felt-tip pen—the tip is completely smashed and ruined now—and as soon as I finish writing this, I am going to slash my wrists and bring an end to this whole endless nightmare. My hand is numb with fatigue now after writing all of this, so I'm going to stop. I'm not going to let them get me. I'm not going to suffer this anguish any longer. I will not let them get me. They are not going to get me.

The Dead Horse Saloon

After walking for what felt like an eternity in the dark, the desolate road curved and Devin could see a parking lot up ahead immersed in the amber glow of an overhead streetlight. He was close enough to read the sign. The red neon and black marquee letters said,

THE DEAD HORSE SALOON
AND GENTLEMEN'S CLUB
Fine Food and Spirits,
Exotic Dancers,
Karaoke on Thursdays at 9:00 PM

There were a dozen cars and half as many motorcycles parked in front of the building. *This is too good to be true*, he thought, as he quickened his pace toward the saloon.

When Devin stepped inside the first thing, he saw was an exotic dancer suspended upside down on a brass pole wearing nothing but a pair of black, patent-leather pumps. A song by Buck Cherry blasted through the speakers. He could smell cheap cologne, stale cigarette smoke, and beer. Blacklights cast a purple hue throughout the bar and a large, glimmering, mirrored disco ball spun above the stage.

A big man with a cleanly shaved head that shone like polished glass stepped in front of Devin. He was adorned in glistening, diamond earrings. He looked like Mr. Clean, Devin thought.

"You got some ID?" Mr. Clean asked.

Devin took out his wallet and showed his ID card. Mr. Clean examined it with a flashlight, grunted indifferently, and then stepped aside and let Devin pass.

The song finished and the dancing girl picked up her belongings from the stage. She disappeared quickly through a backstage door.

The DJ was sitting behind the mixer station near the stage, wearing black Ray-Bans and headphones, a cigarette hanging from the corner of his mouth. He spoke over the PA system in a thick voice enhanced with an echo effect. He had a tone that sounded like Wolfman Jack.

"Alright," the DJ said, "everybody give it up for Holly."

The crowd applauded with whistles, whoops, and shouts of joy.

"And now get ready for Bobbie Blue. She is bootyliceous," the DJ said, followed with a howl.

The crowd applauded even louder in a raucous tumult.

Bobbie Blue came out onto the stage as a song by AC/DC filled the air—it was a song about a highway leading to Hell. She was wearing a fancy costume of leather and lace with boots all the way up to her ass; everything was blue in color, including her lipstick and hair. She jiggled her breasts and ground her hips to the beat, sultry and seductive, slowly removing her outfit piece by piece.

Devin approached the bar and took a seat.

The bartender ambled slowly over, drying a beer glass with a dishtowel. He was chewing on a Swizzle Stick, a cigarette behind his ear, hair slicked back with Brylcreem.

"What'll you have?" the bartender asked.

"I'll have a beer," Devin said.

"Coming right up."

Devin looked up at the big, Samsung, LED television screen behind the bar and watched with mild interest. It was tuned to a local news channel. A blond bombshell news reporter was speaking into a microphone. There were police cars and fire trucks behind her with lights flashing. Red flairs blazed on the street near what looked to be a terrible automobile accident. The paramedics rolled a gurney with a body wrapped in a sheet into the back of an ambulance. Devin could not hear the TV over the loud music, but he could read the closed caption text scrolling across the screen:

. . . AUTHORITIES RESPONDED TO THE ACCIDENT AFTER A 911 CALL WAS RECEIVED EARLIER TONIGHT . . . THERE WERE NO SURVIORS . . .

Suddenly, the scene on the TV changed to what looked like a slow-motion instant replay with blow-by-blow details of the accident. The volume on the TV increased and Devin could hear it perfectly, even over the loud music.

"How in the hell can they do that?" Devin asked. He was amazed that they could replay an accident. Something wasn't right about that, he thought. "Can they do that?" he asked the man sitting next to him.

The man, who bore an uncanny resemblance to Charles Manson, only shrugged, and went back to nursing his drink.

Back on the screen, a white 1967 Camaro raced down the highway, swerving erratically into oncoming traffic and darting straight toward a minivan.

Abruptly, the camera made a quick cut to the perspective of the driver of the Camaro. Devin could see the shocked look in the woman's eyes as she tried to steer the minivan out of the way. A horn blared, tires squealed and screamed, and then the two vehicles collided, the impact tearing metal and shattering glass.

Devin jerked his head back and covered his face, bracing for the impact. He jumped up from the barstool onto his feet, losing his balance and falling backward. The world spun beneath him as he stumbled and crashed into a table where a man and a woman were engaged in conversation, knocking their drinks to the floor. He landed on his ass in a puddle of beer and cigarette butts from an upended ashtray. He looked around at the crowd. The music stopped and the bar became silent. The dancer on the stage stopped dancing. All eyes were on Devin.

He rubbed his eyes and looked back at the TV where a Budweiser commercial was praising the King of Beers.

Mr. Clean came over to help Devin to his feet, saying, "You alright, buddy?"

"Uh, yeah," Devin said. "I think so."

"What the hell just happened?" Mr. Clean said.

"I don't know. I was watching the news and then . . . I fell off my seat. I was watching TV and then the next thing I know I'm on the floor." He scratched his head as he tried to make sense out of it.

"Sorry about that. I guess I just slipped."

"Don't sweat it," Mr. Clean said, giving Devin a hand up onto his feet. "Shit happens."

Devin hobbled back to the bar and sat down.

"Everything is gonna be alright," Mr. Clean said, giving him a firm pat on the shoulder.

"Thank you," Devin said.

The DJ cued in: "Alright. He's alright ladies and gentlemen. Now let's get back to the festivities. Bartender, get that man a beer."

The crowd cheered as the music blared through the PA system and the girl on the stage resumed dancing, jumping up and spinning around on the brass pole.

The bartender put a Budweiser on the bar in front of Devin and wiped his hands on a dishtowel. Devin reached for his wallet, but the bartender interrupted saying, "This one's on the house."

"Thanks," Devin said. He lifted the bottle and took a drink. It tasted strange; watered down. Was this some kind of joke, Devin wondered. He took another drink and decided that the beer was fine.

He watched the girl dancing on the stage and smiled. She was hot. The night was getting better already. This was ten times better than the party he had attended earlier that night. He thought about how the party had ended . . .

• • •

Devin was bored with the party. It was always the same with college house parties. After a while it just lost its appeal. He didn't care for the whole scene. He was getting ready to drop out of college completely and head out to the West Coast to seek his fame and fortune. Fuck school. Who needed it? He looked at the girls sitting across the table sipping sweet mixed drinks, engrossed in idle gossip. He hated it. He hated them. He came to the party to get laid but now he had lost his mojo and didn't care anymore.

"Don't you ever stop?" Devin said to the girls. "I've heard about all I can stand."

"What?"

"Has anyone ever told you that you talk too much?

"Who asked you, anyway?"

"Nobody. Just stating a fact."

"Why don't you just leave if you don't like it?"

"Maybe I'll just do that. I'm sick of you bitches anyway?"

Devin grabbed Tony and ushered him toward the door; they were going out to get some fresh air.

Outside, Tony stood on the grass shaking his head in a befuddled stupor.

"Let's get out of here," Devin said.

"Are you kidding me?" Tony asked. "There are some hot chicks in there and I'm about to score."

"To hell with them."

"I don't get you. We came here to get laid and now you're acting like an asshole. What gives?"

"I'm over all of this shit. I hate this fucking town. I hate these stupid college bitches. This sucks. Let's go."

"That's all fine and groovy for you. But what about me? I was this close to scoring in there." Tony held his fingers half an inch apart.

"I know. But I'm not interested now," Devin said.

"That's just great. It's always about you, isn't it?" Tony said, tossing his beer bottle into the bushes. "Well, you pissed them all off, so it's probably a done deal anyway."

The door to the house flew open and a muscle-bound jock sporting spandex shorts and a tank top came out onto the porch. He looked at Devin and Tony and said, "Which one of you pricks called my girlfriend a bitch?"

Devin and Tony looked at each other and then back at the jock and then at the parking lot across the street. It was at least a hundred yards, and the jock would surely catch them, Devin thought.

One of the girls that had been sitting at the table came outside. "It was him," she said, pointing at Devin.

"I'm going to kick your ass, punk," the jock said, trotting down the stairs like a WWE SmackDown wrestler. He flipped his hat around with the brim backward and flexed his muscles.

"You're going to have to catch me first," Devin said, breaking into a mad dash across the yard.

Tony was right behind him.

Although Devin and Tony had both run with the track team in high school, they were no match for the jock. He was a professional athlete, a linebacker for the college football team and he was much faster. He was primed, pumped, and ready to kick some ass. He was slowly closing in on them.

Devin knew this would result in a painful beating, especially if the jock's buddies caught up and joined in; it might even result in an ambulance ride to the emergency room. He had to think quickly, using brains over brawn. Still running, nearly out of breath, Devin reached into his coat pocket and felt the Beretta 9mm pistol. Desperate times called for desperate measures, he thought. He pulled out the gun and turned around and aimed at the jock. His heart was pounding in his ears.

"You better stop, or I'll blow your damn head off," Devin said. He pulled the slide back and loaded a shell into the chamber, cocking the hammer to prove he was serious.

The jock skidded to a stop, hesitated, considering the proposition, saying, "You don't have the balls, punk. If you shoot me, you'll be fucked."

"Don't think so?" Devin said, taking aim. "Just take another step and find out."

Tony stopped running, turning around to see what was happening. He saw the gun and said, "What the fuck are you doing? The cops are gonna throw us in jail. Let's get out of here."

"Just turn around and walk away," Devin said to the jock. "We are going to leave and that's that. Alright?"

The jock pondered for a moment, shook his head, spat in the grass, and then adjusted his hat.

"Sure. Whatever you say. But this isn't over. Not by a long shot. I'll catch your ass someday and you'll be sorry this ever happened."

"That's fine by me," Devin said. "I'll be looking forward to seeing you again. Maybe next time I'll shoot you for real. Now get the fuck going before I do it right now."

"Okay, okay. I'm going," the jock said, turning and starting back toward the house where a large crowd was gathering on the lawn.

Devin started away, backpedaling, and watched as the jock went back to the house. When the jock was far enough away, Devin turned and ran across the street to his car with Tony close behind. They jumped in the white 1967 Camaro and raced way from the scene, the 350 high output engine revving explosively down the road.

"Man, this is not good," Tony said. "They're going to call the cops."

"They won't catch us," Devin said. "We'll be ten miles away before the cops get here."

Devin pulled out onto the highway and stepped hard on the throttle. The speedometer needle climbed past 100 miles per hour as they shot away into the night.

"Slow down," Tony said. "You'll get us killed."

"Shut up!" Devin said, looking over at Tony. "I know what I'm doing." He accidentally swerved into the opposite lane over a solid yellow line and into oncoming traffic while his attention was diverted from the road.

Suddenly, a minivan came around the corner and impact was imminent. The woman driving the minivan tried to swerve out of the way, her face an expression of terror and shock as she anticipated the impact. There were children in the minivan. Devin could see them. The headlights were bright. The sound of screeching tires was a prelude to a horrendous crash.

"Lookout!" Tony shouted.

"Holy shit!" Devin said, swerving to avoid the collision.

Both vehicles went into uncontrollable skids, crashed into each other with tremendous force, and then spun away like pinwheels. The Camaro smashed into a tree and the minivan flew off the embankment, slamming into the rocks below.

• • •

Devin opened his eyes and looked around at the dark interior of the wrecked car. It took him a moment to realize what had happened. A ticking noise coming from the engine compartment and the smell of burnt rubber and gasoline brought the reality and horror of the accident back with sudden comprehension. He moved and his leg throbbed with a sharp stabbing pain as he turned and looked at Tony.

"Tony . . ." he said. "You okay?"

He saw that Tony was knocked out cold. His breathing was labored, and his chest heaved. There was a large gash on his face and blood bubbled from his lips.

"Tony. Wake up," he said. "Oh man, wake up. Everything is going to be alright. Don't you fucking die on me. It can't end like this."

Tony wasn't dead, but he was very close to it. The blood bubbling from his mouth was proof of that.

"Shit," Devin said. "Wake up, Tony. Oh, fuck me, man. I'm going to get some help."

Devin pried the door open and crawled out onto the grassy hill. He staggered and fell climbing up the slippery embankment. He mounted the summit of the hill and stepped onto the road. He stumbled to the other side and looked down into the ravine where he could barely see the smoking wreckage of the minivan by the light of the moon.

His stomach lurched as he puked on the pavement. He wiped his mouth on his sleeve and began to panic.

Looking both ways, he saw that the road was deserted and desolate, and dark. He reached in his pocket and took out his cell phone. He turned it on only to read: NO SERVICE.

"Shit," he said, smashing it on the ground.

He started walking down the road, limping from the sharp stabbing pain in his leg. He would find help somewhere; the first house he came to would surely have a phone, he thought. After about a mile he grew faint, stumbled, and then passed out cold on the side of the road in the damp grass. Everything faded to black.

When he awoke sometime later, he couldn't remember anything. So, he got up and started walking, completely unaware of the automobile accident or even who he was.

• • •

Devin was startled from the memory when a heavy hand landed on his shoulder, snapping him back to reality. It was Mr. Clean.

"You going to be alright?" Mr. Clean asked.

"Holy shit!" Devin said. His memory came back with complete recollection, everything flooding back into his mind in an instant. "I've been in an accident. I may have killed someone."

It was all coming back to him now. He must have suffered some sort of amnesia or something, he realized, because he couldn't remember any of it until now. The accident he had seen on the TV was real. He was the driver of the Camaro. Somehow, he had survived the accident and made his way to this seedy bar; now he was drinking beer while people lay dying at the scene of the crime. The police, emergency crews, ambulances, and reporters were already there now so what could he do?

He had to do something; he had to own up to his responsibility. He looked around the bar, stood up and shouted at the top of his lungs: "There's been an accident down the road. People are hurt. I need a ride. Who can give me a ride?"

Nobody responded.

He couldn't believe this. This was an emergency and they were all ignoring him.

"Did you hear me? I said there's been an accident and I need some help!"

The bartender came over and said, "Listen, you need to calm down. You're upsetting some of the customers."

"What?" Devin said.

"Sit down and have another drink."

"Didn't you hear what I said?"

"Yeah, I heard you," the bartender said. "But did you hear me?"

Devin felt his temper flaring. This couldn't be happening. This had to be a dream. He was growing more hysterical with each thump of his heart. He ran toward the stage, turned toward the DJ booth, and grabbed the microphone. The DJ didn't try to stop him.

"Listen," Devin said into the microphone. "Everybody listen . . . there has been an accident. I need someone to take me there so I can see if my friend is alright."

The music stopped and the girl, Bobbie Blue, quit dancing. The room was silent for a moment and then everyone began to boo and hiss and throw beer bottles and ashtrays at Devin. The DJ snatched the microphone back.

"Everyone just calm down," the DJ said in his monotonous announcer's voice. "Never mind this idiot."

Devin looked at the DJ in disbelief.

"Go sit down," the DJ said into the microphone. "Nobody wants to hear about your problems."

The crowd cheered.

Devin was speechless. He looked around, dumbfounded, in complete despair. This was insane, he thought. He turned and ran toward the door. It was locked and wouldn't budge. He yanked on the doorknob until he realized it was hopeless and then he fell to his knees and began to sob hysterically. It was too much. He was breaking down. What had his life come to? He was sure this was a nightmare and he would wake up any moment screaming, safe at home in his bed. Please, oh please, he thought, let this all be a dream.

"We got a live one, folks," the DJ said. The music began to play again; it was Lynyrd Skynyrd singing about a free bird. "You'll only find this kind of fun at the Dead Horse Saloon . . ."

Devin sat on the floor, his head spinning in circles as tears rolled down his cheeks. It was hopeless, he thought.

The bartender picked him up from the floor and led him to a stool at the bar. Devin resisted at first, but Mr. Clean assisted and together they sat him down on the barstool. The bartender put a bottle of beer in front of Devin and said, "Relax. Everything is going to be alright. Don't worry about it. There isn't anything you can do now."

"Let's get back to having some fun. What do you say?" the DJ announced.

The crowd cheered again.

Another pretty girl came out onto the stage and began dancing, taking off her clothes. The patrons went back to business as usual.

Devin didn't know what to do. He watched the girl dancing. It was like an LSD trip. His entire life flashed before him at high speed. Images of people and places that he loved. He thought about the people involved in the accident. The lady and her children. Tony. They were probably all dead. He shook his head, a solitary tear rolling down his cheek. "What have I done?" he said to no one in particular. "Oh God, what have I done?"

"He can't help you now," a voice said, bringing Devin out of his stupor.

"Huh? What?" Devin said, observing that it was the guy that looked like Charles Manson. "What did you say?"

"It's too late for that," the man said.

"Too late for what?"

"Help from God. He can't help you now."

"What the hell are you talking about?" Devin said.

"Look," the man said, pointing toward the window by the door, "out there."

Devin swiveled around on his bar stool. He stood up and walked slowly to the window. He couldn't believe what he was seeing.

Outside, in the parking lot, standing like zombies, Devin recognized Tony and the woman and her two children. They were covered in blood and lacerations, flaps of skin and hair hanging askew. They looked in through the window, pointing accusingly at Devin. He could feel guilt swelling in his chest and throat.

"It can't be," Devin said, putting his hand against the cold glass. "What are they doing out there?"

Suddenly, Tony began to glow with a bright white intensity, and then the woman and children started to glow as if they were illuminated by floodlights with millions of fireflies swarming around them. They changed to a translucent, vaporous, green hue, and their forms began to melt and merge, wavering, waxing, and waning, like a candle flame in a gentle breeze. They swirled around, faster, and faster, merging, becoming one and turning into a fantastic green glowing tornado, rising into the sky. Leaves and debris swirled around in the wake of the twister. It reached high into the night sky, illuminating the clouds.

Hurricane force winds emanated from the cyclone. The clouds overhead roiled and rumbled, lightning bolts licking the gaseous twister, snapping, and crackling with electric intensity. A horrendous thunderclap shook the glass under Devin's hand, and then a tremendous flash like an exploding atomic bomb followed, blindingly bright. He put up his hands to block the piercing light and closed his eyes.

"Oh my God," Devin said.

When he opened his eyes, the parking lot was empty except for the swirling cyclone of debris that slowly settled back to the ground. It was dark again, and the streetlights seemed sinister now, like the glow from a haunted house jack-o'-lantern. It was silent in the room behind him. He stood motionless, staring out into the parking lot, afraid to turn around. He could feel all the eyes in the bar on him; everybody in the room was watching. He felt the tiny hairs prickling along his spine.

The DJ broke the silence over the PA, saying, "Wow. Now that was quite a light show, wasn't it folks?"

Devin still didn't turn around. He was looking out into the parking lot where the cyclone had been. Terror filled his veins like ice water.

"It's time to get back to business," the DJ said. "Everybody give it up for Jessica Fox."

The crowd applauded. Music blared through the speakers with Rob Zombie singing about a living dead girl.

"Did you guys see that?" Devin asked, turning around.

When he turned and looked at the customers in the bar he was filled with absolute dread. The patrons of the bar had transformed. They were all pale and withered and crawling with maggots. The girl dancing on the stage was a corpse. She gyrated her hips, spun around and then did the splits. Her jaw fell off and landed on the floor. She rolled her fishy white eyes and quickly reached down and picked it up, snapping it back into place. The guy that looked like Charles Manson had changed into a demon, serpentine, with horns, and claws. He looked at Devin and laughed.

Devin swooned and almost fainted right then, but he managed to stagger to the bar.

"Welcome to the club," the demon said. "You are our newest member."

"What?" Devin said. "I don't want to be a member. I just want to go home. This can't be real."

"Oh, this is real," the bartender said. "This is your home now. You are one of us. Forever. Nobody ever leaves the Dead Horse Saloon."

Devin looked at the bartender. He was all festering sores and maggots. A beetle was crawling around in an empty eye socket.

"No. I am not."

"Take a look for yourself," the bartender said. He pointed to the mirror behind the bar.

Devin looked and was struck with overwhelming horror when he saw his reflection. He was staring into the eyes of a mangled corpse.

"No," he said. "That's not me. No way."

He turned and ran to the door, grabbed the handle, and yanked hard. His bloody hands slipped from the brass knob. The door was locked and wouldn't budge. He pulled the doorknob with all his might, pushing and kicking, beating his fist against the door. It was of no use. The door wouldn't budge. He looked out the window and noticed that all the vehicles parked in the lot were rusty and broken down from years of disuse. The lot itself was overgrown with weeds and spindly trees. The neon sign was no longer lit and now the marquee displayed three words:

CLOSED FOR ETERNITY

The Angel's Ballad

Alex Ramsey saw the sign that read YARD SALE and stepped hard on the brake. He brought the black 1969 Pontiac Firebird to a screeching halt in the middle of the busy street.

"What are you doing?" Lucas Kirby said.

"Over there," Alex said, pointing a finger. "They're having a yard sale. Let's go check it out."

"A yard sale?" Lucas said, skeptically. "Since when did you become interested in yard sales?"

A car honked its horn behind them alerting them to the fact that they were holding up traffic.

"One man's trash is another man's treasure," Alex said. "Do you want to go, or not?"

The car behind them honked again. Alex could see the driver in the rearview mirror shaking his fist angrily.

"I guess so. If you insist." Lucas said.

Alex pulled over and let the impatient motorist behind him pass; the driver sped past with a roaring engine and his middle finger pointing long and high into the air—flipping them the bird—his face a twisted expression of rage.

"Jesus," Alex said, as he parallel parked in front of the house where the yard sale was taking place. "Some people are just ticking time bombs. That guy has got some issues." He turned off the engine.

It was midsummer in June of 2019, and the weather was fine this time of the year in Longview, Washington. Cumulous clouds floated lazily in the blue sky and the sun shone down warmly. Overhead in the trees, robins and goldfinches were fluttering about merrily chirping out birdsongs. It was a picture-perfect late afternoon for a yard sale. Alex and Lucas climbed out of the car and looked at a handful of people milling around the items that had been stacked neatly on tables, shelves, in boxes, in organized rows around the yard. There were elderly people, couples, children, and some teenage girls—Alex and Lucas spotted them right away—milling around, looking at the items for sale.

The most interesting individual of all was an elderly man in a wheelchair. He was watching over the people in the yard and he had a small card table next to his wheelchair and on the table, there was a small adding machine and what appeared to be a cashbox. As they approached the stairs that led up to the yard, a young girl went to the old man and gave him five dollars for a china tea set.

"Thank you very much, miss," the old man said, snatching the bill from her dainty hand. "Will that be all for you today?"

"Yes," she replied. "Thank you."

The old man lifted his arthritic hands, shaky and knobby knuckled, and took a pencil from his ear, licked the lead, and clumsily wrote out a receipt on a carbonless notepad. He struggled to rip the page loose, finally pulled it free, and then gave her a copy. "Please do come again," he said. "I'll be here for a few more days, or until everything is gone."

"Okay," she said, walking away with her prize in a box.

Alex watched the old man, curious and amused. Lucas became lost among the vast array of items in the yard; his attention was instantly caught by a box full of 45 rpm vinyl phonograph records.

"Wow," Lucas said aloud to no one in particular. "Look at all of these. . . ." He thumbed through the records and found such rarities as: The Beatles, Elvis, The Rolling Stones, and other rare collectibles. He couldn't believe his eyes and that these gems were right within his grasp and for sale at such a low price. The price on the box said, All Records $1.00 each. He estimated that there were probably two hundred or more records in the three boxes, and he wanted to buy them all. "Some of these will be worth a fortune on eBay," he said, looking around to see if anyone else had noticed the treasure he had found. No one was paying any attention except for Alex and the old man. Alex walked over to where Lucas was standing and flipped through the stacks of records.

"I thought you didn't like yard sales," Alex said.

"I wasn't expecting anything like this," Lucas said. He already had a handful of records he intended to keep.

The old man rolled up stealthily on his wheelchair and surprised Alex and Lucas when he spoke: "Hello, boys. Those are some fine specimens there, don't you think? Those records are all in mint condition."

"What, er, huh?" Lucas said, embarrassed, feeling as though he had been caught stealing.

"Those records," the old man said, pointing with a bony finger. "I hate to get rid of them—but . . . everything must go."

"Why so cheap—" Alex started to say but was suddenly cut off by Lucas.

"Never mind that," Lucas said. "It's a fair enough price." He looked at Alex and scowled. "Why don't you look around and see if you can find something *you* like." He motioned with his head as if to say, *go away . . . you're blowing this for me.*

"Alright," Alex said, catching the hint. "I'll just look around then." He looked at an old tool box on the table in front of him and feigned interest.

"You boys from around here?" the old man asked.

"We sure are," Alex said, just as he was preparing to walk away. He stopped and looked back at the old man, and said, "Born and raised right here in Longview. We go to the Mark Morris High School every day, except on weekends, of course."

"Wonderful. So did I," the old man said. "I was an honor roll student. It's my alma mater. It is the best high school in town."

"That must have been a long time ago," Alex said. He was wondering how long ago that would have been; he did the math in his head and came up with at least sixty years ago.

"Yes, I'm old," the old man said, winking at Alex. "Seventy-eight, to be exact. But that don't mean nothin. I've lived a long and happy life. I don't expect a young whippersnapper like you would understand, anyway."

Lucas went back to digging through the records and found a Jimmy Hendrix record titled "Little Wing." His heart jumped in his chest; this one was a rare find.

"Well, it is a nice day for a yard sale," the old man said. "You two take your time and look around and see if you find anything that strikes your fancy."

"Sure thing," Alex said, bemused. "We'll do that." He saw that Lucas was engrossed in looking at the records so he went his own way and looked around lazily at the other items in the yard, only mildly interested now; he was ready to leave—the old man gave him the creeps for some unknown reason.

Lucas, on the other hand, was finding all kinds of treasures that he intended to turn over for a tidy profit on eBay. There were antique scales and weights, a large box full of model train sets, some military memorabilia—all of which he knew was worth a fortune on eBay (he couldn't help but wonder why the old man didn't put the stuff up for auction himself, but, oh well, one man's loss was another man's gain) and he would reap a tidy profit. There was one item, however, that Lucas noticed suddenly, and his jaw dropped when he looked at it: six-string nylon acoustic guitar unlike any other he had ever seen. It was made from a solid cedar top with mahogany back and sides and a clear gloss finish. It had a rosewood fingerboard and bridge and stylish rosette inlay. It glowed warmly in the afternoon sun. The mother-of-pearl tuners and gold hardware blazed like a heliograph reflecting the sunlight, blindingly bright and causing Lucas to squint. He hurried over to the guitar and strummed the strings. The guitar emitted a beautiful sound like notes plucked on a harp. It was in a hard-shell case that was lined with plush purple crushed velvet. He had to have this guitar—there was no way around it. He picked up the guitar and strummed it gently. He didn't really know how to play guitar all that well, but he did know a few chords and he was an accomplished pianist and he could read music, so he played a few chords and it issued such a melody and harmony that even the birds in the area seemed to stop and listen.

"This is awesome," he said. "Alex . . . look at this."

Alex was holding an old bamboo fly-fishing rod and real. He looked over at Lucas and said, "What have you got there?"

"Come and look at this," Lucas said. He turned the guitar over, looked for a price tag, but he found nothing. It was of no importance, however, because he was willing to pay handsomely for it—almost any price, no matter how high it might be. He could not find a name brand, make, or model on the guitar. He had an idea that the guitar was custom-made and that only added to his desire to have it.

The old man noticed that Lucas had taken a keen interest in the guitar and he quickly rolled his wheelchair over to where Lucas and Alex were standing and admiring the guitar.

"She's a beauty, ain't she?" the old man said.

"Sure is," Lucas said. "But you don't have a price tag on it."

"I'm sorry," the old man said. "It must of plumb slipped my mind. I've been busier than a one-legged man at an ass kicking contest lately, what with all of this, and it's really been hard to get anybody to help out with the work involved. A yard sale is a lot of work."

"You're doing all of this by yourself?" Alex asked, incredulously.

"No. Of course not," the old man said. "I'm a cripple, you know? There ain't no way in blue blazes that I could have done all of this by myself. I've got family and friends helpin out." He licked his lips.

"Anyway," Lucas said. "How much do you want for this guitar?"

"Hmm," the old man said, contemplating. "It's a rare one, and it's worth a pretty penny. It's handmade, you know, custom made by a luthier all the way down in Paracho, Mexico back in nineteen-forty-five, I think." He scratched his head. "I can't remember now, exactly. I suffer from chronic C-R-S."

"What's that?" Alex asked.

"Can't remember shit," the old man said, bursting into a fit of laughter that sounded like dry thorns crackling on a fire. "Oh, that's a hoot. I just love that one. But it's true. I can't remember anything, really. It's kind of nice, if you ask me. I don't have too much to worry about anymore. C-R-S. Do you get it?"

"Uh, yeah," Alex said, looking on in surprise at the old man. "I get it." He raised his eyebrow in astonishment. He was thinking that the old man might be a liar and that the guitar was just a piece of crap made from balsa wood in China and that the old man probably really suffered from Alzheimer's and was a chronic bullshitter. "Hand made in Mexico, you say?" Alex quizzed. "Let me see it." He took the guitar from Alex and examined it closely. He couldn't find any labels, marks, or numbers that might identify the make and model of the guitar.

"It's a one of a kind," the old man said. "I wouldn't lie to ya. Got no reason to lie. If you don't want it . . . don't buy it."

The old man was visibly offended by Alex.

"It's beautiful," Lucas said. "I've got to have it. How much do you want for it?"

The old man scratched his head again, lost in deep thought, and then after a moment his face lit up with a smile and he said, "Make me an offer I can't refuse. How much are *you* willing to pay for it?"

Lucas dug out his wallet and began counting his money.

Alex was growing increasingly suspicious of the old man and now he looked at him as nothing more than a shyster. This whole scenario reminded him of a movie or a novel he had read once, but he couldn't quite put his finger on it. It was just an odd situation—or so it seemed to him.

"What did you say your name was?" Alex asked the old man, as if it was suddenly important.

"I didn't," the old man replied, "But, if it makes ya happy, my name is Stewart P. Ward." He extended his hand in a friendly gesture. "And what might your names be?—since we are being all right and proper and getting acquainted all of a sudden."

"I'm Alex Ramsey," Alex said, shaking Stewart's hand, "And this is my best friend, Lucas Kirby." Alex noticed that the old man's hand was cold and clammy, and it felt like a freshly caught rainbow trout. He quickly let go and wiped his hand on his pant leg.

"You are a feisty one, aren't you?" Stewart said, looking Alex in the eye.

"Well, just looking out for a friend, is all," Alex said. "In fact. Maybe I should check online to see what that guitar is really worth. This is two-thousand-nineteen, after all, and we do have the Internet . . . so I'll just take a look on my phone and see what I can find."

"You do that," Stewart said. "I guarantee that you will find that I am telling the truth."

Alex took his Android cell phone from his pocket and tapped the screen, bringing up Google Chrome.

"Just a second here . . ." Alex said. "Here we go. Guitars . . . yep. What is the model number on that one? Any ideas? I couldn't find one, so that leads me to believe it's a knockoff."

"A knockoff?" Stewart said, alarmed. "You are insulting me, son. I told you it is a one-of-a-kind. Handmade in Paracho, Mexico. Look that up on your fancy phone."

"Alex, what are you doing?" Lucas asked.

"Just doing a little research. Checking the facts. We'll see how much a guitar like that goes for on eBay or Amazon. He probably peeled the Made in China stickers off to disguise the fact that it is a cheap guitar."

"Tsk-tsk," Stewart said. "I don't think I like your tone."

"Here we go," Alex said. "Guitars . . . handmade in Paracho, Mexico. Here is one listed for only three hundred dollars, brand new. So, the one you have here can't be worth that much . . . especially at a yard sale."

"You are a real thorn in my side. You do realize that, don't you?" Stewart said, looking at Alex.

"How much are you asking for that guitar?" Alex quizzed. "It better not be too expensive, because this *is* a yard sale, and it *is* used, and we don't even know if it's authentic, at this point."

"I don't know," Stewart said. "How much you got?"

Lucas had finished counting his money and looked up, saying, "I've got forty-eight dollars and seventy-five cents." His face was twisted into a confused grimace and he was thinking that this might not be nearly enough for such a fine guitar. "Is that enough?" he asked.

Stewart pondered for a moment. He scratched his stubbly chin and said, "She is a right nice guitar and she did cost me a pretty penny . . . but I can't play her anymore because I got terrible arthritis these days—" He held out his bony hands with knobby knuckles protruding to demonstrate. "—And unfortunately, I need the money more than anything at this point. I got the cancer and don't have much time to live. Trying to get rid of everything quick . . . so . . . you can have her for forty-eight dollars and seventy-five cents, I guess."

Alex made a surprised guffaw and rolled his eyes saying, "This thing isn't even worth that much. I don't think so, anyway."

Lucas said, "Obviously you don't know the value of guitars." He handed the money to Stewart. "Consider it sold."

Stewart took the money and struggled to stuff it into the cash box with his arthritic hands. "I will write you a receipt," Stewart said, rolling away on his wheelchair. He went to the table and grabbed the pencil and notebook and awkwardly scribbled a receipt. It took a moment because he kept dropping the pencil and couldn't hold the notebook down with his crippled hands. He finished the receipt and handed it to Lucas.

Alex looked at Lucas and said, "Are you crazy? Your stepdad is going to flip out when he finds out you spent all your money on an old guitar."

"It's not really any of his business," Lucas said. "It's my money, after all. I earned it. Plus, it's less than fifty bucks. Big whoopee. My shoes cost more than that."

Suddenly, Alex was reminded of the tale of "Jack and the Beanstalk," for some odd reason, perhaps because much like that story, there would be an upset mother—and one very angry stepfather—when this transaction was over and Lucas went home with his guitar, which would really be nothing more than magic beans to them.

"I don't think you should buy that guitar," Alex said. "Something isn't right about this."

"What could possibly be wrong?" Lucas said. "I like this guitar and I aim to keep it—no if, and, or buts about it. There is nothing wrong with it."

"I guess not," Alex said, defeated. "If it makes you happy . . . then I guess you should go for it."

They looked at Stewart as he examined the receipt. He seemed lost in thought. After a moment he chuckled to himself and then looked back at Alex and Lucas.

"Is that going to be all you boys are buying today?" Stewart asked.

"I got this fishing rod," Alex said.

"I want those records too," Lucas said, "but I don't have enough money with me."

"I'll be having this yard sale until everything is gone," Stewart said. "So, you can come back in a day or two for those records."

"But what if they are already gone by then?" Lucas said.

"I'll put them to the side for you and mark them as sold," Stewart said. "Just come back and get them when you get the money. Don't leave me holding the bag, though. I must sell everything as quickly as possible. I got bills to pay, you know."

"I sure appreciate that," Lucas said.

"Now you take care of that guitar," Stewart said. "She kept me company through some great times in my life . . . but she also got me through some hard times, too. Sometimes playing the blues on her was the only thing that kept me from losing my mind.

This statement made Alex apprehensive. Something about losing one's mind—or Stewart in particular—didn't sit right with him. There was something unsettling about the old man, but he couldn't put his finger on it.

"Thank you so much," Lucas said. "I will take good care of it—"

"Her," Stewart corrected. "She's a girl."

"Okay," Lucas said. "I'll take good care of her."

"I'm sure you will," Stewart said, smiling. He winked at Lucas with a look that said he knew things were going to be just fine.

"We should get going, now," Alex said. "I have a hot date tonight, so I hate to break up this little party, but . . . ."

"Fine," Stewart said. "You boys come back and see me later."

"Yeah. Right," Alex said. "You betcha."

Lucas gathered up the guitar, put it away in the hard-shell case and they turned and began to walk back to the Pontiac Firebird parked on the side of the road.

Stewart shouted at them as they walked away: "The Lord be with you boys. May he watch over you and send his angels to watch over you both. Take care boys, and God bless you both."

"Alrighty then," Alex said, hopping down the stairs and simultaneously pulling his car keys from his pocket. "That is one strange old dude."

Lucas was following happily along, smiling brightly as he approached the car. "He seemed fine to me," Lucas said. "And what an awesome deal he gave me on this guitar."

Alex opened the car door and climbed inside. He put the glimmering key in the ignition and twisted it, turning over the starter motor until the engine responded with a roar. Lucas opened the passenger side door and put the guitar in the backseat and climbed into the passenger seat and shut the door behind him. Alex put the car into gear and pulled out onto the road; Lucas looked back and waved at Stewart—the old man smiled and waved back, as he watched them drive away.

"I'm kind of hungry," Alex said. "What do you say we stop at Applebee's and have a burger?"

"I think that sounds like a great idea," Lucas said. "We can celebrate my new guitar."

"Not what I was really thinking, but if you say so."

"I say so," Lucas said. "You know . . . I'm not sure I want to leave my guitar in the parking lot when we go inside."

"The doors will be locked."

"What if someone breaks the window out?"

"Just quit it," Alex said. "No one is going to steal your guitar. Okay? You're being paranoid."

"Alright," Lucas said. "I just don't want to lose her before I even get a chance to play."

Alex rolled his eyes and sighed. He was beginning to see a trend: Lucas was becoming obsessed with the guitar. They pulled into the Applebee's restaurant, parked, and locked the doors, and then went inside, and enjoyed a juicy hamburger, French fries, and a Pepsi cola. All Lucas could think or talk about was the guitar and this vexed Alex to no end.

• • •

After finishing their burgers and departing Applebee's, they drove through town, past the Mark Morris High School, then out into the suburbs of Longview, past frame houses and gated communities and farms and orchards where you could pick your own fruits, berries, and vegetables. It was a stunning day and the sun was just beginning to set over the horizon filling the sky with hues of blue, pink, and gold.

"I can't believe you bought that guitar," Alex said.

"Why not?" Lucas said.

"Because," Alex said, shrugging. "I don't know. You just don't seem like the guitar playing type."

"And what does that mean, exactly?" Lucas asked.

Alex thought about this for a moment and then said, "You just seem too . . . bookish."

"And what is that supposed to mean?

"Just what it means," Alex said. "You're a not really a rock-and-roll kind of guy."

"Bookish? Rock and roll? That's ridiculous," Lucas said.

"Yes. Bookish," Alex said. "You read lots of books and you get straight A's in school. You are not the typical rock and roll stereotype I would expect to see playing a guitar."

"So, what are you saying?" Lucas asked. "I'm a nerd?"

"I didn't say that," Alex said.

"Yes . . . you did," Lucas said. "In a roundabout way—that is exactly what you are saying."

"Not a nerd, exactly," Alex said, turning the steering wheel sharply. "Just . . . bookish. It's not a bad thing, by the way. You wear Coke bottle glasses and you aren't really a hit with the ladies, if you know what I'm saying."

"Oh. I see what you're getting at," Lucas said. "Just because I don't have a girlfriend you think I'm a nerd," Lucas said, angrily. "And now that I've bought a guitar you think that I am trying to perpetuate some sort of rock and roll cliché, or something. I'll have you know that I play the piano very well, thank you, and I know enough chords on the guitar to play most songs. You know that already. So, why do you have a problem with it?"

"See what I'm talking about?" Alex said. "Perpetuate. Who uses words like that?"

"I do," Lucas said, defensively. "It's just the way I talk. Is something wrong with that? I use the appropriate words that suit the ideas I wish to express. Sorry you don't understand all of them."

"Now you're just being a smart-ass," Alex said. He sighed and turned the steering wheel sharply and pulled up in front of Lucas's house. "I understand what the words mean, but it just makes you sound so . . . pretentious. I just think you need to lighten up a little bit. You're just so anal retentive sometimes."

"Pretentious? Retentive? Look at you using big words. That's a good one," Lucas said. "And all this coming from you, Mr. C average, or should I say three point oh? And speaking of girls, what about you and your failed relationship with Christina? Are you going to tell your 'hot' date about Christina?"

"I'm still mixed up about that relationship," Alex said. "What can I say? Everybody knows I'm still in the middle of a break-up with Christina. We just aren't close anymore. I'm not telling anyone about it. It's nobody's business."

"You should be over all of that by now," Lucas said. "She's ancient history. Isn't she? Get on with life."

"Yeah," Alex said, sighing deeply. "So, you say. Some things are hard to get over—including Christina Bishop."

"I understand," Lucas said. "Anyhow, I better get inside and take care of my homework before Steve gets home."

"What are you going to tell him about that guitar?" Alex quizzed.

"I don't know yet," Lucas said. "He really shouldn't care too much. He likes music. I don't see why he should care about me buying an old guitar at a yard sale. It was my own money, after all." He said this to reassure himself, but they both knew that the truth was that Steve—Lucas's stepfather—would probably be very angry about the guitar. The fact was that Steve was angry about everything all the time and anything that Lucas or his mother, Theresa, did usually was ground enough for an insane rampage of anger, violence, and aggressive behavior that would leave a wake of destruction in its path. Steve also was a terrible alcoholic and often drank excessively and would terrorize Lucas and his mother with violence and physical abuse.

"I hope everything is going to be alright," Alex said. "If not . . . get a hold of me."

"It'll be okay," Lucas said, halfheartedly. "I can handle it."

"Well," Alex said. "All I'm saying is if that asshole gets out of hand . . . you need to do something about it. He can't keep on hurting you and your mom like he does. It just isn't right. He deserves to go to jail."

"Don't worry about it," Lucas said. "I appreciate your concern—I always have—but it is something that is bigger than just calling the police. My mom loves him, and she isn't going to just have him arrested. You know that. And she would never forgive me if I called the police and had him arrested."

"That just sucks major ass," Alex said. "If you ask me, he needs his ass kicked in a big way."

"I know how you feel," Lucas said. "But it's all in God's hands now. He is the only one who can stop it."

"Sure. Whatever," Alex said, displeased with the thought. "I don't think that is going to happen in this lifetime. God hasn't been making too many appearances lately."

"Everything will be fine," Lucas said, reassuringly. "God is alive and well. Don't you forget that. Pretty soon I'll be eighteen and after graduation I'll be leaving for college and then I won't have to deal with it anymore."

"That's good for you," Alex said. "But what about your mom?"

"I don't know," Lucas said. "Hopefully she'll wake up and realize that he is a worthless piece of shit and she'll leave his sorry ass."

"Not soon enough," Alex said.

"It's always the same old situation, no matter how many times we talk about it," Lucas said. "It never changes or goes away."

Alex sighed again and said, "That's too bad, bro. I'm so sorry for your situation and bad luck in life."

"Nothing you can do about it," Lucas said. "It will work out in the end. I've got faith—aren't you going to be late for your date?"

Alex looked at his watch and said, "Holy shit. You're right. I've got to go, man."

"See you later," Lucas said, getting out of the car.

"See ya on the rebound, dude," Alex said.

Lucas grabbed the guitar and his duffle bag from the backseat, shut the door, and then watched as Alex backed out of the driveway and then shifted gears and shot down the street. He could hear the souped-up engine in the Pontiac Firebird roaring as it faded into the distance. He opened the front door and stepped through, entering the house.

• • •

Lucas was greeted by his mother in the living room.

"Hey," she said. "How was your day?"

"It was okay," Lucas said.

She gave him a kiss on the cheek.

"What's that?" she asked, pointing down at the guitar case he was holding in his hand.

"It's a guitar I bought at a yard sale," Lucas said, setting down his duffle bag full of schoolbooks. He placed the guitar case on the couch and opened it, taking the guitar out and displaying it to her.

"Wow," she said. "That's nice."

"It's awesome," Lucas said.

"How much did it cost?" she asked.

"Fifty bucks," Lucas said. "Can you believe that? Fifty bucks for such a beautiful guitar as this?"

"I guess that's a good deal," she said, her tone had a hint of disapproval. "But I thought you were saving your money for a car? You know Steve isn't going to be very happy about that."

"He'll understand," Lucas said, optimistically. "When I explain how good of a deal, I got he can't help but like it. Not to mention that it was handmade in Mexico. It's a one of a kind. It's probably worth a lot more than fifty dollars."

"How do you know that?" she said, looking at him with piercing blue eyes.

"Stewart—the old man at the yard sale told me," Lucas said. He turned the guitar over. "There are no stickers or labels or anything to say where it was made . . . and besides that, you can't even touch a cheap used guitar at the pawn shop or on eBay for fifty dollars—at least not one in as good of condition as this one—and it came with a hard-shell case, too. All that for fifty bucks. That's a steal."

She sighed, bewildered, and said, "You better keep it out of sight for the time being. Let me talk to your father—"

"He's not my father," Lucas said, bitterly.

"—about the guitar," she finished.

"He'll never be my father," Lucas said. "You know I don't like it when you try to put words in my mouth. I will never recognize him as my father, or call him that, ever!"

"I understand how you feel, honey," she said, sweeping his bangs away from his eyes, delicately, with her fingers. "But you know that I love him, and that he really loves both of us—"

"Bullshit!" Lucas said. "He's too hateful to love anybody—including himself."

He could tell that she wanted to slap him, tell him to stop talking in such a manner as this, but she refrained; he knew that she loved him too much to hurt him; the truth was that her husband did enough hurting for everyone in the household and she was powerless to stop it.

"Don't say that," she said. "Please don't talk about him like that."

"I'm going upstairs," Lucas said. "I'll be doing my homework." He closed the guitar case, picked it, and his duffle bag up, and went upstairs to his bedroom.

• • •

Inside his bedroom he felt better; this was his sanctuary away from everything; sometimes he would sit there in silence and meditate in solitude, and other times it was his only retreat and refuge away from his tyrannical stepfather. Many times, he had overheard fights between his mother and Steve; sometimes there were just arguments, and other times there was physical confrontations. He hated it; he wished he was someplace else, anyplace else in the world as far away from Longview and Steve as he could get—and soon he would make this a reality—but as for now he was stuck in this terrible dilemma. His room was decorated much like any typical seventeen year old boy would have done; there were posters of famous rock bands and musicians, a Dell computer sitting atop a cherry wood desk with a colorful screensaver depicting fish in an aquarium, complete with audio effects that sounded like air bubbles in water and the crashing of surf on the shore, there was a bookshelf full of books, a lighted globe of the Earth, a lava lamp, and model aircraft suspended from the ceiling by monofilament line. It was his place and he spent a lot of time there.

He set down his book bag and took out the guitar from inside the hard-shell case. He was absolutely amazed by the astonishing crafts-manship and detail that had been given to the guitar. He put his fin-gers on the strings and fretted a chord, strumming and plucking with his other hand, his fingers caressing the strings ever so gently and lovingly. He felt joined to the guitar as if he and it had become one.

Outside his window a gust of wind blew through the trees toss-ing the branches and leaves about as if they were dancing to the music he was playing. The resonance of the guitar in his room and the acoustics were excellent and the sound was rich and deep and pleasing to his ear. He played various combinations of the chords he knew. The songs he played had melodies and harmonies inspired by classical musicians from the Baroque period such as Bach, Pagani-ni, and Mozart. The moment was pure bliss. He would have contin-ued playing the guitar forever but then he noticed the papers inside of the hard-shell case. He hadn't noticed them before, so he reached down and pulled the pages from within the pocket in the purple plush velvet lining. There was a whole stack of loose pages, some joined together with a paperclip, other single, some stapled together, but they were all musical in nature. He took the stack out and spread the papers out on his desk. Some of them were chord diagrams and instruction on how to fret the chords and how to read the diagrams, and others were bits and pieces of songs. Some of the songs had lyrics; some of the songs were written by hand in pen or pencil and others were Xerox copies or printouts from a computer; some of the songs used standard musical notation, and some of them were in a tablature notation that used graphs and numbers to represent notes and strings; some of the songs were nothing more than cheat sheets with chord diagrams over the lyrics, and on some of the pages there was nothing more than the alphabetical letter that represented the progression of chords over the lyrics.

Lucas was fluent in most of the musical notation, and he was amazed at some of the complexity involved in the melodies and harmonies. He recognized some of the songs as old ballads and blues riffs, and folk songs, but some of them appeared to be completely original and were simply amazing in their form and composition. He wondered if these sheets of music had come from the hand of Stewart—the old man in the wheelchair at the yard sale. It seemed like a logical conclusion.

It was puzzling to Lucas, however, that the old man was letting go of such a fine instrument and his original compositions—but he knew that stranger things than this had happened. He had heard of a case where a man purchased some old books and papers from a Goodwill thrift store and that the boxes contained an antique map of the world and some original musical compositions by the likes of Back, Beethoven, and Mozart, that were all worth a substantial amount of money. Why in the world had the old man let the guitar go so easy? Lucas wondered. He had said he needed the money because he was sick with cancer. That might explain it. It just seemed odd, but it was to Lucas's advantage and he wasn't going to make too much of a fuss about a good thing such as this.

Maybe he would revisit the old man tomorrow and buy the records and bottles and other items he had been looking at today. He thought that would be prudent—but he would need to get into his savings and that meant that he would have a confrontation with his stepfather—Steve—and that might get ugly. There had to be a way that he could please all the concerned parties and walk away from it better off than he had begun. He knew that if he catered to Steve's greedy nature, he could probably convince him that it was a good investment and that after he sold most of the items on eBay that there would be a handsome return and profit margin and that this would undoubtedly appeal to his stepfather's capitalistic point of view. It was risky—especially since he had already bought the guitar without first consulting Steve—but it was worth the gamble and Lucas was certain that his calculations were correct and that his instincts were true and it would all work out in the end—unless he aroused

Steve's anger and incited a tyrannical rampage—and for that he would just have to wait and hope.

Lucas turned his attention back to the sheet music on his desk; he shuffled through the pages noting the specifics with some of the composition such as tempo and key. Some of them had strange key signatures and odd tempos that reminded him of funeral dirges or death marches, and others had somber undertones in the accompanying lyrics. Some of them were inspired by Mississippi Delta blues players such as Muddy Waters and John Lee Hooker, and some of the ballads had amazing lyrical and poetic compositions that were every bit as beautiful as anything Shakespeare, Shelly, Poe, or Frost had ever penned yet as funky and hip as Bob Dylan or Jack Kerouac. He thumbed through the pages, occasionally fretting a chord, or playing a melody from some of the staffs and notes until one piece in particular caught his attention. The title on the page was catchy: "The Angel's Ballad." The music and lyrics were even of more interest. Some of the verses were heavenly as if they had been taken straight from "The Book of Psalms" in a *King James Bible* and the melodies and harmonies were equally as beautiful as anything ever composed during the Baroque period of classical music.

The wind picked up outside the window again; a ferocious gust shook the trees blowing any loose leaves down to the green lawn below. A scrap of newspaper blew up and lodged on the chain link fence and the clothes on the clothesline swayed and danced on the breeze, as if ghostly spirits had dressed up in the shirts and pants hanging out to dry and were dancing to the music Lucas was playing. He could see his dog, Sam, a black Labrador Retriever, at the edge of the fence barking hysterically at something in the cypress, juniper, and other evergreen shrubs that decorated the perimeter of his back yard. Sam was a good dog, but sometimes he went crazy when a squirrel, raccoon, or cat came into his territory and he would bark insanely unless he was brought inside the house until he forgot about the whole ordeal. He must have spotted something because he was presently at the fence doing cartwheels and running in circles barking in all of his excitement at whatever it was that he had spotted.

Lucas strummed another chord and let his fingers walk down the strings following the notes on the page. He hummed along with the melody. It was simply divine. After playing it for a while it suddenly became second nature to him, and the notes and chords flowed effortlessly from his fingers and the guitar. He closed his eyes and envisioned heaven in all of its glory with hills of green, skies of blue, clouds drifting lazily over golden streets and palaces and walls made of alabaster and pearl, a place where everyone was at peace and angels flew around in the sky with wings spread wide playing harps and singing praise; it was a majestic vision—even though he knew that some of it was stereotypical and trite—he enjoyed it nonetheless.

When he opened his eyes there was a face staring back at him through the bedroom window. It was a beautiful face, an androgynous, angelic face with big, soporific eyes.

"What the—" he said, startled, jumping up from his chair and nearly dropping the guitar.

He blinked and the face was gone as quickly as it had appeared. He rubbed his eyes with his free hand. His heart was beating wildly in his chest like the galloping hooves of a racehorse. Surely it was his imagination playing tricks on him; perhaps it had been his own reflection looking back at him. He was sure that he had to be seeing things because his room was on the upper floor of the house and anyone on the outside would have to climb up on the roof and then would be forced to lean over at a precarious angle in order to get a peek into his window. He shook his head and rubbed his eyes again. He leaned over his desk and peered out the window to get a better look.

• • •

When Lucas went outside the air was brisk and cold. It was on the verge or raining, and the first few drops were spattering against his face. He went around the house to where he had observed Sam and stood, looking on curiously.

Sam, the dog, was now jumping about and barking up at Lucas's bedroom window as if he too had seen the peeping Tom. Lucas was sure he was imaging all of this, but he decided that it warranted further investigation, so he left his bedroom and went downstairs through the kitchen and patio door out into the backyard where he stopped on the deck and looked around. Sam was jumping up and down excitedly and doing backflips as he barked at the wind.

"Come here Sam," Lucas said. "What is it boy?"

Sam ran to Lucas, tail wagging and tongue protruding from his mouth, strings of drool dripping to the ground. He jumped up with his muddy paws onto Lucas's clean white shirt.

"Get down," Lucas said.

Sam dropped down onto all four paws and ran in a circle; he acted as if he wished he could tell Lucas something—if he could just speak, he had something of the utmost importance to say—very important but he lacked the vocal capacity to put it into words; he ran this way and that way and then stopped to see if Lucas was following.

"What is it?" Lucas said, becoming aware that Sam was trying to coax him into following along. "What do you see, boy?"

Lucas followed Sam around the corner of the house to where the dog was sniffing around anxiously. Sam sniffed here and there and then stopped and sneezed. A large white feather drifted down on the breeze and landed near the dog. He sniffed it and sneezed again. *AH-CHOO!*

"What is that?" Lucas said as he walked over and picked up the feather.

It was unlike any feather he had ever seen before: it was large and white like a swan feather, but it had a brilliant colorful sheen like alabaster or mother-of-pearl, and it was blindingly bright in the afternoon sun. It was remarkable, yet painful to look at because of its brightness.

"Wow," Lucas said. "It's beautiful."

Sam let out another sneeze: *AH-CHOO!*

"Wonder what kind of bird it came from?" Lucas said. "Looks like a goose feather, or a swan."

Sam lost interest in the feather and trotted away, stopping to sniff the air and then decided that he had better things to do like poop and then dig a hole near the fence.

"You stop that," Lucas said, scolding Sam again. "Quit that digging. You know Steve will kick your but for that."

Sam ran away around the house with his tail between his legs. He found a Day-Glo orange ball that was laying in the yard and insisted that he wanted to play fetch. When Lucas didn't respond Sam tossed the ball up in the air and played catch by himself.

Lucas looked up at his bedroom window and wondered if he

was going crazy. He was certain that he had seen something like a human face looking in at him through his window—and his dog, Sam, had acted like he saw it too—but what, or, better, who had it been? The face seemed to be that of a pretty girl in Lucas's memory, but perhaps that was just his imagination filling in the blanks. It was beginning to seem like a hallucination now, however, and Lucas wondered if he might be losing his marbles. There wasn't anybody around and there were no signs of a prowler, so he decided to forget about it and went back inside, anxious to get back to the guitar. He went in through the patio door.

• • •

Inside, he was taken by surprise when he saw that his stepfather, Steve, was home from work and standing in the kitchen—he had been watching through the sliding glass door.

"What are you up to?" Steve asked.

"Nothing much," Lucas said, closing the sliding glass door. "Just checking on Sam."

"What was he barking at?"

"I don't know," Lucas said, looking at the feather he was still holding in his hand. "I think there may have been a bird flying around out there—"

"What kind of bird?"

Lucas was struck by the odd idea that he was playing twenty questions with Steve all of the sudden.

"I don't know," Lucas said, "but I found this feather outside—"

"Let me see that," Steve said, snatching the feather from Lucas's hand. "That's one hell of a feather. It would have to be a giant swan or something and we don't have those kinds of birds around here. Are you trying to pull some silly shit with me?"

"No. I found that feather outside," Lucas said. "I thought it might have come from a bird—"

Steve smacked Lucas on the back of the head with his palm. "Don't back talk me, boy."

"I wasn't," Lucas said, realizing that he was trapped; no matter what he said, and that silence would also get him into equally as much trouble as a smart remark. "I just thought that—"

"That was your first mistake," Steve said. "You're not old enough to *think* about anything important." He handed the feather back to Lucas. "That ain't no bird feather from around here. How dumb do you think I am?"

"Thank you," Lucas said, taking the feather from Steve's hand. "I'm sorry—"

"Stop it with all of that queer bullshit," Steve said. "I just came in here to get a beer—not to hear any of your silly wisecracks."

Lucas was thinking about how much he really loathed this man that his mother loved so much; he truly detested this man; sometimes he fantasized about a world in which the asshole did not exist at all. He didn't truly understand why his mother tolerated Steve's antics other than she was blinded by what she thought was love, or she was just scared of him. Lucas couldn't understand why Steve disliked him so much, either, or why the man had to be so mean. It was as if he was inherently evil and chose to be an asshole just for the sake of it. There had been numerous occasions in the past where Steve seemed to make progress and then as quickly as a gunshot at a track meet—ready, set, go—bang, the moment was lost. Steve would instantaneously revert to his insidious wickedness and would inevitably ruin the moment, especially when he was drinking. The worst part about all of it was that his mother always came to Steve's rescue and would defend him, and always justified his actions in some trivial way. In her eyes the man could do no wrong and she would defend him jealously, even after he had beat her senseless in an insane rage and, even once or twice, after he had nearly killed her.

It was a big crock of shit as far as Lucas was concerned, and he was over it.

"May I go now? Lucas asked, cautiously. He was always on edge around Steve, walking on the proverbial eggshells.

Steve was digging through the refrigerator frantically searching for a beer. He found one, turned, closed the refrigerator door, popped the top off the bottle, took a drink, belched, and then wiped his mouth with the back of his hand. He looked at Lucas with disdain and said, "Yes. Get out of my sight you little worm." He then yelled to Theresa that he was out of beer and needed to go to the store to buy some more.

Lucas left the kitchen in a hurry, still as always, wondering what his mother saw in the man. He was just glad to get away from him, never wanting to be near him for too long because it usually resulted in some form of abuse, be it of the physical or mental variety. He passed his mother in the hallway and she had difficulty making eye contact with him; it was obvious that she didn't like the way her husband treated her son, but she was powerless to do anything about it. They didn't exchange any words as they passed each other but he could tell that she wanted to say she was sorry for the way Steve acted.

Lucas went upstairs to his room and closed the door behind him.

• • •

He sat down at his desk and examined the white feather he had found in the yard. It truly was beautiful, as far as feathers go, with colors that seemed remarkable and incredible. He decided to look on the Internet on his computer to see if he could find any information about feathers that might be like the one, he now possessed. After searching for a while on Google, he located some feathers that were like the one he had found, but none that were a perfect match. The closest matches he could find were goose and swan feathers, which were prized for use in the past as quill pens.

He already knew that much.

Quill pens could be an explanation that worked for him, though— the feather obviously didn't come from a bird flying around his house so it must have been imported by human hands—and he decided that maybe somebody had lost a quill pen in the neighborhood and the wind had blown it into his yard.

In any case, Lucas put the feather away in his pen and pencil holder—a Ball caning jar—and decided that he should get his homework done because it was getting late. Dinner would be ready soon, he knew, and he would have to do the dishes afterward.

He looked at his recently acquired guitar and had an urge to pick it up and play it, but he resisted and began doing his homework instead, which took almost an hour, and after that he played a video game— Diablo III: Ultimate Evil Edition—on his Xbox game console until it was time for dinner. He heard his mother call him downstairs when dinner was done.

• • •

Lucas went downstairs and sat at his usual spot at the dinner table; Steve was already seated at the head of the table and was busy shoveling peas, mashed potatoes, and meatloaf into his mouth; Theresa was making a fresh pitcher of lemonade at the sink, stirring it with a long plastic spoon, lemon slices and ice cubes swirling around in the yellowish liquid inside the glass container—she brought the pitcher to the table and poured a glass for Steve, then Lucas, then one for herself. She sat down and placed a cloth napkin on her lap.

There was an awkward moment of silence—this wasn't unusual, but it was always uncomfortable—and Lucas or Theresa would have to say something because Steve didn't talk much when he was eating, and he wasn't much of a conversationalist in the first place.

"So how was your day?" Theresa said to Steve.

"It's always the same, every day," he replied. "The whistle blew at the factory and I was happy as hell to get out of there. Nothing changes. It sucked, really."

She put food on her plate and ignored his rude statement.

Lucas broke the tense moment saying, "Finals are coming up in a couple weeks."

Steve grunted; Theresa smiled but said nothing.

"I'm hoping to make the honor roll this semester," Lucas said. He suddenly remembered the guitar and—with certain trepidation—he felt his testicles shrivel up into his abdomen as he thought about a confrontation with Steve that would inevitably take place in the near future in response to the guitar, he had purchased from the yard sale. He looked at Steve, who was staring blankly as if he was in a trance, looking directly at the candles and the centerpiece on the table. He chewed his food like an automaton, reminding Lucas very much of a dairy cow chewing its cud. Lucas hoped that his mother wouldn't bring the topic up yet, at least not right then, because there would surely be an outburst of rage from the presently sedate Steve after he heard about the guitar. Lucas put some potatoes on his plate, constructed a channel in the mound and then poured on some beef gravy, creating a semblance of a volcano, and then he helped himself to some peas and meatloaf.

Theresa looked at Lucas with a knowing gleam in her eyes as if to say, *don't worry, son . . . I've got it under control.* She then looked at Steve and said, "So . . . what do you have planned for this weekend, honey?"

Steve grunted, washed down his food with a long drink of lemonade, let out a long belch, and then said, "I think I'm going out to the hayfields with the guys to shoot some skeet and train the dogs with decoys. I'm taking Sam out to give him a workout."

"Oh, okay," Theresa said. "That sounds like fun. Maybe Lucas would like to go." She turned and looked at Lucas—he looked back at her as if he had just been caught doing something extremely naughty, his face turning several shades of pale. He felt like a fish hooked by the lip and his mother had been the one to bait the hook. He didn't dare say that he didn't want to go because that would ensure that Steve would insist that he go; he didn't want to say that he wanted to go because he still might end up going. It was a lose-lose situation, and he was trapped.

Steve hiked his leg and cut a long, loud fart.

Theresa said, "Steven. Where are your manners?"

"More room out than in," he said. "That's what I always say. I don't think he should go. I don't think the guys would be comfortable—and besides we all agreed that we would leave the women and children at home this trip."

Lucas, relieved to be off the hook, looked at Steve and wondered how the man had made it this far in life with such basic social skills and etiquette; he knew that Steve only had a basic education and whenever his intelligence was insulted he would go crazy and throw a fit; he was fond of saying, "I know stuff." However, Lucas knew of one topic in which Steve was both knowledgeable and astute: he knew almost everything there was to know about cars, motorcycles, and mechanics in general—and he should, after all, because he was a certified mechanic and he worked at a local GM assembly plant where they put together engines and vehicles on an assembly line. He also enjoyed building hot rods in his spare time. Lucas knew that he could always count on this as an ace in the hole to bail him out of a bad conversation, and that Steve would always take the bait and jump into the conversation eager to show off his knowledge and to fantasize about dream cars.

Lucas swallowed a mouthful of food and said, "I saw an eighty-eight Camaro for sale today."

Steve chewed thoughtfully on a piece of Texas toast, saying

nothing.

"It was really nice," Lucas said. "They only wanted two thousand dollars for it."

"That's too much," Steve said.

"It's an Iroc-Z, though," Lucas said, pleading his case, but aware that too much of an argument could bring an ensuing disaster.

"Uh-huh," Steve said. "That was a very nice vehicle—Dale Earnhardt drove one of those back in the day. Two thousand dollars is okay for one of those—if it isn't all beat to shit—that is."

"It was in really good shape," Lucas said. "I looked it over—and it only had one hundred and twenty thousand miles on it."

"That's a lot of mileage," Steve said. "But if the body is good then the engine can be rebuilt. It might be worth looking into. Where did you say you saw it?"

"It is right down by the high school," Lucas said.

"Maybe we should go over and take a look this weekend," Steve said. "After I get back from my trip out to the hayfields, that is. How's that sound?"

"Awesome," Lucas said, feeling that the ice was melting between them and that he had gained some common ground with Steve. He thought about bringing up the topic of guitars, but then reconsidered, deciding not to press his luck. It was always a dangerously touch and go situation with Steve.

"Maybe Sunday," Steve continued, getting up from the table. "Might even go fishing—just you and me. What do you think?"

"That's wonderful," Theresa said, for want of anything better to say. She was always glad at moments like these when the two most important men in her life seemed to be getting along, no matter how fleeting or short-lived were the moments.

Lucas looked at his mother—she was glowing and radiant. She was such a wonderful mom and she was so sweet—he loved her very much. On impulse, without thinking, Lucas said, "I bought a guitar today." He thought that now was the best time to bring up the subject.

Theresa dropped her fork.

There was an uncomfortable silence that seemed to last for an eternity.

"How much did you spend on it?" Steve asked, nonchalantly. "You know you were supposed to be saving up your money for a car."

"It was only fifty bucks for the guitar," Lucas said, surprised that Steve was being so docile about the whole thing. "I still have plenty to buy a car with."

"I thought your mom and I were clear that you were supposed to ask us before you spent any money—especially on something as useless as a guitar."

"Yes. But—" Lucas said.

"Don't make excuses!" Steve shouted. "I have a good mind to ring your scrawny little neck the next time a sound comes out of it. So, you better watch your mouth right now."

"Please, Steven," Theresa said, rising to Lucas's defense. "Don't make such a big deal out of this. It's just a guitar—a very nice guitar."

"Don't you get started either," Steve said, pointing his finger in her face. "I won't stand for both of you teaming up on me—the last time I checked . . . I was the one paying the bills around here. I'm the one who makes the important decisions. Right?" He slammed his fist down on the table for emphasis.

Silence ensued for a beat.

"Well," Steve said, demanding an answer. "Don't everybody speak at once. I make the important decisions . . . right?"

"Yes, dear," Theresa said, mechanically. "Now, please calm down. You're making a mountain out of a molehill."

Lucas was terrified and enraged at the same time; he as afraid of the man and enraged that his mother was such a pushover. He was helpless to do anything about it, however, even if he wanted to; but he had fantasized about inflicting some wicked physical injury on Steve before but lacked the testicular fortitude to act out this fantasy; he just didn't know exactly what to do about it. The point was moot.

"I think I'm old enough to make my own decisions," Lucas said, sounding like the cowardly lion from the *Wizard of Oz*. The words spilled from his mouth before he could take them back; he was speaking from somewhere deep within himself that he never knew existed. It was like steam pressure had built up inside and now he needed to let it out. "I'm not a little kid anymore and I deserve some respect. I earned that money on my own and—"

"Boy," Steve said, clenching his fists. "You had better not bite off more than you can chew. Right now, you are about this close"—he held up his hand with his index finger and thumb only a millimeter apart— "to really pissing me off. And we both know what happens when I get pissed off, don't we? I suggest you shut your ever-loving pie hole before I decide to close it for you. Capeesh?"

Lucas nodded, all his steam was gone and now he was terrified at the repercussions that would follow from his outburst.

"He's right, you know," Theresa said, still feeling the maternal urge to defend her son.

"Don't you tempt me, woman," Steve said, raising his hand up in the air as if he meant to strike her. "I'm not in the mood at all. Now, I'm going to leave before I lose my temper and wind up doing something I might regret later."

Steve went to the refrigerator, took out a beer, and went into the living room where he flipped on the television and sat down in his leather La-Z-Boy recliner. He opened the bottle of beer and took a long drink then belched loudly. This was an image of Steve that Lucas would never forget.

Lucas and Theresa began cleaning up the dinner dishes without saying a word. After dinner the leftovers were put away and all the dishes were finished. Lucas kissed his mother on the cheek and said, "Goodnight." He went to the bathroom, and then went upstairs. He could hear his mother and Steve arguing—presumably about the guitar—so he crept stealthily up the stairs, careful not to step on the stair that squeaked, in the hopes of getting away unnoticed. When he got to his room he went inside and carefully closed the door behind him.

He was tempted to play the guitar but decided that it would be terrible timing to do that, so he fed is goldfish, turned off his computer, slipped into bed and read several chapters from a novel by Kurt Vonnegut about aliens from a planet named Tralfamadore. He grew sleepy after that, so he turned off his lamp and closed his eyes, falling into a deep sleep where he had a dream about dying and going to heaven where he was floating around and playing a guitar.

• • •

The following Saturday, Steve was hanging out with his buddies; they went out to the hayfields shooting shotguns at skeet and training their young retrieving dogs—one of which was Sam. This outing usually included driving their monster mudder trucks through the bogs on the outskirts of town and making a dirty, muddy mess of the landscape, themselves, and their vehicles. This was an event that had been a ritual of Steve's since time immemorial.

Out on the hayfields, Steve, Billy, and Norton pulled their trucks, a Ford, a Dodge, and a GMC Sierra, into the field by the lake and parked. They got out with their shotguns, decoy ducks, skeet targets, and canvas training throwing dummies for the dogs. Steve had brought Sam, and Billy and Norton each had two dogs, for a total of five dogs: one golden Labrador retriever, Sam, two black Labradors, Jack and Sparky, and two German shorthairs, Poo and Blitz.

"So, how's that stepson of yours doing these days? Is he still a pussy?" Billy asked Steve.

"Yes," Steve said. "His mom has got him so spoiled. I don't know what I'm going to do. Hopefully he'll move out when he turns eighteen. That's really all I can hope for, to tell the truth."

Norton opened a cooler in the back of his truck and pulled out cans of Coors banquet beer. He passed the cans around. They all drank their beer, looking like something out of a King of The Hill cartoon. This was how they liked to spend their free time. If they weren't shooting their guns at helpless animals or killing fish, then they were wrapped up in events that centered around such activities which included cleaning and loading guns and bullets, shopping at Cabela's, and when there wasn't anything else to do watching Babe Winkelman and Buck McNeely on TV; or, if hunting and fishing momentarily lost its appeal—which never happened—they would sit around watching ESPN or any other type of sporting event that they could find, including heavyweight boxing and the Ultimate Fighting Championship, mixed martial arts fighting, or, in a pinch, professional wrestling.

"Yep," Billy said. "That's how it goes. You gotta put up with a brat when you marry a woman who already has kids."

"It's not that bad, is it?" Norton asked. "I get along just fine with *my* stepson."

"It is that bad," Steve said. "I can't get along with that kid no matter how hard I try. He is just a little sissy. I am always trying to make him toughen up. I think he is like a girl sometimes."

They laughed at that thought.

"Maybe he is," Billy said. "Maybe he will get a sex change soon, and you will have to call him Lilly, or something."

"I hope not," Steve said.

"Aw, just give him some time," Norton said. "He'll man up eventually. Kids are just like that when their young."

"I guess so," Steve said. "Now let's get to working these dogs. I didn't come out here to talk about my stepson. I'll have to deal with him when I get home, so enough."

"You got it, buddy," Billy said.

They loaded up their twelve-gauge shotguns and went out into the field with the skeet and a hand clay pigeon thrower.

"You're up first, Steve," Norton said. "I'll throw and you shoot."

Steve assumed a shooter's stance and said, "Pull."

Norton threw a clay pigeon up in the air and in an instant, Steve fired his shotgun and blew the orange disk into bits and pieces in midair. They repeated the process, taking turns shooting and throwing.

After the shooting was done, they focused on the dogs. They would throw the canvas dummies out into the water where they had placed the decoy ducks, and then let the dogs chase after them, bring them back, and then do it again, and again, and again. The trick was in the repetition. The dogs would learn through receptiveness and the sound of the guns would trigger their response.

"Let's have a drink," Norton said, producing a bottle of Jim Beam bourbon.

"Don't mind if I do," Steve said, taking the bottle, and twisting the cap. He poured a long drink down his gullet and grimaced at the burn in his throat. "Oh, yeah. That's what I'm talking about." He handed the bottle to Steve.

"Thank you kindly," Steve said. He took a drink, then another. "Mmm. That's good."

They passed the bottle back and forth until they were good and drunk. Nothing mixed better than guns and booze, in their opinion. You could get drunk and howl at the moon and just let loose and have a good time, safety be damned. Nobody ever got shot by accident just because they drank a little whiskey, they would argue. This is what men did; and they were proud of it. They were men's men and they did things that were manly, including smoking cheap cigars, cussing, farting and a lot of scratching wherever they might be itching. These activities were full of male bonding and beer drinking and the best part of all was that it was just "the guys" and no wives or snot nosed kids were involved—the wives and kids were usually overjoyed to be excluded and see them go away.

After a while, Steve and his friends were drunk and decided that getting into the mud in their trucks sounded like a good idea. They collected their dogs and other belongings and headed over to the dirt road that led into a tremendous muddy pit of ruts, puddles, and bogs.

Steve went in first in his GMC and kicked up mud and grass everywhere in a rooster tail. He was so drunk now that he was almost seeing double. It was good fun, though, and he turned up the radio to listen to some Hank Williams Junior full blast while he drove like a madman through the muddy pits and hollows. He held on tight to the steering wheel and stepped down hard on the accelerator. This was going to be a blast. He didn't care about going home. That would come later. For now, he was just going to enjoy the day with his buddies. That was good enough for him.

• • •

Lucas woke up that morning, stretched and yawned, rubbing his eyes, and reacquainting himself with the waking world and its surroundings. He was hungry and he knew that his mother would make him a scrumptious breakfast, which usually consisted of scrambled eggs, toast, ham, juice, milk, peaches, and anything else he might desire. He climbed out of bed, dressed in casual clothes, and sat down at his desk, turned on his computer and waited for it to start up. He would check his e-mail first, simply out of habit, or maybe login to Facebook for a while, and then he would go downstairs. This was a Saturday morning ritual. The computer clicked and whirred as it powered up, the familiar operating system logo flashed across the LCD screen saying that it was loading, please be patient, one moment please. . . .

Most of his e-mails consisted of spam with advertisements for Viagra and pornography; he never understood how he had been targeted for these spam messages and reasoned that the unscrupulous spammers just targeted everybody with an e-mail address at random with brute force tactics. There was one e-mail message from Alex that contained some crude jokes and then invited him to join in on the fun. He clicked on the link and it took him to YouTube where there was a video recorded by a man talking to his mom—off screen—about a strange, ugly cat he was filming in his yard that reminded him of his grandma.

Just then, Lucas received a text message on his iPhone. It buzzed, vibrating on his desk. He picked it up and read the message from Alex.

Hey. You alright? Basically, just wanted to see if you still wanted to go back to that yard sale. I wouldn't mind picking up some of those old records. I looked into it, and those things are worth a mint on eBay. It was just an idea. Maybe? Let me know. Later, bro.

Lucas read the message and then sent him a quick reply.

Yes. I'm fine. Thanks for asking. I do want to go back to the yard sale, but it might not be a good idea right now. I want to play my guitar for a while today. I'll get in touch with you later and we can talk about it. TTYL.

Lucas looked out his bedroom window and saw that it was the beginning of another magnificent sunny day and he decided that after breakfast he would go out into the backyard and play the guitar on the patio. With this in mind, he gathered up the sheet music and put it into the guitar case, closing it and snapping the brass latches; he picked up the guitar case and left his bedroom, and went downstairs.

• • •

Lucas joined his mother in the kitchen; she was drinking coffee and watching a home improvement show on a small flat panel TV mounted on a wall. There was a newspaper spread out on the table in front of her.

"Good morning," Lucas said.

"Are you ready for breakfast?" she asked, looking at the guitar case in his hand.

"Yes," he said, setting the guitar down. "I am starving."

She got up and began cooking his breakfast, still watching the TV as she moved around the kitchen.

"Steve is not very happy about that," she said, looking at the guitar. "But I think I've got him calmed down enough to leave it well enough alone."

She dumped liquid scrambled eggs into a frying pan; they sizzled and sputtered in the hot lightly oiled pan.

"That's good," Lucas said. "I don't understand him. Why does he have to be such an . . . *asshole* all the time?"

She looked at Lucas for a moment as if she wanted to cry, and then she said, "He's just a typical man. Hopefully you will strive to be different and be a peaceful loving kind of man. He can't help himself."

"You're always making excuses for him," Lucas said.

"Just leave it alone," she said, exasperated. "Please don't let it ruin such a lovely day."

There was another uncomfortable silence—which was getting increasingly common these days, Lucas thought—and then she placed his breakfast before him on the table. The plate of food was steaming. He tore into the food with a vigorous gusto.

"I have some errands to run this afternoon," she said. "So if you need anything let me know before I leave"—she looked at the clock, saw that it was almost noon—"and that means within the next fifteen minutes or so, okay? I have to get ready, now."

"Mm-hmm," he hummed with a mouthful of eggs.

"Good," she said. "Will you be alright by yourself?"

"Yes, Mom," he said, feeling like a little kid again. "I'll be fine—I'm not six years old anymore. Go do your thing . . . and don't worry about me. I'll be fine. Promise."

He mopped up the traces of eggs from the plate with a piece of toast, popped it into his mouth, and then licked the plate clean, washing it all down with a glass of orange juice.

She saw that he was finished and picked up his dirty dishes, quickly washed them in the sink, and then dried them and put them away.

"I thought you were in a hurry," Lucas said, as he watched her put away the dishes.

"I am. I just didn't want to see those dirty dishes in my clean sink," she said, drying her hands with a towel. "Now I'm really going to get ready this time."

"I'm going out into the back yard to play my guitar for a while," he said, getting up from the table. "Oh, I almost forgot. Alex sent me an email asking if I wanted to go back to that yard sale for the records and bottles today. Is that alright with you?"

"You might want to ask Steve," she said, hesitantly. "You know how he is about things like that. And with you buying that guitar already . . . I don't know."

"I want you to tell me 'yes' or 'no'," Lucas said, visibly bothered by her response. "I don't feel like I have to ask *his* permission for anything, anymore. He's not my dad and he never will be!"

She slapped his face hard enough that it echoed through the kitchen.

"You watch your mouth, mister," she said. "That man has done a lot for you over the years and I won't have you disrespecting him in my presence. While you live in this household you *will* give him the respect that he deserves. Got it?"

Lucas had a look of shock on his face as if he had just been shot by a high-powered pistol and was only now realizing it. He felt tears welling up in his eyes; they were tears of anger and sadness; anger because he hated the man and the way he treated his mother; sadness because she was so easily persuaded by the Steve's pessimistic attitude, and that she loved him more than she loved her own son.

"I'm sorry," she said, hugging him. "I don't know what came over me. I love both of you so much and I just can't stand to see you hating each other like this. Why can't you two just get along?"

"Because he is mean," Lucas said, tears rolling down his cheeks. "Because he doesn't know *how* to be nice . . . and because he hates me and is jealous that I am your son and not his son."

She held his head against her bosom and hummed the melody from "Somewhere Over the Rainbow" as performed by the Hawaiian musician, Israel Kamakawiwo'ole. She used to sing it to Lucas when he was a little boy and he was afraid of the dark at night, and even though he was now almost eighteen years old, it still felt good to both. She was truly sorry for the terrible mess that had become of the relationship between her son and her husband and herself; she loved Steve—and she certainly loved Lucas—but she intended to grow old with Steve and be buried in the plots they already had picked out in the cemetery.

"Sometimes I wish I had never been born," Lucas said. "And I'm sure *he* feels the same way. My *real* dad would never have treated me this way."

"You can't say that," she said. "You were just a baby when your father died—"

"But he was my *real* dad . . . and I'm sure he would have treated me better than this," Lucas said.

"You don't have it that bad," she said.

"He is abusive," he said. "And you let him get away with it." He pushed her away. "I have kept quiet all these years because I didn't want to hurt *you*—but this is ridiculous!"

He was right, and she knew it; there was no argument against what he had just said. She sighed, defeated.

"I'm going outside now," Lucas said. "Don't worry about me. I'll be okay."

He grabbed his guitar and went out through the sliding glass door onto the patio.

• • •

The sun was shining down on his face, drying the tears that still lingered at the corner of his eyes. He sniffled and wiped his nose on the back of his hand, rubbing away the moisture from his eyes. He was still upset by what had just taken place, but it had become such a common occurrence lately that it came as no real surprise and the emotions tended to go away rather quickly.

His mother stood inside the glass window watching him. Tears rolled down her cheeks. She stood there for a moment—maybe five minutes—and watched him as he sat down and took out the guitar from the case. He was seated comfortably in the patio furniture as he produced some sheets of paper that appeared to be sheet music. He began to play, strumming the strings, but she couldn't hear the music through the glass; she touched her hand to the glass, five fingertips leaving heat prints with misty rings, as if she thought she could feel the vibration of the music with her fingertips. After a short time, she turned away and got ready to go on her weekend errands, but there was still a sadness in her heart that just wouldn't go away.

Lucas breathed in the fresh air and felt the sunshine on his skin.

He saw that his mother had been watching him and that she was now gone. He tried his best to put all sorrow out of his mind and immersed himself in the beautiful sound emanating from the guitar. At first, he just played some random chords, warming up, but then he became more focused and tried some classical compositions that were always a little more challenging and proved to be more difficult. After messing around with random snippets, he decided to try one of the songs that he had found inside of the guitar and that had been of interest to him when he had first seen it. The one that he was most interested in was "The Angels Ballad." He took the papers and set them out on the table so that he could easily read them. He was amazed at the sheer genius and artistry of the composition; it was almost like something not of this earth; like music from another realm, and the lyrics that accompanied the sheet music were also mesmerizing—although Lucas wasn't much of a singer or songwriter and he had never been too keen on folk ballads—he could appreciate the verses that made up the stanzas:

> *The heavenly angels sing a song of praise,*
> *With blessings cast upon the sons of man,*
> *With adoration throughout their days,*
> *To guide the rulers and comfort the damned,*
>
> *To see the weary traveler on his way,*
> *Watching over the children, the lion, and the lamb,*
> *A comforter in times of sorrow and distress,*
> *The angels are always there to assist,*
>
> *And love is a desire that they must wrest,*
> *For theirs is a free will and one damning wish,*
> *Will set them as mortals to the test,*
> *To walk as mortal man with lust and sin,*
>
> *Angels of a stately nature do envy humankind,*
> *Even though they are set apart to protect,*
> *The faithful, the sinner, and the blind,*
> *The choirs in heaven they do direct,*

With a tendency for earthbound desire so inclined,
A temptation even to those so true and elect,
If ever an angel shall fall from grace,
There is always that one choice they can make,

To live as a mortal and die in his place,
Like a man whose heart doth break,
To stare into the beauty of an angel's face,
Would cause mere mortals to pine away,

The love that endures throughout all time,
Is the love of an angel singing a heavenly hymn,
And though it is truth by heavenly design,
The love of an angel will endure to the end,

And when an angel chooses to live as man,
Never heavenly wings will they possess again,
Seraphim, cherubim, long to know the hearts of man,
To know the knowledge and spirituality of man,

Free will, sin, and evil concern man and angel alike,
Yet angels see only the good of God and cannot sin,
Man does that which is evil but good in his own eyes,
Doing evil for the sake of evil is not in man's design,

Yet somehow freewill has made man so inclined,
Angels are burdened with the task to guard mankind,
Aiding in man's salvation is their task at hand,
Although they may desire the fruits of men,

And they cannot sin or become human,
The work never ends for guardians by sword and rod,
Angels dance to the delights of music of the spheres,
The angles dance to a ballad of music of the spheres.

Lucas played the song through in its entirety, even attempted to sing some of the verses, but mostly he concentrated on the melody of the ballad. It was a reoccurring theme, catchy and beautiful, like something one would expect to be composed and played by the likes of Yanni, Dido, or Enya. He closed his eyes and let the music take him away. The birds and other flying insects seemed to quiet down, gathering around to listen to the music. It was as if nature had stopped to listen and it had become so silent that a proverbial pin could have been heard if dropped—something distracted him and brought him out of his enchanted trance. The sound of a twig snapping. He heard it over the music, and when he opened his eyes, he was so shocked by what he saw that he nearly dropped the guitar and wanted to get up and run.

There was a beautiful girl standing in the grass of the backyard lawn and she was looking at him intently. She looked like one of the fairies or nymphs from a Nene Thomas painting. She was very beautiful, Lucas observed, dressed in a long flowing gown that appeared to be made from silk or satin; there were jewels around the sleeves and bust area of the gown. She stood looking at him with large, hypnotic eyes that seemed to radiate color like fire opals, the color constantly changing like a mood ring. Her hair was long and radiant of a chestnut color, her skin was milky white and smooth, and her cheeks were blushing with a rose hue.

She looked at Lucas and said, "Please don't stop playing that music."

"Who are you?" Lucas asked, confused. Abruptly, he was reminded of the face that had appeared in his bedroom window the night before when he had played the music for the first time. "Where did you come from?"

"That's not important," she replied. "I am here because I heard the music you were playing . . . it's so lovely. I must hear it again. Please play it again for me. Won't you?"

"Uh, sure," Lucas said in complete disbelief. "I—uh—guess I can play it again."

He started playing the song again from the very beginning and watched, amazed, as the girl began dancing around the yard like a ballerina, hovering over the grass as deftly and delicately as a figure skater on ice. She was like something right out of a romantic fantasy painting or a figure from a Baroque period painting like Venus. Lucas was taken by her beauty and he couldn't keep his eyes off the mysterious dancer in his backyard.

Without warning, from behind, Lucas heard the sliding glass doors opening and he turned to see his mother looking out at him.

"I'm leaving now," she said. "Are you sure you don't need me to get you anything from town?"

Lucas turned and looked at his mother. He was shocked, caught unaware, as if he had something to hide. How was he to explain the strange—and very attractive—girl dancing around in the backyard?

"No. I'm okay," he said. "Uh—everything—I'll be fine. Just go do your thing."

He turned around to where the girl was standing in the yard, wondering how on Earth he was going to explain this, but she was gone, without a trace.

"Are you sure?" his mother asked him.

"Yes," he said, very confused.

"Okey-dokey," she said. "Call me if you change your mind. I should be home in a couple of hours."

"Yes, mom," Lucas said. He was curious to where the girl had disappeared. "Have a nice day."

She looked at him for a moment as if she had something profound to say and then sighed.

"I love you," she said. "Please forgive me for—"

"I love you," Lucas said. "Don't worry. I understand. Apology accepted. Now go have a nice time in town."

"Alright, honey," she said, kissing him on his head. "I'll see you later then."

And with that, she closed the sliding glass door and was gone.

Lucas watched her leave, listened to her Honda Accord starting, watched as she drove away down Maple Lane and out of sight. Lucas saw the black Firebird coming in the opposite direction down the road and smiled. He knew his best friend would come and visit unannounced, because he often did, and he couldn't wait to tell Alex about the beautiful, strange girl who had appeared in his back yard when he started playing the guitar.

• • •

Alex decided to pay a visit to Lucas just to hang out for a while. He pulled into the driveway and parked his Firebird. Lucas was waiting for him, watching from the front porch, waving as he pulled up at the house. Alex turned off the engine and climbed out of the car.

"Hey Lucas," Alex said.

"What's up?" Lucas said. "I just had the strangest thing happen."

"What? What's going on?"

"You are not going to believe what just happened . . ."

"No? Try me," Alex said. "I might believe it."

"Well," Lucas said, his eyes wide with excitement. "While I was in the backyard playing that guitar I bought at the yard sale—it's too strange . . . and you're not going to believe me when I tell you."

"Spit it out, already," Alex said.

"I was playing this music that was written down inside the guitar case and all of the sudden this—this beautiful girl appeared in the yard. She was dancing to the music. I don't know where she came from. She was just . . . just there all of the sudden."

"When did this happen?"

"Just a while ago. I was out there after breakfast this morning and she came out of nowhere."

"You don't know who she was?"

"No. I have no idea."

"Was she cute?"

"Yes. She was beautiful. Like an angel."

"Well let's go back there and take a look."

"She's not there now," Lucas said, scratching his head. "She appeared when I played the guitar, though. Maybe she'll come back if I play again."

"You are right," Alex said. "I'm not sure if I believe you."

"Well, let's go back there and see what happens."

They went to the backyard and sat on the patio furniture.

"I was sitting right here," Alex said. "I found this sheet music in the guitar case and I started playing it and when I looked up, there she was . . ."

"Go ahead, then," Alex said, dubious. "Try it again. See if the music makes her come back."

"It won't work now," Lucas said. "I have a feeling she won't come back because you're here."

"Sure," Alex said. "Whatever you say. Are you sure you're feeling alright? I'm starting to worry about you."

"I'll give it a try," Lucas said, picking up the guitar. "You have to believe me. I'm not kidding."

"Just play the song."

"Okay, here it goes," Lucas said, putting his fingers to the strings.

"Keep your fingers crossed."

"They're crossed. I'm waiting."

Lucas began playing the ballad again, messing it up at first, and then starting over. He plucked the strings and read the sheet music, mouthing the words to the lyrics as he went along. He hoped that the girl would appear, but he knew in his heart that it was useless while Alex was sitting there.

The girl did not appear.

Lucas finished playing the song and then stopped and looked out to the backyard, longingly.

"And . . . nothing," Alex said. "Are you sure you're not making this up? I mean, you do have quite an imagination with the fiction you've been writing since the first grade, but this is pushing it a bit. Don't you think? Now you are imagining girls appearing from thin air?"

"I didn't imagine it," Lucas said, defensively. "She was real."

Alex surveyed the yard.

"You don't have to believe me, I guess," Lucas said. "But that doesn't mean it didn't happen."

"What girl in her right mind would just come into *your* yard and dance around while you played the guitar? You said you didn't recognize her, right? She isn't a neighbor, then?"

"I've never seen her before," Lucas said. "But she was real. I'm telling you. I was scared at first, because she was just . . . there all the sudden. After a moment though, I felt totally comfortable in her presence. I felt attracted to her in some strange and amazing way. Her eyes were all fiery and magnificent. I was instantly in love."

"You are on one now," Alex said. "I don't believe you."

"I guess it does sound strange," Lucas said. "I'm not lying, though. Why would I do that?"

"Maybe you need an imaginary friend to cope with your problems. I don't know. You tell me."

"You know what," Lucas said. "You can just go away if you are going to ridicule me. I was having a great experience until you showed up. In fact, you scared her away."

"Oh, I see," Alex said. "It's my fault your imaginary girlfriend is not making an appearance. Okay, that makes sense."

"Are you gaslighting? I really saw her. Don't believe me if you don't want to. That's your choice. But you don't need to make me feel stupid or crazy for my experience."

"Look, man," Alex said. "I've known you practically all your life. I care about you. I'm worried about you and your imagination. You've always been a bit peculiar when it comes to making shit up . . . but this takes the cake."

"I'll tell you what," Lucas said. "When she comes back I will take a picture with my iPhone and send it to you. How does that sound?"

"Okay, you do that. I'll be waiting."

"I really don't have to prove anything to you, you know?"

"No. You don't. But you can't expect me to believe such a far-fetched story as this."

"It's not your concern," Lucas said. "Why don't you just go home and leave me alone, fi all you're going to do is make fun of me."

"Fine. I'm just going to leave you alone with your guitar and your imaginary friend now."

"Good," Lucas said. "You do that. And don't come back unless you are ready to apologize for treating me like this."

Alex walked away and went back to his car. He was angry, but he still loved his friend. He hoped in time they could work it out. He started his car and pulled away from the house.

• • •

Later that day, across town, Alex drove back to the house where the yard sale had taken place and spoke with the old man, Stewart. He was sitting on his porch in his wheelchair, drinking a cup of coffee and watching traffic drive by on the street. When Alex walked up on the sidewalk and entered the yard, Stewart got a bemused look on his face.

"Hello," Stewart said. "I got rid of all the merchandise from the yard sale . . . so there's nothing left, I'm afraid."

"That's not why I'm here," Alex said.

"Well, what brings you back over here, then?"

"I've got a question about that guitar you sold to my friend, Lucas."

Stewart had a faraway look in his eyes, as though he was trying to remember something but could not quite recollect what it was, or why he was thinking about in the first place.

"Yes. Go ahead," Steward said. "What do you want to know?"

"I've got a feeling you weren't being honest about everything. There is something wrong with your story."

"You calling me a liar?" Steward said, sitting forward in his wheelchair. "I've got no reason to lie. I'm dying. Why would I lie at a time such as this?"

"What? You're dying?

"I thought I told you I had cancer at the yard sale."

"I guess you did. Anyway, I'm sorry to hear that."

"No worries. I'm ready to go. I've had a good life."

"Well, when you said that guitar was made in Mexico . . . hand-made by craftsmen. I swear I thought it looked like a cheap guitar made in China."

"Oh, yeah?" Stewart said. "What do you know about guitars? Are you an expert?"

"No. But, I do know that it is easy to take advantage of someone who is . . . gullible."

"Are you calling your friend gullible?"

"He is, kind of, in a way," Alex said. "I just want to make sure you're not taking advantage of him with that guitar. He really loves it, you know. And I don't want to see him get hurt in any way. That includes old men and yard sales with cheap guitars."

"No. Absolutely not." Stewart said. "That guitar is a handmade work of art. It's an antique, too. It has great value, especially for someone like your friend who can really see the beauty in it. And make sweet music with it, too. That may be something you will never understand. I knew your friend would be able to appreciate it, though. I've got a good sense for people. I could tell he was special. That guitar will change his life. Besides, forty-eight dollars is a steal for that guitar."

"What makes you so sure of that?"

"I know, personally, what that guitar can do. You wouldn't believe me if I told you. But your friend will understand. Believe that."

"If it's so special," Alex said. "Why did you get rid of it?"

"You're not too bright, are you boy? Didn't you listen to what I said. First of all, I'm dying. I'm not long for this earth anymore. Second of all, I can't play it no more," he said. He held up his hands to show knobby and twisted knuckles and fingers that looked like grotesque, crippled claws. "The arthritis got so bad after a while I couldn't play the guitar anymore. So, I just quit. If your friend can play it then he should. It's a special guitar."

"Oh, I see," Alex said. "I'm sorry about your troubles, and all. I didn't mean to come over here to burden you. Like I said, I'm just worried about my friend. He has taken a keen interest in that guitar and I'm afraid he may be obsessed with it."

"That's going to happen," Stewart said. "You can't stop it. It's out of your hands at this point."

"What does that mean?"

"It means what it means," Stewart said. "That guitar has a special power to bless the right person who plays it. It's magic."

Alex coughed into his hand, saying "bullshit" into his fist.

"Go ahead and call it bullshit if you want. But it's true. It has a special power and brings good fortune to the right player."

"Okay, now I know your crazy. I don't believe in all that nonsense."

"You don't have to believe it. It's not your concern. I can tell you this, though: your friend will find everything he ever wanted—or needs—when he starts playing that guitar. Mark my words."

"I think I should be going now," Alex said.

"Yes. Maybe you should. Good day to you, boy."

"Good day to you, sir."

With that, Alex turned and walked away from the old man.

• • •

Lucas began to think about the dancing girl. Where had she gone? Who was she? Why did she appear when he played the guitar? Maybe she was a new neighbor that had just moved into the neighborhood. He had never seen her before; he was sure of that. He was struck by the notion that he might be losing his mind. What was this sudden and strange appearance of the pretty girl in his yard? Where had she come from? Perhaps Alex was right, and she was just a figment of his imagination and he was lost in a delusional fantasy. He had imagined her; that was the only logical explanation. Hadn't he thought he had seen—her—someone peeking in through his window last night? Strange as it was, she had been peering at him through his window, there could be no doubt of that, he thought. He knew he had caught a glimpse of her outside his bedroom window.

The entire situation had a certain surreal quality to it, almost as if he was dreaming. He rubbed his eyes, shook his head, and breathed in deeply, pinching himself to make sure he was awake. Maybe his mind was playing tricks on him; she seemed so real though, and he hoped that she would come back again.

He focused his attention back on the guitar and began playing again, fretting the chords and finger picking the strings. He was once again engrossed in the music, hoping, waiting for the dancing girl to appear, but there was nothing . . . she didn't appear.

It was hopeless, Lucas thought. The girl would never return.

He played a different song, something with a more upbeat tempo and wondered why he was such a loser.

"What am I doing?" he wondered, aloud. "I'm sitting here dreaming about an imaginary girl. I am really losing it. Get a hold of yourself, Lucas." He spoke to himself as thought that would remedy the situation.

He played the "Angels Ballad Again," this time with more passion and precision than ever. He could only wish and hope that the pretty dancing girl would reappear.

He waited, played again, then waited some more.

Nothing.

The wind blew across the lawn, ruffling the grass and pulling dried, dead brown and gold leaves along in its wake. It blew the sheet music askew beside him and scattered it at his feet. He collected the loose pages and stacked them neatly by his side. He was getting ready to pick up the guitar and sheet music when he decided he would try again, one more time. He hoped upon hope that it would work this time. He said a little prayer to God in thinking that maybe He might favor him and bring the girl back.

Still nothing.

"This sucks," Lucas said. "Where are you? If you appeared once, you can come again. Please come back."

He strummed the guitar strings once more, a final attempt, and played the song again.

As if in reply to his pleading and prayers, finally, as if by some magical process, and to his astonishment, the beautiful dancing girl did reappear, stepping softly and silently from behind him. He was startled again, even though he had been expecting her.

"That is such a lovely song," she said, doing a pirouette across the patio. "Every time I hear it I just want to dance."

Lucas was now watching her and taking in every detail. He stopped playing and stared longingly, completely overwhelmed by her beauty.

"There you are," Lucas said. "I thought you would never come back. I was beginning to think maybe I was going crazy and had imagined you."

"Please don't stop," she said, standing with one leg raised in mid-stride.

Lucas saw that she wore no shoes and that she had very delicate ankles and bare feet. He also saw that there was a set of wings folded neatly behind her back. The wings were nearly concealed, but he could see that they were composed of bright white feathers very similar to the one he had found yesterday. Between the wings and her lovely countenance, he was stunned and speechless.

She looked at him with her enchanting, soporific eyes, expectantly, blinking with large eyelashes, saying, "Please play that song again."

"What—who are you?" he asked, stammering.

"My name is Karina," she said. "Although I have many names. But that is not of any real importance. Is it?"

"Uhm . . ." Lucas was at a loss for words. "I—uh—don't know . . . what do you mean?"

"Are you going to play so I can dance, or what?" she asked.

"Oh—yeah," Lucas said, putting his fingers back to the strings on the guitar. He began to play and watch her as she danced.

Karina drifted lightly down the stairs and floated across the grass, her bare feet hovering over the lawn, not touching the ground, her wings unfolding and flapping. She spun in a circle, her silky garment fluttering as she moved, her long flowing hair radiant in the afternoon sun as if flowed and bounced in strands and curls over her shoulders. She was magnificent. If Rembrandt or Degas could have envisioned that moment it would surely have been one of the finest representations of beauty ever captured with paint on canvas.

Lucas could have—and would have—played and watched her dance for eternity, but suddenly she stopped, became distracted, and turned to look at something, sniffing the air, as if she sensed some impending doom.

"I must go now," she said. "There is danger coming soon."

"What? Why?" Lucas said. "What danger?"

Be careful, Lucas," she said. "There is danger present. You must not lose your faith or hope or, especially, your courage."

"What do you mean?" Lucas said. "Where are you going? Faith? Hope? Courage? What is that supposed to—"

She rose up into the air, her wings flapping briskly, and then she flew away out of sight and was gone. The sight of this was shocking enough to cause Lucas to feel both fear and amazement as his heart pounded in his chest. The sight of a girl with wings was unreal and unbelievable, yet he was witnessing it, and he was frozen solid in his seat.

• • •

Lucas heard a familiar sound, the throaty roar of a GMC Sierra pick-up truck coming down the road. Steve was home. Could this be the danger that the dancing girl had spoken of, Lucas wondered.

Steve pulled the truck up in the driveway in front of the house. Lucas heard the doors shut, heard Steve talking to Sam, heard the gate on the chain link fence open and then he saw Sam run wild and excited into the back yard, sniffing and doing his signature cart-wheels, peeing, and then kicking up sod with his hind legs. Sam saw Lucas and ran up to him, jumping up onto his legs, nearly knocking the guitar from his hands, licking his face.

"Sam," Lucas said, patting the dog's head. "How are you boy?"

Sam sniffed Lucas, sneezed, and then ran back toward the gate where Steve was standing in his camouflaged jumpsuit with a shot-gun slung over his forearm.

Steve and Lucas made eye contact—Lucas could tell that there was going to be trouble. Steve looked mad about something and Lucas could tell that he had been drinking—heavily from the looks of it, not to mention that he was holding a nearly empty bottle of Jim Beam whiskey in his left hand.

"Well, well, well," Steve said, his speech slurred. "Look what we have here . . . ."

Lucas had the urge to get up and run but he felt trapped, imag-ining that this was what an animal must feel like right before it gets ran down in the middle of the road at night entranced by bright head-lights and squished by tires that bring certain death. He wanted to speak, say something to ease the tension, but he didn't know what to say.

"If it isn't Garth Brooks," Steve said. He took a long drink from the whiskey bottle, finished what was left of it, and then quickly closed the distance between Lucas and himself. He tossed the empty bottle down in the grass. He said, "You know what I think. . . ?"

Lucas didn't want to know what he thought, and didn't care either, but he knew that he was about to find out. The situation looked like it was about to get out of control; Steve was not only drunk and dangerous, but also, he had all the appearance of a crazed lunatic with one eye twitching wildly out of control. Lucas didn't reply because he knew that the question was rhetorical and that there was no correct answer needed or warranted.

"I think you are a smart-ass little punk," Steve said. "That's what I think." He came within striking distance of Lucas, leaned down until their faces were only a few inches apart—Lucas could smell the foul stench of booze on Steve's breath. "I think you are a spoiled little brat and I would love nothing more than to wring your little pencil neck and snap it off." He made a wringing motion with his hands and then finished with a gesture that suggested the breaking of a stick.

Lucas shrugged and leaned back, feeling like a coward, and thinking that he wished he could be anyplace else on Earth right then. He was worried about the guitar more than anything, including his own safety. He said, "Please don't hurt me or my guitar. Just let me put the guitar away so it doesn't get damaged."

"What?" Steve said, appalled. "What did you say?"

"I—" Lucas began to say, but he was quickly cut off by Steve.

"You listen here," Steve said, leaning even closer, so close that their noses nearly touched. The reek of whiskey was intolerable. "You listen here, you little piece of shit. I've had it with you. I've had all I can take."

Steve reached out and snatched the guitar away from Lucas— who struggled to keep the guitar in his hands with all of his might, but to no avail—and after ripping it loose, he raised it over his head like an executioner raising a double bladed ax before bringing it down on the culprit's neck on chopping block. He held the guitar high up in the air, swaying drunkenly, the shiny gloss finish glinting in the sun, and said, "As for this thing . . . I think we will just finish it right now."

"No. Please don't," Lucas said, pleading, when he realized what Steve intended to do with the guitar. "Please don't break my guitar."

"I've got no use for this, and neither do you," Steve said. "It was a waste of money and will most certainly be the ruin of your life. Music is of the Devil. It accomplishes nothing."

With a sudden sweeping motion, Steve swung the guitar down like an ax, aiming for the concrete slab that made up the patio, where seemed to calculate that the guitar would be smashed most effectively.

Lucas screamed for him to stop.

Without warning, overhead, the angel named Karina suddenly appeared and she moved with Supernatural speed to interfere with Steve's plan to destroy the guitar.

"No. Don't," Lucas screamed at her, realizing that she was going to intercede. "He's insane. Watch out!"

Steve was caught by surprise, but he had quicker reflexes than might be expected from an intoxicated man, and he spun around and then three things happened almost simultaneously: firstly, Steve saw Karina—a girl with wings flying overhead—as she swooped down on him and he raised the shotgun up while letting the guitar fall to the ground; secondly, the guitar broke in half, the neck disjointed from the body—Lucas dove after the guitar but it was too late; thirdly, Karina grabbed Steve by the shoulders and said, "Speak no more," right at the same time that he pulled the trigger on the shotgun. There was a loud explosion as buckshot and gun smoke blasted through the air; the gunshot was deafening. Karina was thrown backward as the shotgun blast hit her sending feathers out in every direction around her heavenly body. At the same time a bright blinding electric blue light exploded from her fingertips and hit Steve with the force of a lightning bolt, knocking him backward; both of them were thrown in opposite directions and they both landed on the grassy lawn, lying deathly still and without movement. Sam—the dog had been watching intently from a distance—let out a loud squeal and ran for cover under the bushes making a high pitched *yark-yark-yark* sound as he went with his tail tucked between his legs.

"Oh no," Lucas said as he watched from his vantage point on the ground. "Please, God. No."

Lucas got to his feet and ran over to where Karina was lying in a mess of feathers and gun smoke. She did not move.

"This isn't happening," Lucas said, reaching down to touch her. "This can't be happening. You can't die. You're an . . . an angel."

Karina showed no signs of life.

Steve moaned on the other side of the yard.

Lucas reached down to Karina and ran his hand along her face, then down her neck, wondering if she had a pulse. Did angels have a heart and a pulse? he wondered. There should have been a lot of blood, too, but he saw none. He began to weep uncontrollably.

"Karina," he said, grabbing her limp hand. "Please wake up. You can't be dead. It's just not possible . . . is it?"

A dash of hope struck his heart as he thought he saw her move. One of her eyelids flickered, her lips trembled, and then both of her eyes opened wide, looking up at Lucas.

She said, "I'm okay, Lucas." She sat up, bracing herself with her arms behind her, palms down in the grass. "Do not worry about me." She looked across the yard toward Steve. "It is he who you will want to be concerned with right now. He needs your help and compassion."

Lucas turned and looked at Steve as he squirmed around, moaning in agony.

"Go to him and assist him," she said. "Show him kindness. He will trouble you no more."

Lucas took a step toward Steve, then stopped and looked back at Karina. She was now up in the air, hovering, pointing toward Steve. She said, "Remember, Lucas. You should love your enemy and not gloat when he stumbles . . . he needs your help. Go now and help him."

"But why—" Lucas said.

"Don't ask why," Karina said. "Just do it. Do it because you possess the ability to love others, even those who harm you."

"What will happen—" Lucas said.

"Go!" Karina said, with thunderous force.

Lucas looked away in the direction where Steve was now sitting up in the grass, and then back toward Karina, unsure, and he saw that she was gone.

"Great," Lucas said. "Just great. I finally meet someone special and then something like this has to happen."

He walked over to Steve and was shocked to see that his countenance had changed; it was as though he had aged tremendously in a
matter of minutes and had turned into a very old man. His hair had
gone completely white as snow, his eyes were as white as eggshells,
his skin had taken on the appearance of that of a wrinkled prune.

Lucas reached down and helped Steve to his feet, which was a
cumbersome task, and together they hobbled across the patio and in
through the sliding glass door. Inside, Lucas helped Steve sit down
on the couch. It was obvious that Steve was blind and that he could
not speak—and he would never speak again for the rest of his days.
He had been turned into a deaf mute by the events that took place
that day in the backyard when he tried to kill an angel.

• • •

Afterward, Lucas had to explain to his mother what had happened,
and, as you might imagine, it was a hard story for her to believe.

"He's in a better existence, now," Lucas said to his mother. "He's
been touched by an angel. I think he will be much nicer after this."

"But how do you know this to be true?"

"I watched it happen."

"An angel. You've seen an angel?"

"Yes. I do believe that is what I saw. And she is beautiful."

"Where did she go? And how do you know she is a girl."

"I don't know that answer to that, but I'm sure she is a girl. She
comes when I play the guitar. But now that Steve has broken the guitar, I'm afraid I will never see her again. The guitar had the power to
summon her when I played that special song."

Oh, Lucas," she said. "You have such a wild imagination. We
need to call the ambulance and have them come and look at Steve. I
don't think he is well."

"He'll be fine, mom," Lucas said. "But I will call the ambulance
for you."

Eventually, after a visit to the Longview Emergency Room, and
several follow-up doctor visits, she accepted that Steve had become
an invalid and she took care of him after that. The doctors couldn't
explain what happened to him with science or medicine and could
only scratch their heads in amazement and disbelief. They would
now have to survive on a meager income provided by the social

security disability that Steve would receive since he wasn't able to work any longer.

She was forced to seek employment to supplement their income, but she didn't mind. She still loved Steve and in some strange way she thought that it was a blessing in disguise because now he couldn't abuse her or Lucas anymore and he was as submissive as a lamb, and now she knew that they would truly grow old together—if destiny would have it that way, depending on how long he could live in such a condition—and that they would live happily ever after. As long as he lived, she would stay by his side.

• • •

Lucas, on the other hand, was perplexed . . . not only had he lost the guitar, but also, he had lost contact with the beautiful angel named Karina. She would not visit anymore since he didn't have the guitar.

At first, he just gave up, but later he went to visit the old man, Stewart—the yard sale guru—from whom he had originally purchased the guitar. He wanted to ask him about the guitar and the girl, Karina. Perhaps Stewart knew more than he was letting on. Lucas was dismayed when he discovered that the old man had passed away after losing a battle with cancer—although he had left the records and bottles behind with a relative with specific instructions that they should be given to Lucas if he ever returned for them. Stewart expected that Lucas would come back eventually and had left him a note.

Dear Lucas,

I know you may be confused by what is happening now. After you purchased my guitar and witnessed its power you are probably wondering what the heck is happening to you. By now you have discovered that it is special. I'm sure of that. If not, well then never mind. If you don't know, then carry on with your life anyway. I only hope you are blessed with what the song, "The Angel's Ballad" brings to you. I'm not going to be around much longer, so take care of her. She will take care of you, too. I am going back home now, up to the Pearly Gates and my mission here is accomplished. Fare thee well, my son, and God bless you.

Lucas read the note, not quite sure what it all meant, but he was sure that Stewart had been placed into his life for a reason and that Karina was part of the plan. Why had he died from cancer? Why would God allow such a terrible thing to happen? It didn't seem fair. He knew he would have to accept it.

Later that day he received a text message from Alex:

Hey bro. What you doing? I am really sorry about how I treated you. I know you love that guitar. I'm not worried about your story or the girl you spoke of. It's your business. As long as it makes you happy. I just want to be friends. I love you like a brother. Please don't ever forget that. Maybe we could hang out later. Let me know. OK. TTYL.

Lucas sent a text message in return:

It's all good, bro. I'm not mad at you. I don't expect you to believe a crazy story like this. I guess the old man, Stewart, had cancer and he died. He left me some things from the yard sale. Maybe you can come over sometime and check it out. I'll hit you up soon. Take care, bro. Later.

That was the end of the whole affair, or so Lucas thought. . . .

• • •

Lucas later realized that he still possessed the sheet music with the ballad that had seemed to summon the angel, and on a hunch, he purchased a new Martin D-35 dreadnought acoustic guitar with the money he had been saving up for a car and he went out into the backyard and began to play "The Angel's Ballad."

At first, nothing happened, but after several attempts, he was amazed and delighted when Karina made an appearance, much in the same fashion as she had the first time, dancing around the yard once more, to the irresistible sound of the music from the song that Lucas played. She loved the music with such passion, and he shared that same passion, so they were truly a match made in Heaven. They fell in love—a love beyond human comprehension—and they spent most of Lucas's time on Earth together in performance of the dance to "The Angel's Ballad." There was one final dilemma, however, and that was the fact that he was mortal, and she was immortal and not capable of physical intimacy. Their bond was restricted by this barrier, but not diminished by something so trivial as carnal desire. The physical desire Lucas felt for her reduced with time and their love grew stronger on a spiritual level, and nothing would interfere with such a pure and innocent love that transcends physical existence . . . but that is another story altogether. Suffice it to say, theirs was a happy conclusion.

A Case of Mistaken Identity

I had gone into the Circle K store for a cup of coffee and a Krispy Kreme doughnut, a regular stop on my way to the night shift at the plant. It was just after 10:00 p.m. and Abdul, the night clerk of the store, had put on a fresh pot of coffee for me, as usual. He knew just how I liked and was always eager to please.

When the Honda Civic pulled up in front of the store I didn't think much of it. It was one of those modified cars that look straight out of the movie *The Fast and the Furious*, complete with spoiler, hood scoop, and low-profile tires. It was obviously a work in progress because it was covered in primer and in need of a fresh coat of paint. It was loud, too. We could hear it all the way inside the store when it pulled up. It had one of those fart-can mufflers that increase the volume of the exhaust pipe.

The kid driving the car looked a lot like Marshal Mathers, the famous musician. There was a girl sitting next to him, and she was young and pretty. Neither of them looked older than eighteen. He got out of the car clad in a hoody over a wife beater t-shirt and extra baggy pants. He was sporting gold chains around his neck. He came in through the door and Abdul was instantly on guard, watching his every move.

I noticed that he was just over five feet tall by the measurement tape you see in every convenience store today. The kid didn't look around and went directly to the back of the store, obviously in a hurry, knowing exactly what he was after.

I put my doughnut and coffee on the counter and pulled out my wallet to pay for my goods. Abdul was looking over my head. His eyes were wide, and he had a nervous look on his face.

"Busy night?" I asked, trying to get Abdul's attention.

"Huh? Can you hold on for a moment, please?" Abdul said in broken English.

"I guess so. I'm not in that big of a hurry."

Abdul reached for the phone and punched in a number. He watched the kid in the round convex mirror at the back of the store. His eyes never left the kid that owned the Honda. Abdul didn't want to let on what he was doing, but I had a pretty good idea that he was calling the police. He looked at me and rolled his eyes, motioning with his head over to the wall where a bunch of papers and some photos of missing persons were tacked to the wall. Next to that was a police composite sketch of a man in a hooded sweatshirt that looked a lot like the kid at the back of the store. It stated that this guy was wanted and there was a reward for the arrest and conviction of the suspect. I saw the resemblance and knew exactly what was happening. I began to get nervous.

Abdul stepped back for a little privacy and spoke into the phone. I couldn't hear the complete conversation, but it amounted to a call for help, and Abdul was growing more nervous by the minute. He hung up the phone and came back to ring up my bill.

"Sorry," Abdul said, ringing up my purchase.

I swiped my credit card and waited for the receipt. It seemed like it took forever for the cash register to spit out the little white piece of paper. Abdul ripped the receipt from the machine with too much force, pulling extra paper from the spool. He ripped it in half and handed it to me with a shaky hand.

"Thank you and please come again," he said.

"You alright?" I asked. "You need some help?"

"No. That's okay. Thank you."

"Okay then," I said, picking up my coffee and doughnut. "I'll be seeing you later then."

"Have a good night."

"You too."

I turned for the door and went toward the exit, but I couldn't help looking over my shoulder to see where the kid was in the back of the store. I could see his blonde head over the top of the shelves. I had to look in the mirror to see him, and he appeared to be looking intently at some item I couldn't make out. Suddenly I realized that I should be getting the hell out of there before the situation heated up even more. I went through the door and looked directly at the young girl sitting in the Honda. She looked back at me. She was a pretty little thing, and I couldn't help wondering what she saw in someone like the Eminem clone in the store. I shook my head and went to my car.

I was fumbling with my keys, placed the coffee on the roof and held the doughnut in my mouth, as I found the right key and unlocked the car door. I was just about to get into the car when three police patrol cars screamed into the parking lot. If I was going to get away from the action, I had to hurry. I grabbed my coffee off the roof, spilling it over my fingers and burning them, and climbed into my car. I dropped my keys, scrambled to pick them up, and then jammed the key into the ignition just as all hell broke loose. I watched like a captive audience from the seat of my car, doughnut still hanging from my mouth, as the events unfolded.

The kid burst through the door and saw the police cars in the parking lot. He had his hands inside the hoody pocket, and his pants were sliding down his hips exposing his Calvin Cline underwear. His eyes were as wide as the chrome rims on his Honda Civic. He stood stone still for a second as he considered his options.

The police had assumed aggressive shooting position behind their patrol cars and commanded him to put his hands up in the air. He still had them inside the hoody pocket, and he was obviously concealing something, maybe a gun.

I could tell this was going to get ugly. What should I do? I wanted to drive away, but I was trapped in by the patrol cars—read, white, and blue lights flashing like some insane rave party. Just my luck. I thought about starting the engine and was getting ready to turn the key in the ignition when one of the cops screamed at the top of his lungs, telling the kid to get down on the ground.

The kid didn't move. He just stood there like a statue, frozen in fear, his feet itching to make a run for it, and his pants sliding even further down his hips.

Without warning, the kid took his hands out from his pockets, and he was holding something in his right hand. At first, I was sure it was a gun. The police must have thought the same thing. They opened fire and shot the kid multiple times in the chest. The gunshots were deafening even inside my car. It was like a terrible dream. The fireworks from some hellish nightmare. I could see the black holes on his T-shirt and the blood making a pink misty cloud as the bullets ripped through his chest and shattered the glass on the storefront.

The item in his hand was a small box . . . something he had just shoplifted from the store. It fell on the sidewalk next to the kid as he collapsed to the ground in the throes of death.

The girl in the Honda jumped out and screamed, running toward the kid dying on the sidewalk. She fell on her knees and grabbed the kid's face. She was screaming at the police as they closed in on her, yanking her kicking and thrashing off the ground and putting her in handcuffs. One of them ran over and kicked the box away from the kid, making sure it wasn't a weapon. The box skittered toward my car and I could see what it was then. It looked like a self-pregnancy test kit. I recognized the box because my girlfriend, Tonya, had recently used one of the kits when she thought she might be pregnant—to her dismay, the test results were negative. I couldn't help wondering if this girl would have different results. Maybe she would have the dying kid's child and carry on his legacy.

Abdul came out from his hiding spot inside the store and peeked through the broken glass window to see if it was safe.

The kid was dead and the sound of an ambulance approaching broke through the night.

When Abdul came out of the store he talked to the police.

"Is this the guy?" one of the officers asked.

"No," Abdul said. "I think that was not him."

"Are you sure? You called and said you recognized him."

"I'm not sure—but it looked like him," Abdul said. "But now I think it wasn't him."

The cops took the kid's driver's license from his wallet and compared it to the composite sketch. The girl was screaming at the police, crying and kicking, demanding to be let free from the handcuffs.

"Johnny never robbed this store," she said. "He was just getting a pregnancy test for me. We didn't have any money, so he was going to steal it. He's never done anything wrong before. You guys shot the wrong person."

I was questioned and told them everything I saw. It was truly one of the most horrendous things I have ever witnessed. The tragedy of it all is that it turned out to be the wrong guy. Johnny Jamieson was shot dead for stealing a pregnancy test kit and matching the profile of someone who had robbed the Circle K convenience store.

The police agreed that it was a case of mistaken identity.

The Green Glass Eye

Although it was over thirty years ago, back in the late summer of 1985, I still remember the events of the night I saw a real ghost as if it were yesterday. It is only now, after all this time, that I can actually come to terms with the event. It all started when I was on vacation in Washington state, with my wife, Tabitha, who was fast asleep upstairs in room 313 on the third floor of the Queen Charlotte Hotel. I decided to venture down to the lobby to do a little reading before turning in for the night. I was enjoying a nice cup of Earl Gray tea and nearly three chapters into a novel when the old man with the black eye patch interrupted me and started up a conversation.

"Do you mind if I sit down?" the old man asked.

I looked at him for a moment, taking in his features, examining his potential as a threat. He was wearing a black wool Greek fisherman cap and green knitted sweater over which he wore a navy pea coat. He wore blue denim trousers, black rubber boots, and he was smoking a briar wood pipe. He didn't look like he posed much of a threat—in fact, he looked a like a fisherman off a boat from the pier. I thought he looked harmless enough.

"No. Not at all," I said. "Be my guest."

He sat down and looked around the spacious lobby, removing his black wool cap and running his fingers through his scraggly gray hair. "This is a nice hotel," he said, putting the cap back on his head. "I've stayed here many times."

"It is very nice," I agreed.

The lobby of the Queen Charlotte Hotel was nearly empty except for a couple checking in at the reception desk, the clerk, myself, and the old man with the patch on his eye. There was a fire crackling in the fireplace, colorful fish swimming about in an aquarium, a light drizzle outside brought spatters of rain down gently against the large picture windows that looked out across the sandy beach and shore of the Pacific Ocean. The lobby was decorated with a maritime motif complete with anchors, steering wheels from ancient ships, fishing nets, glass float balls, buoys, and starfish. It was cozy, I thought. The furniture was modern leather and oak, lamps and chandeliers hung overhead, vending machines and video games sat against a far wall. It was a nice, clean, well-lit place to read a book.

"What is that you are reading?" he asked, pointing at my book.

I showed him the cover of the book. I was reading *The Strange Case of Dr. Jekyll and Mr. Hyde* by Robert Louise Stevenson.

"Oh, well good for you," he said. "You don't see too many people reading the classics these days."

"I don't know about that," I said.

I put a Queen Charlotte Hotel business card between the pages of my book to mark my place and set it aside.

The old man lit his pipe with a stick match, puff-puff-puffed and then blew out a cloud of smoke, sighing contentedly.

"My name is Jack," he said. He blew out a smoke ring. "Jack Fargo is my name."

"Nice to meet you, Jack," I said. "My name is Niles Porter."

"Very nice," Jack said. He leaned forward, offering his hand. I reached out and shook it; he pumped my hand twice and then quickly let go. "Nice to meet you as well, Niles Porter." The smoke from his pipe caused him to squint with his one good eye. "I'm thinking that you aren't from around these parts," he said, tapping the bowl of his pipe in an ashtray.

"And you would be right in assuming that," I replied. "I am from Springfield, Illinois, actually."

"Oh. I see," Jack said. "Very nice. They grow lots of corn there in Illinois. Got lots of soybeans, and cattle too. It can be nice over in the Midwest if you're into that kind of thing."

"I call it home," I said.

"It's a little too dry—landlocked you might say—for my liking, though," he said. "I prefer to be by the ocean, myself. Give me the salty sea and waves and wind and sand and I'm a happy man." He nearly sang the last sentence. "So, what brings you to these parts?"

"My wife and I are here on vacation," I replied. "It's a nice little romantic getaway for us. And we have relatives here, too, so we try to get out this way whenever we can find the time." My throat was suddenly dry, so I took a sip from my tea. I put the cup back down on the coaster. "We like to come here around the time of the Fog Festival, too. It's a fun time of year around here."

"Oh, yes," Jack said, a distant look in his eye. "That it is, indeed. The Fog Festival is quite a lot of fun. I always enjoy all the festivities that come with it. The beach parties. The food. The music. Wonderful fun."

Jack and I watched as a hotel worker crossed the lobby and placed a fresh log on the fire in the fireplace. He stoked the coals and then quickly departed, smiling as he passed by us.

"Just out of curiosity," Jack said. "Why did you choose that book to read? It's one of my personal favorites . . . Dr. Jekyll and Mr. Hyde. I love that story."

"Oh, I don't know," I said. "It was in a collection of books I ordered off the Internet. It came with *Dracula* by Bram Stoker and *Frankenstein* by Mary Shelly in a three-book set. I just thought it would be fun to reread the classics of horror. I do a little writing myself, and I really like the horror genre."

"I see," Jack said. "Forgive me for being so nosy. I was just curious." He puffed on his pipe once more. "You like scary stories? What if I told you a ghost story that involves this very hotel?"

"I do love a good ghost story," I said. "You have a ghost story to tell?"

"I thought you looked like the sort who could appreciate a good ghost story," Jack said. "That is why I stopped when I saw you sitting here." He paused for a beat. "How much do you know about this hotel?"

"I know a little about it," I said. "My wife and I have been coming here for a long time. I know it was flooded back in the 1920s and that it was rebuilt."

"True. True," Jack said. "But did you know that it is haunted by a ghost?"

"You're telling me this hotel is haunted by a ghost, for real?" I asked. "Give me a break . . . nobody really truly believes in ghosts

. . . do you think?"

"Maybe not," Jack said. "But I still believe in ghosts."

"Okay, then," I said. "I guess it's up to you to convince me. Let's hear your story."

"Indeed," Jack said. He puffed thoughtfully on his pipe again for a moment and then continued. "This hotel has a very rich history. How much do you *really* know about it?"

"I know it used to be a boarding house for fisherman and migrant workers, and that it was flooded in a terrible storm in the 1920s—as I've already said—but other than that . . . I know very little about it."

"That is more than most people know about it," he said.

"Well, I just read the brochure," I said, picking a brochure up from the table and showing it to him. "I also did a little research on the Internet, too."

"Very good," Jack said. "Unfortunately, that isn't the whole truth, exactly. There is some disinformation involved with the history of this place, and there has been somewhat of a cover-up to conceal the hotel's jaded past. The general public isn't informed of all of the finer details, but the locals and old folks—most are dead now—still remember some of the juicier morsels of truth."

"So, what is your angle in telling me all of this?" I asked. I was suddenly suspicious of this peculiar old man who reminded me of someone from an old movie or book like *The Old Man and the Sea* by Ernest Hemingway.

"I have no angle," Jack said. He sounded perturbed and offended. "I just thought you might appreciate a good story about a local legend around these parts. If I am intruding and have upset your better judgment, I apologize . . . I will go about my business and leave you to your book—"

"It's okay," I said, reassuring him. "I'm sorry. Don't get offended. I was merely inquiring into why you want to tell me this story—but never mind. I *do* want to hear more about it. You have my undivided attention."

"I believe the truth should be told," Jack said, sitting back in his seat. He took a deep breath. He seemed to be lost in thought for a moment, pondering some long-forgotten time and place . . . the memories flowing back into his mind's eye. After a moment, he began to tell his tale.

"It all started back in 1912 when the hotel was first built. It wasn't really a hotel then. It was more like a boarding house for—as you have said correctly yourself—fishermen and migrant workers. And that is what it appeared to be, at first glance.

"But first, before I get into that . . . I need to tell you more about the community.

"Back then, around the turn of the twentieth century, this town, North Point, was nothing more than a stopping point for small shipping and fishing vessels. It had not yet become the thriving little community that it is today. It was a place filled with wild and unruly people and there wasn't much of a lawful presence back then. There was a sheriff and a deputy, but they were corrupt and easily persuaded to look the other way for a small fee.

"North Point, at that time, boasted a saloon—known as Charlie's Saloon—and a general store, a jail, and this here hotel. There were a few houses here and there, and the town population was roughly around a hundred souls back then, depending on the season—in the wintertime it dropped down to about twenty people.

"Anyhow, this hotel wasn't always called the Queen Charlotte. In fact, back then it was simply called 'Ruth's Boarding House.' And most everyone around town just called it Ruth's, and most everyone knew about Ruth and what her business was, but nobody seemed to give it much concern. Let's just say that she had a small group of girls that she kept around, and they could keep a lonely deckhand company for a while—if the price was right.

"Nobody really got too offended—not until Reverend James Peters came to town, that is, but I'll get to that later. Nobody seemed to mind what was going on at Ruth's and it was one happy, booming economy. The money was rolling in over at Ruth's and Charlie's Saloon. Business was good.

"Soon a road was built that connected North Point to Aberdeen and then people started to travel out at their leisure. Automobiles weren't that big yet, but people were showing up in Model-A Fords, Studebakers, and REO speed wagons full of tourists and potential clients of Ruth's as time went by, more often than not, and North Point became a regular destination for sightseers and thrill seekers alike.

"Charlie's Saloon offered dancing girls—most of whom were employees of Ruth's—and poker along with home cooked meals and it was always packed to the rafters on weekends. Charlie even had a couple spare rooms located in the back of the saloon in case someone was in a hurry and didn't want to walk the hundred yards to Ruth's. Things seemed fine all over in North Point, except for the likes of a scoundrel—or so some people called him—by the name of Duke Carter.

"He was considered to be a despicable character—although nobody really knew why because he was actually a pretty decent fellow if you got to know him—and it seemed that nobody really cared for him, personally, but his money was as good as anyone else around these parts, so the townsfolk tolerated him. He was also pretty handy with guns, knives, and his fists, and he had been rumored to have shot a few people that crossed him and used them for fish bait on his fishing boat—this was never proven, but it did propagate a certain dread when he was present. He kept a boat down in the harbor aptly named: *Magdalene*. Everyone assumed he had named it after the lady in the Bible, although nobody really knew for sure. The sheriff—Tom Jones—was afraid of Duke and let the scoundrel pretty much have the freedom to do mostly anything he wanted to do.

"Duke liked one of the girls that worked for Ruth and he was always following her around and trying to court her, but she didn't seem all too interested in his propositions.

"Her name was Mary and she was young and pretty, no more than nineteen years old, long black hair, beautiful blue eyes, alabaster skin, and a curvaceous figure that turned most every man's head that passed by her. She had been working for Ruth only a short while when she had the misfortune of meeting Duke Carter.

"Duke requested Mary every time he was in town and she obliged because business was business, but aside from giving him what he had paid for, she had no use for him, and she fled from his presence whenever possible. She was repulsed by the ape of a man. What vexed her most was the fact that Duke had a fake glass eye. He had lost his eye in a bar brawl when someone cut him with a broken bottle and was forced to replace it with a glass eye, the matching color to his other green eye. Mary was so repulsed by the hideous green glass eye that she insisted that Duke wear a patch over the glass eye whenever they were together. He grudgingly obliged, but sometimes in the heat of passion he would forget, and she would see the green glass eye and it would fill her with such dread that she would tremble and shake and her countenance would become distraught for days at a time.

"Mary tried to get away from Duke on several occasions, but each attempt eventually ended in failure. She had nowhere else to go—Ruth knew this and always took her back with open arms—and after a time she surrendered herself to the disheartening fact that she was stuck in a terrible situation and there was no other way out; taking Duke's marriage proposal was beginning to seem like her only option.

"Duke and Mary were engaged only weeks later, and she began spending more time with him. He was intent on making an honest woman out of her and if she was going to be his wife she would have to learn how to work and earn her keep. He took her down to his boat, *Magdalene*, and put her to work mending nets, tying fishing lines, cleaning fish, and cleaning the boat. After a while she was beginning to feel like a slave more than his fiancée.

"She told him that she didn't want to be his slave anymore and that she would rather go back to working for Ruth. She said he could have his stupid engagement ring back and that the wedding was off.

"Of course, Duke was not going to stand by and watch her leave without a fight. He grabbed her right then and there and tried to shake some sense into her.

"'Why are you doing this?' he asked, holding her by her shoulders. 'I love you. Don't you see that?'

"'I'm just a whore to you,' she said. 'You have never loved me. You only love my body and the fact that I am an indentured servant to your every beck and call.'

"'Don't leave me,' he said. 'Please don't leave me. I'll do anything for you. You have changed my life. Can't you see that? I love you, Mary.'

"She struggled and broke loose from his grip and turned away from him. She hurried up the walk that led away from the marina and the boat and she quickly made her way back to Ruth's, where she tried to hide from Duke and get back to business as usual."

Jack paused his narration and looked at me intently. He emptied his pipe, reloaded it, lit it, then puffed on it until smoke was billowing over his head. He reached into his coat and took out a sterling silver whiskey flask with a stag's head on it.

"All this talking has made me thirsty," he said, taking off the cap from the flask. He put it to his lips and took a long drink. "Would you like a nip?" he asked, handing the flask to me.

"No thank you," I said. "I quit drinking a long time ago. Alcohol has done nothing but destroy everything and anything that was ever good in my life. I've been sober now for five years."

"Oh, I see," Jack said. "That's a shame—I mean too bad for you. But I understand. Every man has to know his limitations."

"I've heard that somewhere before," I said. "Clint Eastwood, isn't it? And it is true. Life is much better for me now that I don't drink. It took a lot of trial and error, but I finally got it right."

"And that is only right and proper," Jack said.

I was anxious to hear the rest of the story, so I urged him on by saying, "What happened next?"

"I was hoping you would ask that question," Jack said. "It's good to have an eager ear to hear your stories. So, what happened next was . . .

"After Mary went back to Ruth's Place, she tried selling her goods to other gentlemen but none of them wanted to cross paths with Duke so the whole situation resulted in a draw. Mary wasn't bringing in any money, so Ruth put her to work in the kitchen cooking and cleaning, and in housekeeping, making beds and cleaning rooms.

"Duke stopped by to see Mary all the time and eventually she warmed up to him and they began seeing each other again, frequently.

"And then, one day, the unthinkable happened—Mary bedded down with a fellow from out of town. He was a deckhand on a boat that had pulled into port during a storm. He had been warned that Mary was spoken for and that messing with her would surely result in a nasty ending, but he didn't seem to mind or care and said that he wasn't afraid of the guy everyone was afraid of by the name of Duke. Well, that was his first and last mistake.

"Later that night Duke pulled into town and soon enough the gossip got back to him about Mary having been with another man. He was furious. The perpetrator was down at Charlie's Saloon playing poker, getting drunk, and bragging about the fun night he had had with Mary and said that he would fix Duke's clock once and for all, if need be.

"It came as no surprise that Duke went immediately to the saloon looking for the man who had stolen his pride. When he got there all heads turned to watch the showdown.

"'You the one that's been messing around with my girl?' Duke asked, pointing a finger at the man, caught unaware, who was sitting at the poker table.

"'What if I am?' the man replied.

"People started to move out of the way as they saw that a show-down was in the works.

"'I guess you need a little lesson on what happens to guys that go messing around with another man's woman.'

"'And who's going to teach me?' the man said, standing up. 'You don't look like much of a teacher . . . so, I'm guessing you need to go get some help.'

"This last sentence so enraged Duke that he charged at the man with his fists up in the style of Marcus of Queensberry rules, like a prize fighting pugilist, but the man had no intentions of playing by the rules and he quickly pulled a long shiny Bowie knife from his belt and held it out in front of him, waiting for a good opportunity to strike. He stabbed at Duke with the knife and sliced his outstretched fist, flaying the skin on his knuckles to the bone. Duke was surprised by this sudden turn of events and was caught off guard, allowing his opponent time to trip him and kick him in the ass which sent him crashing to the ground in a jumble of chairs, tables, poker cards and chips, and beer and whiskey glasses. Duke rolled over on his back in time to see the assailant lunging down at him with the knife raised high over his head, glinting brightly in the light, razor sharp and deadly, and it looked like Duke had finally met his match and was about to meet his maker, but that was not the way it would turn out. He had a .38 snub-nosed revolver in his belt, and he brought it out in time to put a bullet right through the other man's forehead. The fight was over just like that.

"The dead man crashed to the ground like a felled oak tree. He landed next to Duke, prostrate with his hands out to his side, the knife falling from his hand and bouncing across the wooden floor. A pool of blood formed on the floor around the dead man's head as red as port wine. Duke got to his feet, put the gun back in this belt and quickly left the saloon. He wasn't worried about being arrested for murder—and that would never happen anyway because it was later found to be a case of self-defense—and he hurried over to Ruth's to have a word with Mary.

"He crashed through the front door of Ruth's and stormed through the lobby—the interior of the building was much different back then; it was much smaller; the lobby was nothing more than a glorified living room. Ruth was sleeping on the sofa in the lobby and awoke, startled when Duke entered the room.

"'Where is Mary?' he said. 'I need to see her, now!'

"'She don't want to see you, Duke,' Ruth said. 'Oh my God,' she said, looking at Duke's hand. 'You're bleeding all over my carpet!'

"She jumped up from the sofa and went quickly to the bathroom and brought back a bath towel.

"'Here,' she said, grabbing his hand. She rolled the towel around his hand tightly. 'What in the world happened to you?'

"'It's a long story," Duke said. 'I need to see Mary this instant.'

"'Fine," Ruth said. 'I guess I can't convince you to go away. I'll go get her. Keep in mind that she might not want to talk to you though.'

"'I know,' Duke said. 'Just go get her, please.'

"Ruth went upstairs and quickly returned with Mary. They came downstairs and Ruth went right to work cleaning the bloodstain on the carpet while Duke talked with Mary.

"'What's this I heard about you and that man, Mary?' he said, sternly.

"'It ain't none of your business,' Mary replied. 'I'm a grown woman and I can do whatever I want or see whomever I want to. You don't own me.'

"'Why did you do this to me?' he asked, sounding sincerely hurt. 'I thought we had something special.'

"'*You* had something special,' she said. 'I, on the other hand, had nothing at all. *Nothing*!'

"Duke's anger had subsided by then and it gave way to grief. He looked like a schoolboy who had just had his heart broken by the prettiest girl in school. He was a portrait of sorrow and pain. 'I love you. Don't you see that?'

"'So you say,' Mary said coldly. 'I think I'm just a possession to you. You need to forget about me, Duke. Just go away. I can't do anything for you or give you what you need.'

"'Yes, you can,' Duke said, nearly weeping.

"'No, I can't,' she said. 'I'm done talking about it. Now, goodnight.'

"She turned away and went up the stairs without looking back.

"Ruth finished cleaning the carpet of blood and stood up. She said, 'You need to give it some time, Duke. She's really upset with you, and rightly so. I must tell you that I don't like my girls getting too serious with the gentlemen they meet, and you are no exception. I think you believe that you love her . . . that's a very sweet thought . . . but you must separate fantasy from reality and see which is which. If you two are meant to be together it will happen in its own sweet time. But for now . . . you need to just let it cool off.'

"'I guess you're right,' Duke said. 'She is just so special to me. I've never felt this way about a woman before.'

"'I know, honey,' Ruth said. 'Just give it some time. What you need to be worrying about more than anything right now is getting your hand fixed up. Why don't you go wake Doc Thomas up and have him look at that hand?'

"'I'll do that,' Duke said. 'Tell Mary that I love her. Okay?'

"'Alright,' Ruth said, halfheartedly. 'I'll do that for you. Now, go get your hand stitched up.'

"Duke left Ruth's that night and didn't return for over a month. He went to Doc Thomas and got his hand stitched up. The sheriff, Tom Jones, got a hold of him shortly after that and questioned him about the shooting at the saloon; no charges were filed because it was self-defense; all the witnesses had told the same exact story as Duke, so that was the end of it all—even though Tom would have loved to have been able to arrest Duke—he was still leery enough to leave well enough alone.

"Time passed by and Duke decided he would try to win Mary's heart back again. He bought her flowers and cards and clothes and had them sent to her over at Ruth's. He never made a personal appearance, however, because he now felt bashful and ashamed for how he had treated her, and for killing the man in the bar.

"There was a new problem for everyone in North Point, however, and it made everybody forget about the shooting at the saloon: Reverend James Peters had moved to town and was building a new church building not too far from the heart of town where he could keep a close eye on everything. He was of the Southern Baptist faith and he had sworn to clean up North Point and be rid of all the filth and sin and vice that was running rampant there. He had waged a personal war against Ruth's and Charlie's Saloon and any other miscreants that resided in town. He was going to give them God's message and save their souls. He did a good job too because business at Ruth's and Charlie's Saloon began to decline rapidly after the Reverend arrived on the scene.

"This was Duke's time to act, or so he thought. It was obvious that times were changing in town and the 'good old days' were ending, and now would be the best time to steal Mary away and take her off into a better life. He made his move and went to Ruth's to have a talk with Mary.

"At first, Mary was reluctant, but after listening to Duke talk for a while, she thought that what he was saying made a certain sort of sense and that sooner or later—probably sooner than later—Ruth was going to go out of business.

Duke and Mary began seeing each other again and everything should have been eternal bliss forever and ever amen, but that wasn't the case. One night, Duke was up in Mary's room and they were making love and suddenly she saw Duke's green glass eye and she became extremely distraught.

"'Stop,' she said. 'Get off me.'

"'What is the matter?' Duke asked.

"'It's your eye,' she said. 'It's hideous. You know I don't like it.'

"She got up from the bed and went into the bathroom to get a drink of water. When she came back out, her hand was shaking, and she spilled water on the floor.

"'I told you to wear your eye patch whenever we make love.'

"'I forgot,' Duke said. 'And I didn't bring it with me tonight.'

"Not wanting the mood to get away, he massaged her shoulders and kissed her gently on her neck and ears. He knew that she could not resist this, and she began to moan with pleasure. It wasn't long before they were back on the bed and picking up where they had left off, however this time Mary had turned off the lamp so that she could not see Duke's hideous green glass eye. She closed her eyes and tried not to think about it, just go with the pleasure and enjoy the wonderful sex, but when she opened her eyes again, she noticed that a ray of moonlight had found its way into the room and landed perfectly on Duke's face.

"He was in the heat of passion, oblivious to anything other than the intense sensation burning in his loins and the thrusting motion of his hips. His eyes should have been closed—and his one good eye was—but the green glass eye had a bad habit of sticking open because it was dry and the eyelids would catch on the glass; it was open and looking right at her, dead and horrible, with all of its artificial, lifelike semblance, and it repulsed her in such a manner that her entire body filled with such a horror and revulsion that she became rigid and thought she would vomit. She tried to push Duke away, but he was in the throes of ecstasy and he kept up his pumping motion with a maniacal, increasing tempo, thinking that her rigid body meant that she had reached climax. She begged him to stop. He did not. She felt a terror and loathing so dreadful as the green glass eye glared at her that she screamed out in horror, pushing his face away, begging him to stop. He was nearing orgasm now, and he had no intention of stopping. She could stand it no longer, the revulsion had reached an unbearable state and she reached out without thinking, her reflexes within her very being acting on impulse, and she grabbed the first item that her hand touched on the nightstand. Her hand grasped a metal ice pick and she picked it up and jabbed it with brute force into the object of her dread, stabbing madly at the green glass eye. Duke climaxed explosively at the very instant that the ice pick poked into his eye socket and deep into his brain. He died in the midst of an orgasm. The comb was enough to kill him instantly. Mary had no intention of killing Duke; she had only reacted by striking out at the object of her loathing and terror; the very thing that caused her revulsion and such vexation was the target of her aggression, not the man himself.

"Duke fell limply onto her and his body quivered and shook in the throes of orgasm and death. She began to scream at the top of her lungs and did so until somebody came to her room and found the gruesome tableau.

"Ruth came to the room and asked what had happened. When Mary regained her composure, she recounted the events that had led up to Duke's death and it was quickly decided that nobody would say a word to anybody about what happened that night. They would deal with it on their own; get rid of the body, and hopefully nobody would ever miss Duke—and they were fairly confident that would be the case. They concealed the body in the attic of the boarding house until they could come up with a plan.

"The very next day Ruth had concocted a plan to cover up Duke's death that was sure to work. She decided that at night they would take the body—stealthily, of course—and bury it below the church which was currently under construction right down the street. Soon the church would be finished, and no one would be the wiser."

Jack paused at this point in his story, staring at me in silence for a moment.

The story was beginning to get a little too farfetched for me at this point. I coughed into my hand and took a drink from my tea. It was cold by now, but it was wet, so I drank it anyway.

"They were going to bury the body beneath the church?" I asked. "That's blasphemous."

Jack looked at me and stared long and hard. He didn't say a word, just looked at me, and then took a drink from his silver whiskey flask.

I looked back at him uneasily; the glare he was giving me made me very uncomfortable. I was looking at him and was suddenly struck by the idea that he very much resembled the "Duke" character from the story he had been telling me—right down to the patch over his eye. I wasn't sure I believed all that Jack was telling me, for it did seem a bit too fantastic to be true, but I was willing to humor him and listen to the rest of his tale. I figured that he was just one of those old men who liked to tell stories.

"So, you're telling me that this really happened?" I asked.

"That's what I'm saying," Jack said, relighting his pipe. "Every word of it is true. I wouldn't try to fool ya with something as farfetched and make-believe as this. I promise you that every word I have said is the God's honest truth. Cross my heart, hope to die, stick a needle in my . . . eye."

"Hmm . . ." I said, incredulously. "Okay. I can give you the benefit of the doubt . . . but I'm curious about you. Where do you come from, and how do you fit into all of this?"

Jack squirmed uncomfortably, shifting in his seat; he was visibly shaken by my question.

"I am merely the storyteller. It is not important where I come from or even who I am. It's the tale that is important, not who tells it."

"True," I said. "And again, I have heard that before, too. I can't remember who said it right off hand. But you are right. I was just curious to know a little more about you, Jack."

"Alright," Jack said, puffing on his pipe. "If you insist . . . I have lived here in North Point for most of my life. I was born in Poland during the Second World War and my parents migrated here to North Point. I am now a commercial fisherman and I own a fishing boat named *Angel Made* that I keep down in the marina at peer number thirty-five. I am not married. I live alone in a house outside of town. I come here every now and then to stay when I need a room for the night and wish to leave quickly in the morning. This hotel is closer to the marina than my house—which is over five miles away and sometimes I just enjoy the comfort of the Queen Charlotte Hotel. I know the owner and he gives me super rates on my room." He finished saying this and eyed me coolly, as if daring me to challenge him. "And that, as they say, is the rest of the story. Are you satisfied with this little digression?"

"Sure," I said. "I wasn't trying to get into your personal life . . . I just wondered about you and why you would volunteer such a story as this."

"Because it needs to be told," he said. "But mostly it needs to be *heard*. I figured since you are a reader ghost stories . . . that you would appreciate it, especially since it is a *true* ghost story."

"Okay, Jack," I said, trying not to sound patronizing. "It's your story. You can tell it however you like. You have my complete and unadulterated attention. I really do want to hear the rest of it . . . so . . . go ahead. What happens next?"

"Well . . . it's pretty much cut and dried from here on out," he said. "Ruth and her girls were now in quite a quandary with Duke's dead body lying in the attic getting ripe, and Mary stricken with guilt and remorse for having killed him.

"That night they rolled Dukes body up in black plastic, tied it up with twine, and carried him, ever watchful so that they not be seen and keeping to only the darkest paths, to where the site for the church construction was and they quickly went to work digging a hole. After a while they had a deep enough hole, so they rolled the body into the awaiting earth and quickly filled it in with dirt. They raked over the ground to conceal any tracks or traces they might have left over during their nocturnal undertakings.

"As luck would have it, the very next day the construction workers came in and began building the foundation of the church. They made a lot of progress in the next couple of days.

"When the girls returned to Ruth's that night, Mary went back to her room and while she was removing her earrings one of them fell to the floor and rolled underneath the bed. She kneeled down and reached under the bed, feeling around for the earring; her hand grabbed something round and smooth and when she pulled her hand out to see what it was, she was shocked to see that it was the green glass eye in the palm of her hand. She was too frightened and terrified to scream. It was as though her heart had stopped completely. She stood up and the room seemed to spin around, making her dizzy. She took a deep breath and braced herself with one hand against the wall. When she had regained her composer, she acted swiftly, wanting to be rid of the green glass eye.

"Moving quickly and deliberately, she found an orange Mayfair Tea can—she loved black pekoe tea—full of little knickknacks and dumped them out on the bed. She dropped the green glass eye into the empty tin can and quickly replaced the lid. The tin can rattled and clanked as the object inside rolled and jostled around.

"She hurried downstairs and into the basement where the coal bin and furnace were and decided she would put the entire tin can into the furnace, hoping it would burn, not knowing if it would be hot enough, but it was worth a try. The basement was dark and damp and she didn't like it down there with the bugs and cobwebs and earthy smell, so she hurried down the stairs, fumbling with the latch on the furnace, and right about then a large rat crawled out from the shadows screeching and startling her. She jumped back, stifled a scream by biting her fist and dropping the tin can on the ground. She turned to run back up the stairs. Something made her turn back around and stand her ground though, and she bent down and picked the tin can back up with both hands. The rat was coming toward her, squeaking and screeching, whiskers twitching and glinting, yellow teeth snapping and gnashing. It showed no fear. She threw the tin can at it to scare it away. The rat ducked and scurried down into a hole in the wall. The tin can bounced across the floor and spun around like a top and then fell down into the exact same hole where the rat had made its exit. Mary wasn't about to stick her hand down into the hole, so she figured that it was hidden well enough. Just to make sure, however, she found several loose red bricks and dropped them down into the hole, sealing it off, she hoped, forever.

"Mary didn't do so well in the following days. She was terribly distraught, and she paced about nervously, her spirits extremely melancholy. Ruth and the other girls tried to console her, telling her it would be alright, but nothing seemed to calm her, and she kept ranting and raving about seeing Duke's ghost and that it was following her around and wouldn't leave her alone.

"Finally, one night she went to the marina and climbed aboard Duke's boat, *Magdalene*, and she set sail out to sea and was never seen nor heard from again.

"Nobody even noticed that Duke was missing, and nobody really cared or missed him. Life went on as usual and people soon forgot about him . . . and eventually about Mary.

"Reverend James Peters was pleased to open the doors to the First Baptist Church of North Point only four months after Duke went missing. The church was a welcome haven and attendance was strong during the first Sunday service, although there was a foul stench of something that lingered for a while but eventually went away. Reverend James Peters preached about all of the sin and vice that had a grip on the town of North Point, on the entire world, and that what they needed to do was to stamp out all of the lechery and debauchery and fornication that resulted in sin and death.

"Ruth went out of business shortly thereafter and she was forced to put the boarding house up for sale. It took some time before an interested buyer came along—a gentleman from India by the name of Abu Akmed Khalifa purchased it for a song and it was reconstructed and turned into the building that we are presently sitting in right at this very moment."

Jack stopped talking and fussed with his pipe, cleaning it out and reloading it with tobacco. He was silent as if he were done talking, as if that was all he had to say.

I said, "That's it? That is the end of the story?"

"Yep," he said. He lit his pipe with a puff and exhaled out a cloud of fragrant smoke. "That's about all there is to it."

I felt cheated for some reason—maybe because I expected a happy ending or some resolution or denouement other than what he had provided. "And this is supposedly a true story?"

"It is that," Jack said. "Every word of it."

"How did you come to know so much about it?" I asked.

"People talk," he said. "Word gets around. I listen. All I ever did was put two and two together in addition to what I already knew and what I had been told. It's a pretty clear picture."

"Has the ghost of Duke ever been seen?" I asked.

"Not for a long time," Jack said. "Sightings have not been reported in many years."

"Well, it was an interesting story," I said. "I'll give you that. Very entertaining. I thank you for the tale."

"You're very welcome," he said. "It was a pleasure to tell it to you. Now. With all that being said, unfortunately, the time has come for me to go." He stood up and shook my hand. "It was a pleasure meeting you. I hope you enjoy your stay here."

"The same to you," I said, shaking his hand.

"Perhaps," he said, looking intently at me. "Maybe if you are still here in a day or two and we happen to meet again, you can share a story with me." He smiled brightly, almost devilishly.

"That would be nice," I said.

"Goodbye Niles Porter," he said. "Take care."

"You too, Jack Fargo," I said.

I watched him go out through the door and into the rainy night. He vanished into the darkness and was gone, leaving me standing alone in the lobby of the Queen Charlotte Hotel. I was curious. It wasn't until he was gone that I began to wonder more about him. Who was this odd fellow that had just told me such a strange story? Where did he go? Did I really believe the story he had just told me? What if it was true? No, that's ludicrous, I thought.

I decided I would sleep on it for the night and that I should probably go back to my room and check on my sleeping wife. She had gone to bed earlier that evening and I suddenly was concerned about her well-being. I don't know why but I was struck by the thought that she might be in trouble. I went quickly to the elevator and pushed the bright glowing button with the black arrow pointing upward. It wasn't until I got into the elevator that I noticed there was a button with a B—which undoubtedly went down to the basement. For no reason other than curiosity I pushed the B button and felt a chill run up and down my spine when the elevator doors closed and the floor lost gravity as the elevator descended. Stopping at the basement, the elevator doors opened with a clatter and a bell dinged announcing my arrival. I stepped through the doorway and into the hallway. The basement was dimly lit, the walls were painted a yellowish color and the carpet was dark with a floral pattern. To my left the hallway led to a door with a glowing EXIT sign and to my right the hallway branched into a T intersection. I turned right at the T and followed the hallway past a kitchen and a room that had dining tables. There was a small bar down there and I assumed that it was used for catering services. Past the kitchen and dining room there was a doorway that said, UTILITY ROOM. For some unknown reason I was drawn to this door. It was almost as if I heard a voice telling me to open it and go inside.

I opened the door. It turned smoothly on its hinges, inward, silently.

Inside this room there were cleaning supplies, brooms, mops, trash cans, shelves, trays, carts, collapsible tables, and chairs, but what was of the most interest to me was across the room where an old furnace sat up against the wall. This part of the hotel was older than the rest, the foundations showing through, old red bricks and dirt and cobwebs and bugs. It was obvious that this part of the building was very old and the rest of the newer sections of the hotel had been built right over the top of the older sections.

I suddenly remembered what Jack had told me about Mary throwing the can at the rat and then putting bricks down into the hole to cover it. I looked around and sure enough there were some bricks on the ground in a hole, old and covered with dirt and soot. I reached down and started taking the bricks out of the hole, one by one, until all of them were out and in a neat pile. I reached down into the hole and felt something metallic and square. I grabbed the object and pulled it out of the hole. To my amazement it was an antique tin can with the words Mayfair Tea in black on orange script lettering on the label. Below, in smaller sans serif text, were the words Orange Pekoe India Ceylon. A small logo in the lower left corner showed two blue lions facing in toward a gold shield and they were holding up little black waving flags. However, it wasn't the interesting antique tea can that was so intriguing. I had an idea what might be inside. I shook the tin can and something rattled around inside. It sounded like a dense, solid object. It took a moment, but my imagination led me to believe what might be inside the can. Could it really be . . . I felt a streak of electricity shoot up my spine. I opened the lid on the tin can, tipped it sideways and let the object fall out into my hand. There in the palm of my hand, glistening brilliantly was a green glass eye.

Ultimate Masterpiece

William Tremble always wanted to move someplace far away. When he left home, he always had the urge to just keep on going. Never looking back. He was not satisfied with where he resided, ever, period. He knew that there was someplace better awaiting him just around the next corner.

He was a published poet. He was truly gifted, possessing an artistic ability with words that bordered on genius, and he was well known in the literary world. Although he did well, he wasn't rich by any means; he made a nice living with his pen and paper, but it was nothing to get excited about. Sometimes there were lean stretches in his career when he had to eat pork and beans cold from the can, and he would sleep in the backseat of his car, but there were other times when the living was good, and the claret flowed like Niagara Falls. That was how he lived his life: feast or famine. When times were good, he lived lavishly, and when they were hard, he would dig in and brace for it. He knew from experience that eventually his writings would bring in a healthy check with plenty of zeros and things would be fine again.

He had married three times and divorced three times; he had four children as a result of the marriages. The ex-wives and children didn't want anything to do with him other than child support payments. That was fine because he didn't need them anyway, he reasoned. That gave him more time to write. So, he paid the alimony and child support when he could and went to court when he couldn't. Sometimes he would swear off women completely in order to live a life of abstinence and writing, only to turn around and meet someone new and become deeply infatuated. He was a helpless romantic. What else could he do? Unfortunately, he was never satisfied with the women he met because they didn't quite compare to the ideal woman in his mind's eye. There was always a better woman awaiting him someplace, in a distant place where all was bliss, and they would meet and enjoy a happy life together, living off fillet mignon and merlot.

His last relationship was with a woman named Patricia Clark, and she had fallen deeply in love with him. She said she would do anything for him, go anyplace with him, and nothing could ever change that. He loved her in return with the same zeal, treated her like an angel, but he just couldn't take the pressure and expectations that came with settling down into a comfortable relationship. She had cried until her mascara ran down her cheeks, begging him to stay. He had to go, he told her. He just couldn't stay.

It was always the same in the end. He would move on, leaving everything behind, and arrive someplace new and pleasant where he would meet another nice woman and the whole cycle would begin again. The relationship would eventually grow stale, he would become disenchanted, and his wanderlust would begin causing his feet to grow restless and he would inevitably leave.

This time it would be different, however, he thought, because he had learned a lot over the years and had grown from past experiences and, damn it, he was a better man because of it. He was getting tired of wandering, and he was ready to settle down on a nice little piece of ground somewhere peaceful and serene. He also knew that he was nearing the apex of his writing career and soon he would publish a universal classic, one to rival Shakespeare, Shelly, Frost, or Poe. He could feel it; it was his destiny. The ideas had been building up in his mind for a long time, and he had been cultivating them, each new situation or relationship providing fodder for the lines and verses roaming around inside his head. He had written many of them down already, but this next poem would be the *coup de grace*. This time things were going to be magnificent.

Now as he sat in his hotel room, bottle of whiskey on the nightstand, pen, and paper in hand, he was ready to write his ultimate masterpiece. This was the one that would bring him back into the limelight, get him recognized for the great poet that he knew he was. He had an entire notebook full of fresh, unpublished poems, and this would be the one to finish the collection off in high style. He had already contacted his agent and lawyer and had signed all the necessary papers to finish the deal. Everyone would benefit from his next book of poems. It was sure to be an instant success; the publishers were anticipating high returns on their investment.

He opened the notebook and stared at the blank page. The words were in his head, but they were all cluttered and jumbled and scattered. He knew that he could make sense out of the chaos if he only continued to write, anything and everything that came to mind, until eventually the words began to flow rhythmically, effortlessly. He gritted his teeth as he clutched the pen so tightly his fingers turned white and his hand began to shake. He scribbled a line, crossed it out, scribbled another line and verse, crossed it out and ripped the paper from the notebook, smashing and wadding it into a ball and tossing it across the room. He knew he was courting writer's block; however, he had a solution. He knew how to defeat his disinterested muse. He stared intently at the blank page, pondered for a moment, took a drink of whiskey, and then scribbled several lines in rapid succession. When he was finished, he scribbled his signature at the bottom of the page. *Yes*, he thought, *this is it. I've done it.* This would be his ultimate masterpiece.

He reached into the nightstand drawer and took out a Smith & Wesson .357 magnum revolver. He placed the notebook to the back of his head, put the revolver barrel in his mouth, and pulled the trigger. The gunshot echoed through the hotel room. His brains splattered instantly in chunks and rivulets across the ceiling, wall, and on the notebook where he had written his suicide note. His ultimate masterpiece was complete.

The Old Man and the Dancing Bees

Winston Dixon was stung by a bee one morning while tending to his flower garden. He jumped back and clutched his throbbing hand, cursing aloud as he hopped from foot to foot. Ruth Barns, the elderly woman who lived in the apartment next door, had been secretly watching him from an upstairs window; she burst into a fit of laughter as she watched him dance around in pain. He looked up and noticed that she was watching, and it made him furious.

"What are you laughing at?" he said. "Don't you have anything better to do than sit up there spying on me like that?"

"You poor old fool," she said. "I can't help it with you jumping around like that."

"I was just stung by a bee," he said. He held out his throbbing hand for her to see. "Ain't nothing funny about that."

"Okay. You're right. I'm sorry," she said. "Just hold on. I'll be right down." She disappeared from the window. Moments later she came through the security door with a bang and trotted down the stairs. She held a pair of tweezers in her hand. "Let's get that fixed up . . . shall we?" She grabbed his hand and examined the wound. "You have to be careful with bee stings because they contain venom, you know?" She jabbed the tweezers down and plucked out the stinger. "There you go. You're as good as new. Would you like me to kiss it and make it all better?"

"That's quite all right," he said as he snatched his hand away from her. "Thanks, but no."

"Did you say venom?" Winston asked. "The stinger has venom?"

"Yes. Some bees have venom in their stingers," she said. "It's harmless in small quantities, but in larger amounts it can be deadly—especially if you are allergic to it. People have died from bee stings." She leaned closer to him. "You're not allergic to bees, are you?"

"Heavens no," he said. "My hand feels better already."

"Good," she said. "I wouldn't want you to croak on me."

There was an uncomfortable pause in the conversation. Something was troubling her; Winston had known her long enough to read her expressions. She was anxious and nervous this morning, he thought.

"Your flower garden is marvelous," she said, bending down and inhaling the sweetness of a fragrant rose. "May I pick one?"

Winston stiffened; his eyebrows raised in surprise. "Not on your life. You stay out of my flowers."

She looked past Winston, down the street and then back, meeting his eyes. "You know. I was thinking . . ." she said, trailing off and not finishing her sentence.

"What?" Winston said.

"Never mind," she said.

"Spit it out, woman," he said. "I can't read your mind."

After a long awkward moment she said, "You *know* those wannabe gangsters will probably be here any time now, don't you? It's that time of the month again." She stiffened, clenching her fist, her expression becoming one of bewilderment. "Those . . . good for nothing . . . punks," she said.

For a moment Winston was puzzled and then suddenly he realized what she was talking about: a group of young thugs that loved to terrorize the neighborhood; they were always out for a quick buck; they were not afraid to use deadly force; they made regular visits to their selected victims, especially around the first of the month when social security checks arrived in the mail. They had been a regular nuisance to the community. The police were aware of them but were either too busy or undermanned to devote much time and effort into catching the petty thugs, and the victims were usually too scared to talk or become witnesses for fear of retaliation. The young thugs faced little resistance, had little fear of law enforcement, and considered the neighborhood their turf to rule and conquer *carte blanche*.

Winston looked around to see if anyone had overheard their conversation and said, "Just you be quiet. Forget about it. Do as you always do, and everything will be okay." He grabbed her shoulders gently, but firmly, and looked straight into her eyes. "You hear me? They'll kill us if we don't give them what they want."

"It just makes me feel so . . ." she groped for a word. "I feel like a coward—not doing anything about it."

"What *can* you do? We're too old to fight them," Winston said. "And the police are too slow to respond. They'll kill us if we call the cops, anyway."

She contemplated for a moment and then turned and went to the apartment building entryway. She pulled a ball of jingling keys from her pocket and unlocked the graffiti covered door. Before entering she turned and looked back. "Someday they'll have to answer to God for their actions," she said. "It can't be tolerated. I feel so helpless. We can't even call the police or defend ourselves. It's just so . . . ridiculous. I hope they all burn in Hell! You be careful, Winston. It isn't safe to even be out here right now. You should go inside where it is safe—safer than standing out here in the open, anyway."

He remained silent and watched her enter the building.

"Dirty, rotten punks," he said. "What is this world coming too? Can't even go outside anymore. Piss on that. I'm not going to live my life in fear."

He heard a buzzing sound near his feet. He looked down and saw a bee rolling around in distress. It was squirming and buzzing like a jumping jack across the pavement. He raised his foot to stomp on the sputtering insect, held it in the air for a moment, and then decided not to kill it. Killing God's creatures was not within in him—he literally couldn't hurt a fly—unless it was necessary; even when he had to kill an insect, he felt guilty for a long time. He bent down on one knee and examined the bee closely. It was probably the one that had stung him; he could see that it was wounded where a stinger should have been. It looked similar to a honeybee, but it had some unusual colors and markings unlike any he had ever seen. The colors changed with the movements of the bee, iridescent rays of color, shimmering like sunlight refracted through a prism. It reminded him of the fireflies he used to catch at night when he was a boy. The bee buzzed loudly, quivered in the throes of death, then abruptly stopped moving.

Winston dug through the contents of his pockets, found a piece of folded paper—a to-do list scrawled in neat penmanship—and leaned down and scooped up the bee. He was allowing no chance of getting stung again. He felt sorry for it in a strange way. It made him think of his own mortality. He folded the paper around the bee and walked over to the trash can. He was about to throw the paper away when his attention was distracted by a car approaching from down the road; he absentmindedly stuck the piece of folded paper in his pocket, and looked in horror as a 1970 green convertible Cadillac crept along the street like a predatory dinosaur. It had overly large wheels with gold spoked rims; it looked like something a drug dealer would drive.

It was *them*; they had come, just as Ruth feared.

A loud rumbling noise, like the loudest drums from the jungles of Africa emanated from the car; music that was all bass and drums blasted from speakers as big as trampolines. The explosively loud music filled the air, shook the ground, and made Winston's bones vibrate. His heart jumped into his throat, fear playing xylophone notes on his spinal column, paralyzing him. He tried to move but his feet had grown roots.

The white ragtop convertible roof was down, and Winston could see them clearly as they approached. There were five of them: four males and one female. Their heads bobbed to the beat of the music. They were smoking cigarettes and sharing a bottle of cheap wine. The driver had eyes as blue and cold as frozen lakes set deeply into his sunburned face. He wore his blonde hair short and neatly combed back with some type of grease. He wore a white tank top T-shirt, gold chains glittering around his neck. He was slim and muscular, and covered with tattoos that depicted various themes of naked women, booze, drugs, and death. Winston thought the kid had more ink on his skin than the Sunday edition of the L.A. Times. The girl sitting next to the driver was pretty with long black hair and a tan complexion, probably Hispanic in origin. The kid in the passenger seat had skin as black as coal with a blue undertone. He wore designer sunglasses and had a comb sticking from his hair. The two kids in the back seat were either Mexican or Indian, but Winston couldn't tell. All he knew was that they were all *very* dangerous and he would deal with them accordingly; and he knew all too well what was about to take place: they were going to rob him and the other tenants in the apartment building; however, if he paid them to go away there wouldn't be any violence (he hoped) and everyone would be able to sleep easy at night.

The Cadillac pulled up in front of Winston. He could almost reach out and touch them; the smell of cologne and cigarettes filled his nostrils. The music blasted his eardrums and shook his rib cage. The driver parked the car. The girl turned off the music. The young thugs jumped out. They all wore expensive sneakers, baggy pants that sagged and exposed their underwear, and excessive amounts of gold jewelry. Despite the dire situation, Winston found himself musing that they should pull their pants up and wear a belt to keep them up.

"Hey old man," the driver said. He put his hands into his baggy khaki pants. He smiled, exposing teeth like white chips of marble, big and straight like the keys on a piano. "How's it hanging, you old fart? Did you miss us?"

Winston's knees knocked and his hands trembled and shook. He said, "Please don't—"

"Shut up!" the driver shouted into Winston's face. "I didn't say you could talk, did I?" He looked at the other kids for approval. "Did I say this worthless old cocksucker could talk? Huh?"

"Kick the old geezer's ass, Chico," the black kid said.

Chico smiled, then snapped his strong teeth together repeatedly, nearly biting Winston's nose. "What do you think, you old turd? You don't have any teeth left to knock out . . . maybe I could break your arm, or something . . . would you like that?" He glared deep into Winston's eyes. "All you old bastards are the same," he said. "You're all worthless. Pathetic." He pulled a stainless-steel revolver from the front of his pants and pointed it at Winston. "Don't move old man, or I *will* blow your damned head off," he said. "I bet you got a key to get inside, don't you. You could get me inside, huh?"

Winston cringed at the gun barrel hovering only inches from his face; he could see the rifles spiraling down into the deep black abyss where the bullet was chambered. "I don't—I can't—" He stammered.

Chico turned and looked back at the others, snapped his fingers and nodded his head toward the building. "You guys know what to do . . . get the money and kick some ass. Break the door down. We don't need no fucking key . . . Hurry up!" He turned back around. He pulled the hammer back on the pistol and stuck it up to Winston's forehead.

Winston fought back the urge to speak. *Hold your tongue, you old fool,* he thought to himself. A single tear rolled down his cheek. He flashed back to a time in the past when he was much younger and stronger—he might have whipped these punks single-handedly—but that was long ago. Now he was an "old fart" whose crowning glory was growing flowers—flowers that would probably be decorating his grave, shortly hereafter, he mused. The thought made him swoon. He felt the urgency of the situation and needed to say something, anything, to end this atrocity; it was dangerous, even insane, but he felt he had no choice. He said, "I don't have much money—I'll give you everything I have, if you'll just go away and leave us alone. Nobody here has any money. There's nothing but elderly folks on fixed incomes living here."

Chico considered the offer. "You don't have enough, old man," he said. "And I don't take checks or credit."

"I've got cash—just don't hurt anyone. Please," Winston said.

"Maybe . . . maybe not," Chico said. "How much you got?"

He pulled out his wallet, opened it and removed all the bills, and then pulled a handful of change from his pocket. He handed it to Chico. "That is all I have. It's fifty dollars and some change. Just take it and go . . . please."

"Today's your lucky day, old man," Chico said, putting the money in his pocket. "I've got more important things to do than fuck around with you and your lousy fifty bucks." He called the others back; they were in the process of prying open the door with a crowbar. "Let's go, you guys. Let's get out of here."

They all climbed back into the car, except for Chico; he raised the gun into the air, fired two shots and then brought the gun down like a hammer, hitting Winston's skull with brutal force. It knocked him unconscious and he fell to the ground like a wet sandbag. Chico turned and walked quickly to the car, jumped into the driver's seat, and put it into gear. As the car rolled away the music was turned on again, loud bass and drums thumping and blaring into the distance, fading out by degrees as the car drove away.

The witnesses closed their curtains, afraid to go outside

• • •

Ruth, who had watched the whole event, was intimidated and scared but she felt that she had to help Winston. Chester Perkins, an elderly black man with salt-and-pepper hair, was standing in the hallway. He had a massive gunmetal blue Smith and Wesson .44 magnum revolver in his hand. He was confused and scared as paced about waving the hand-canon around awkwardly.

"I seen the whole thing," he said. "We got to help him."

"What's that," Ruth asked, pointing at the gun.

"What's it look like?" Chester said. "It's a gun. And I aim to use it, too."

"It's a little late for that, Chester," Ruth said.

"I got scared," he said. "I didn't know what to do."

"We need to see if he is alright," Ruth said.

They went outside together to see how badly Winston was injured.

• • •

Winston was swimming in a sea of darkness, a black void of nothingness. He could hear familiar voices crying out his name, and somewhere in the distance he could hear sirens. The sounds grew louder. Winston sat upright instantly with a jerk, shouting out like a madman: "Venom!"

He opened his eyes and looked around, stunned.

"What are you talking about? Are you all right?" Ruth asked. "The police are on their way. And an ambulance."

"Venomous—trifling. Why did you call the police?" Winston cried. "Now they'll be back to kill us all."

"What's he saying?" Chester asked Ruth. "Venom? What's that all about?"

"It's nothing," she said. "He's just delirious. We were talking about bees and venom earlier. He's been hit on the head and now he's just cuckoo, repeating gibberish."

"I'm all right," Winston said. "I've been hit harder than that before. Don't you forget it."

Three police cars and an ambulance arrived on the scene. A crowd had gathered around to watch. The uniformed police officers were questioning any witnesses, which were few and next to none. The paramedics helped Winston to his feet. "Easy does it, sir," one of the paramedics said. "It looks like you took a mighty hard blow to the head. You're bleeding quite a bit. We need to get that cut cleaned up. You might need some stitches."

"Nonsense," Winston said. "I'll be fine. Just help me to my apartment. I'm tired. I need to lie down."

"You might have a concussion," the paramedic said. "We recommend that you go to the hospital and let them take a look at you. The police need to ask you some questions, too."

"Fine," Winston said. "Let's get it over with."

They helped him onto a gurney and put him into the ambulance. The ambulance pulled away from the scene and whisked him away to the hospital.

• • •

After several hours of medical examinations, X-rays and questioning from the police, Winston was released into the care of Ruth and Chester. They helped him into a wheelchair and rolled him out through the emergency room doors. They got into a beat-up station wagon and drove away from the hospital. When they got back to the apartment, they helped Winston up the stairs, through the security door, and up two flights of stairs past walls covered with graffiti and gang tags. The numbers on his apartment door were missing leaving a ghostly B9 in the yellowish paint above the peephole. The hallway smelled of urine and sweat and cigarettes. Chester asked if Winston had his keys. He did, in his right pocket. They opened the door and led him into the kitchen, sitting him down in a chair by the kitchen table.

"You're very lucky," Ruth said. "You are also a fool to be confronting those . . . juvenile delinquents all alone like that."

"I didn't plan it," he said, sharply. "They caught me off guard."

"I warned you," Ruth said.

"Somebody has to speak up," Chester said. "Why didn't you tell the police everything you knew about them?"

"And get somebody killed?" Winston said. "You know what

those punks will do if they find out we've been talking to the cops? They'll kill someone—everyone. You can't stop those creeps."

"I'm going to call the police and tell them everything," Ruth said. "I don't care about their threats anymore—something has to be done."

"Are you crazy, woman?" Winston snapped. "It—they can't be stopped. That's just the way kids are nowadays. If you put them in jail they'll just come back someday. And there are always more to take their place. It's an epidemic. The youth of America have no respect for anything—especially their elders—let alone themselves. And they're extremely dangerous."

Chester coughed into his hand and cleared his throat. "I bought me a gun," he said, proudly. "A brand new forty-four magnum. I've got a little surprise for those assholes the next time they come around here. I was gonna go out there this time, but . . . I don't know why I didn't. I'm sorry I let you down, old friend."

The statement agitated Winston; he shook his head in disagreement. "You can't stoop down to their level. Only God can stop those crazy kids . . . and sometimes I wonder if even *He* can or will."

"I'm gonna get them," Chester said. "I don't care what anybody says. Next time I'm gonna put a bullet right in that skinny little punk's chest. I got a bullet for each of them."

"You'll get yourself killed, you know," Winston said, rubbing his throbbing temples. "I need to get some rest now. Just forget about it. Okay? Promise me that much. Please. Now leave me alone and let me get some sleep."

Chester and Ruth hesitated, then said goodbye as they left the apartment.

• • •

Winston awoke late in the afternoon from his deep slumber. His head still hurt, and there was an intense, dull throbbing from the cut on his head. He took two aspirin and washed them down with a glass of cold water. Stretching and yawning, he crossed the kitchen and opened the window to let some fresh air into the room. There was a flower box outside on the window ledge; he breathed deeply, smelling the French marigolds, nasturtiums, and pansies as they swayed in a gentle breeze. The flowers made him feel better.

He decided to smoke his pipe. That always made him feel better. He could think clearly with a good puff of tobacco. Sitting down at the kitchen table, he loaded the pipe with tobacco and then reached into his pocket for a match. He emptied the contents of his pockets onto the table, unable to find a match. He got up, rummaged through the cupboards, and then found a box of Ohio Blue Tip stick matches in a drawer. He sat back down and lit his pipe, inhaling the delicious and aromatic smoke. He looked down at the items he had removed from his pockets and saw the folded paper—his to-do list. He opened the folded paper and the dead bee dropped onto the Formica surface of the table. For a single instance Winston expected it to fly away. He examined the insect closely, marveling at the vivid colors on the wings, thorax, and abdomen. It was curled up in a fetal position. The eyes stared at him blankly, sparkling like two finely cut gemstones. It was an unusual specimen, to be sure; a bee unlike any he had ever seen before. He touched the tiny carcass with the tip of his finger causing it to roll over and over, coming to rest on its abdomen, wings up, hunching down as if ready to spring up at any given moment. He jerked his hand back with rusty reflexes, afraid of being stung again, even though he knew that it was dead.

Unexpectedly, as Winston relit his pipe, a bee flew through the open window, buzzing past his head like a hot bullet. It ricocheted off the kitchen table and hit the mirror hanging on the wall. It became angry at its own reflection, climbing up and down the mirror as it tried to sting the reflection of itself. It left the looking glass and flew around the apartment, inspecting the contents therein, stopping here and there, bounced off the overhead light bulb, and then circled again and again until it noticed the dead bee lying on the table. It dived down like a kamikaze pilot, hit the table and skidded to a halt, wings vibrating, and legs out like landing gear. It marched over to the dead be and nudged it as if it hoped to revive its fallen comrade. The bee bowed its head sadly, and then it looked at Winston with an accusing glare.

"I didn't do it," Winston said. He felt foolish for talking to the bee. "It stung me—I think—but I didn't kill it. I swear I didn't."

The bee folded its upper arms, a cross expression on its face; it tapped a foot as if demanding more information.

"I didn't mean to hurt it," he said. "You've got to believe me."

Winston was sure he was losing his mind. He said, "I'm carrying on a conversation with a bee. I've completely lost it this time. This is nuts."

The bee did a little dance around the dead shell of its brother, like a medicine man in a ritual dance around a fire. A smell like bananas filled the room. Another bee flew through the window, then another and another, each of them joining the dance. Soon there were hundreds of bees circling around the dead bee on the table—and more were flying in through the window. Winston thought he could hear a chant rising from the ever-expanding circle of dancing bees. He rubbed his eyes in disbelief. Taking a second look, he saw the dead bee twitch and squirm, then roll over in a somersault as it sputtered back to life; the other bees stopped circling and joined hands, still chanting. The bee was alive again, reanimated by the strange dance.

Winston felt his heart jump with joy and happiness, a smile brimming on his face.

The bees jumped up in unison, a little cheer rising from the interlocked circle. They each took turns greeting their resurrected brother who was dead but had risen, and then each in turn took flight, zigzagging past the old man and out the window. The last bee to leave was the undead; it flew over to the old man and hovered only inches away from his nose. Winston almost swatted it away as it tickled his nose, but he stayed steady and still. The bee joined its front legs like a priest in prayer and bowed its head in a gesture of gratitude, saluting the old man like a samurai warrior. It made a series of strange squeaks and clicks, barely audible, and then flew out the window and was gone.

Winston had to pinch himself to see if he was dreaming; perhaps he was still fast asleep, and this could all be explained away when he woke up. The pinch hurt. It was no dream. He shook his head, amazed by what he had just witnessed. He knew that bees were intelligent in their own way, but this was beyond anything he had ever seen or heard. He remembered reading somewhere that honeybees lost their stingers and died afterward, but wasps didn't. Maybe they were wasps . . . but he didn't think so, for they didn't look like any wasp he had ever seen. Maybe the bee wasn't dead; perhaps it was just in a coma, or knocked out, or something. Winston was sure, but his curiosity was piqued, and he aimed to find out exactly what kind of bees these were and where they came from.

During the following week he made a trip to the library checking out several books on beekeeping, insects, and anything else he could find on the subject; he rented video tapes and watched them again and again; he consulted experts and quizzed them thoroughly about the specifics on bees. They answered most of his questions but none of them could tell him what kind of bee he was dealing with; it was probably a wasp, perhaps a hybrid, but it might be a honeybee. The experts were a little perplexed at the strange dancing behavior, even amused by the story, treating the old man as if he were senile, even a lunatic. The final answer was yes, bees do dance, but once dead they cannot come back to life. They could lie dormant during cold periods and grow active when it grew warmer, but dead was dead, and that's a fact. Perhaps, they suggested, he should consult a psychologist.

• • •

The bees came back to visit the old man every day; he left the window open and a plate with sugar and pieces of fruit out on the table. After the bees were comfortable with him they would accept bits of sweet stuff from his hand, even landing on his outstretched finger like a pet bird. Golden pollen dust would rub off on his hands with a pungent, fruity odor like bananas. He read about their ability to emit pheromones and mark their territory or send distress signals when they were in trouble; he wasn't sure, but he got the feeling they liked him and were marking him as a friend.

After countless hours of close examination, he still could not pinpoint exactly what species of bee they were, even while comparing them directly to the pictures and illustrations in the books. The closest thing he found that resembled the dancing bees were hybrid honeybees from Africa, also known as Africanized bees, or "killer bees", that had been imported by researchers in the 1950s and 1960s. The killer bees had escaped captivity and mated with local drones. These bees were extremely aggressive and if the nest was disturbed, they would attack in large numbers, stinging anything that moved. A typical colony, he read, consisted of one queen, tens of thousands of workers, and hundreds of drones. They had spread through much of South and Central America, Mexico and had even reached Texas in 1991; they attacked other bees, animals, and humans, even killing when attacking in large numbers.

Winston found it hard to believe that the dancing bees could be so vicious as to kill anything. They fit the description of the killer bees except for the color patterns and they didn't seem aggressive. Perhaps these bees were hybrids, he mused; he was excited by the idea of finding a new species.

Day after day he followed the bees until he had determined that their nest was located somewhere in a condemned apartment complex some three city blocks away. The buildings were scheduled for demolition soon and this heightened Winston's efforts to find the nest, for he knew that the construction workers would exterminate the bees without a second thought. The buildings were boarded up and he had to pry open the plywood that blocked the entrance. The bees circled around his head as he entered the abandoned building. They didn't seem to be bothered by his presence. Up the stairs and down the hallway he found the nest hanging from a sprinkler pipe. It was swarming with what he estimated to be thousands of bees.

Now that he knew where the nest was located it would take some intricate work, he realized, to relocate the nest. He would need special, protective clothing and a container in which to capture the queen; the bees would have to be forced to swarm in order to make them move. He decided that he would gather the necessary items and come back later.

He left the building, pondering how he would go about the dangerous task, when his thoughts were interrupted by a terrible sight awaiting him outside: the 1970 green convertible Cadillac was parked in front of the apartment building. Much to Winston's dismay, the five teenagers were leaning against the car, obviously waiting for him to come out. His heart sank as he stopped and looked down at them. They must have seen him enter the abandoned building.

Chico crossed his arms and leaned back. "Well, well, well," he said. "Look what we have here. What are you doing so far away from home you old geezer? Are you lost? This is my turf . . . and you're trespassing. You know what that means?"

Winston didn't know what to do. He said, "Can't you just leave me alone? I'm not bothering you—"

Before Winston could finish, Chico ran up the steps, grabbed him by the throat and slammed him against the wall. He gritted his teeth and said, "You just fucked up, royally. I don't like you and

I'm going to enjoy tearing you a new asshole." He dragged Winston down the stairs and out onto the street, punching him hard in the face. Blood began to trickle from his nostrils.

"Please," Winston pleaded. "Please don't hurt me."

Several bees buzzed past Chico's head as he continued to beat Winston. "It's time to pay the piper," he said. Shoving Winston to the ground, Chico kicked him in the ribs, and then kicked him in the face, causing his dentures to fly out and clatter across the pavement.

"Please," Winston pleaded again, raising his hands, and begging them to stop. "I'll give you whatever you want. Please just stop hurting me—"

"Whatever I want," Chico said, kicking him again for emphasis. "Hmm, let's see? What could that be?" He kicked the old man with each stressed syllable.

"Maybe to see you dead, you piece of shit. Can you give me that? I want to see you dead!" Chico was enraged; spittle flew from his lips as he spoke.

"Why?" Winston asked. A rivulet of blood ran down his chin. He was lying prostrate on the ground, barely able to lift his head.

"Why? Because we want to," Chico said, stomping the old man's head. "Because we can. Because you're old and weak, and we are young and strong. Because it is what we do. Now you die you old prick. Let's party, everybody." He motioned for the others to join the savage beating.

Suddenly, bees were everywhere, attacking the teenage thugs.

A bee stung Chico on the chest and another stung his face. "Ouch! Shit!" he said. Several more bees stung his arm. "What the fuck?" He swatted at the bees that were swarming around his head. Chico pulled the shiny pistol from his pants and emptied it into Winston's back. The gunshots roared and echoed down the street. The sound of swarming bees grew louder.

"Let's get out of here," the girl shouted, running for the car. She jumped in first, followed by the others. They were swatting wildly at the angry bees.

"Close the top," Chico screamed, jumping into the driver's seat. "Quick, damn it! Close the goddamned top!" The convertible ragtop started to close slowly. "Roll up the windows—now! Shit!" He started the motor, put it in gear and stomped the accelerator to the floor. The tires sparked and squealed, spun out of control, and finally caught traction as the car shot away like a rocket, leaving black smoking lines on the pavement. The engine roared as the car slid around the corner and sped away into the distance.

The bees did not follow; instead, they went back and buzzed over Winston's dead body, circling around and around. They began their strange dance, more bees joining in until there were thousands of bees circling, chanting, jumping up in unison, and then circling again. The chant grew louder and the dance more frantic.

Winston's fingers twitched, one of his eyes rolled around like a spotlight, the other dangled loosely from the socket. As he got to his feet, the bees began to swarm over his body; the queen flew out of the building and landed in his open mouth; she sat inside of Winston's mouth like a pilot in a cockpit. He closed his mouth gently to protect the queen. The other bees covered him in a living, writhing blanket. There were thousands upon thousands of bees covering him until he became a walking human swarm. He had quadrupled in weight and mass, a lumbering *thing* that rippled and buzzed as it lurched away into the oncoming night.

• • •

"Fucking bees," Chico said, rubbing his bee sting wounds. "Can you believe that? They were everywhere. That was crazy."

The others agreed with him. It was wild; eerie; downright strange.

"I need something to drink," Chico said, turning the steering wheel.

He parked haphazardly in front of a little convenience store on the corner of the block. He went inside and picked up a bottle of Canadian whiskey, a case of beer, and a pack of Camel cigarettes. He got back into the car and drove down the road. He turned into the community recreational park and stopped near the basketball court.

The park was empty as the sun began to set. Along the street and around the park, high-pressure sodium vapor lamps began to light up. Palm and oak trees shimmered in the gentle summer breeze as night set in across the city. The group of young thugs got out of the Cadillac and sat on the hood, resting for a minute after all the excitement. Two of them took a basketball from the trunk and played a game of one-on-one, while the others drank beer and whiskey and smoked marijuana and crack cocaine. They were already forgetting about the murder they had just committed; it wasn't the first time they had killed someone (and after the first time it became much easier to do it and forget about it without any remorse). Life and death had neither meaning nor worth to them and the only important things in life were drugs, sex, money, and power. That was the spice of life: to be powerful, respect no authority, and never grow old.

Chico was getting drunk; the stinging pain in his chest and face slowly subsiding as the alcohol depressed his system. He reloaded his pistol and tucked it into his pants. "Rule number one: always reload your gun," he said. This pleased him immensely.

They drank beer and toasted to long life, lots of money, and to never growing old. It was good to be young, they agreed. Very good. Growing old was the end of all things good, they thought.

None of them noticed the dark, lumbering shape that lurked in the shadows just out of reach of the overhead lights. They didn't hear the buzzing sound of thousands of tiny wings as the massive swarm of bees crept closer . . . closer . . . closer . . . watching from the shadows and waiting for the opportune moment to strike.

• • •

Chico was the first to see it and he couldn't believe his eyes when it stepped into the light. It looked like a giant man covered with . . . something . . . like . . . *bees*. It was moving fast toward them, smooth and deliberate, the bees rolling and squirming like maggots on a corpse. Chico pulled his gun from his pants and shot at the swarm, emptying the pistol for the second time that night. The gunshots exploded from the pistol as it spit lines of fire and sparks and hot lead toward the inexplicable thing. It was no use; it didn't stray the monstrous *thing* from its course.

"What in the hell?" Chico said. He threw the useless, empty weapon at the strange swarm of bees and turned and ran.

The bees exploded into the air in a horrendous cloud, dimming the lights as they descended on their prey. The youths ran in different directions, the bees stinging them thousands of times. The girl managed to get into the car and drive away, even while the others tried to get into the vehicle. She ran one of her companions over (one of her last thoughts was that it looked like Chico) the body rolling under the car with a thump. The bees were so thick it was impossible for her to see; she stepped on the throttle and sped away, turned onto a back street by mere chance, the bees stung her all the while until her eyes swelled shut. The bees inside of the car stung her until she was an unconscious, dying mass of swollen flesh. Her foot was still on the accelerator as the Cadillac crashed through a chain link fence, flew over a small embankment, and then slammed into the ground coming to an abrupt stop and bursting into flames.

The other gangbangers were stung to death in the park, their bodies strewn like silent victims of war. The park grew calm and still. The sound of approaching sirens filled the night as emergency vehicles approached the scene from a distance. The bees regrouped on the old man's body and turned him back into a massive, human-bee-swarm again. The steady buzz from the lumbering mass slowly faded as the old man and the dancing bees journeyed away together into the cover of darkness.

Revenge is a Dish Best Served with a Cold Beer

Red brought the chainsaw to work and decided to cut the boss's head off after lunch. Maybe he would hack the fucking secretary into pieces, too. Why stop there? He would just work his way through the building and carve them up at random as he went along. They were all a bunch of shits anyway and they would get what they deserved. He put the chainsaw in a guitar case to keep it disguised. It was going to be a grand time at the office today, he thought with a grin.

When he got to work that morning, curious coworkers asked what he was doing with the guitar. He told everyone that he was going to play some music later. Someone asked if they could see it, and he had to think quickly, couldn't let anyone blow it for him. He told them, "No!" He never let anyone see his ax before a performance.

At his desk, Red logged onto the network and browsed the Internet. He posted a blog about how pissed he was at the system and everybody in it. He fucking hated the world. He was a self-professed cynical misanthrope and fuck anyone that tried to argue. Screw all the assholes and let them rot, that was Red's final thought on the whole thing. At the end of the blog post he said he was going to get even by making hamburger out of everyone, grill them up and serve them with a side of pickles, tomato, onion, lettuce, and mayo, and eat them with some Bush's baked beans. It was a joke, of course, but after a while it began to sound like a good idea. He was getting hungry anyway. Maybe they could have an early lunch at the office.

Carl, the company computer guy, came over to Red's cubicle and stood with his arms crossed and foot tapping as he looked at the computer screen.

"What ya up to?" Carl inquired.

"What's it look like?" Red replied.

"It looks like you're wasting company time on the Internet," Carl said, examining his cuticles. "You know that's against company policy."

"Yeah, I know that," Carl said, grinding his teeth. "So, what's it to you? Why do you care?"

"It's my job to monitor the computers and the users," Carl said, leaning on the cubicle. "And you are a user on a company computer . . . so that means you're in my domain. I'm going to have to file a report."

"You know what?" Red said. "It just so happens that I've got a surprise for everyone today. I was going to save it until after lunch . . . but you've convinced me that there is no better time than the present—for a present."

"A surprise?" Carl said.

Red picked up the guitar case and set it on the desk. "I'm going to play everyone a song."

"How nice," Carl said sarcastically.

Red opened the guitar case and pulled out the chainsaw. Carl's eyes bulged in horror as Red yanked the starter chord and the chainsaw rumbled and sputtered to life. Red revved the throttle and the chainsaw screamed and growled, hissing, and puffing out clouds of oily blue smoke.

"What the hell— " Carl began, but was quickly silenced when Red hacked into his neck and chopped off his head. Blood and meat splattered Red's face and the walls of his cubicle.

It was complete chaos and pandemonium as Red chopped through the cubicles and lopped off heads as he went. Screams and shouts of terror harmonized with the chainsaw roar and echoed through the office building in a diabolical cacophony. Red was oblivious to any pleas for mercy. Blood ran in streams and pooled on the floor.

The boss came out to see what was causing the commotion and his eyes widened in terror as Red descended upon him, swinging the chainsaw like a samurai warrior, slashing, chopping, grinding, and whittling the corpse limb from limb.

The massacre only lasted for a few minutes and no one could escape. Red was too quick and too pissed to let anyone go free and he had blocked all the doors in advance. Each of the coworkers became meat and offal as Red carved them up like a master butcher.

After everyone was dead, Rex went out the back exit into the lounge area and fired up the gas barbecue grill they kept for company picnics. He slapped four generous ground meat patties onto the grill and cooked them medium rare. He took a Pilsner beer from the boss's stash in the refrigerator and sat down at the picnic table and dined contentedly on the burgers. It was a fine day after all. The sun was shining on his face and his stomach was full. The beer was exquisite. He would sit and wait for the authorities to arrive and savor his accomplishment. Things couldn't have worked out better, he thought, with a satisfied grin as he popped the cap off another cold beer.

Pyromance

Keith Chapman, a young man in his mid-twenties, was a guitar player. He was also a singer in a band named Spasmodic Jerks. Although this was his primary source of creativity, he had other darker artistic outlets and adventures. Today he was excited and invigorated. In the back of his Ford pickup, he had several red plastic jerry jugs full of gasoline, a propane torch, a box filled with Molotov cocktails, a box of hand grenades, and a box of dynamite. He was going to have some fun tonight.

On June 15, 2019, at 4 a.m. he was driving down the back streets of Paynesville, California, looking for a good place to burn to the ground. The town was asleep, and that was good, for that meant there would be less witnesses to see him performing his art. He considered himself an artist: fire was his medium and the world was his canvas; he would burn anything to the ground if it felt right; his art was his *raison d'être*.

It was summer and a particularly dry season for Paynesville, so Keith didn't have to look far for possible places to burn. All he needed to do was toss a cigarette butt out the window into a field of grass and that would be enough to cause a three-alarm fire. But that wouldn't be good enough. That was sloppy, accidental, left up to chance. He was an artist and he would create a masterpiece beyond comparison.

Oh, and to think of the victims, so innocent in their sleep, so unaware of their surroundings, as they wandered through their dreams.

That was a fringe benefit.

Keith was struck with a wonderful idea as he drove toward Richmond Estates on Hillside Drive. There were many large and luxurious houses where he was going. Rich men had built their dreams there. What better place to create his work of art? A true craftsman picks only the best raw material. There could be no settling for second best. A man's house is, indeed, his castle, and that castle would soon be Keith's *pièce de résistance*.

He turned off Vine Street onto Hillside Drive and cruised past the expensive houses and mansions, watching for the right one to appear. The street was lit with sodium vapor lamps. All the houses were amazing works of contemporary architecture with lots of glass, wood, brick, and steel. Some of them had four car garages where he knew there were parked Porsche, Ferrari, Maserati, Jaguar, Mercedes Benz, and Rolls-Royce automobiles. The homes were surrounded by fabulous landscapes with rock gardens, water fountains, statues, and exotic trees. Not one of them was without a swimming pool. Most of the houses and estates were surrounded by fences and walls—behind which well trained dogs marched back and forth waiting to chew the limbs off any intruder—and undoubtedly there were alarm systems wired into every nook and cranny.

Despite all the security devices, the inhabitants of Richmond Estates were careless. They lived under an illusion of protection and safety. Although they knew that they were potentially at risk of being robbed and victimized, it had not happened enough to mention—a total of nine times in the history of Paynesville—and none of them thought that it would ever take place. It was something they thought about, but it had lost all immediacy and danger. The good life had made them sluggish; and to the skilled criminal the houses and their inhabitants were ripe for the picking.

Keith was not interested in robbing anyone. That would be far below his standards. He considered himself an artist, not a criminal. What he did was not out of selfishness, greed, or want of ill-gotten gain, but for the sake of beauty and life. To him, fire existed for a purpose. In the forest it made the old trees release their seeds so that saplings could be born. It created heat which had many purposes. It was the substance of the sun, the source of light. Fire was a purifier and a cleanser, a substance to baptize the soul. Keith believed that those who were fortunate enough to be burnt alive were the lucky ones, for their souls had been cleansed and their sins destroyed. Others, however, were not so lucky. And if he could have his way, he would go out with a bang and a blaze.

After driving nearly to the end of Hillside Drive, he found the house that he would set on fire. It wasn't an extremely large house, but it didn't have a fence and it wasn't exposed by too much light. He drove down the road and parked near a vacant lot behind a grove of trees and brambles. He removed a rusty toolbox and a can of gasoline from the back of his truck and crept back down the street toward the house.

He made quick work of the task, nailing the windows shut as quietly as possible, tying rope around the doorknobs, and fastening them to a fixed object so that the doors could not be opened from inside, making sure that there could be no escape from the house, and then sloshing gasoline on all of the walls. He made a trail of gasoline out to the yard. Lighting a book of matches, he tossed them down onto the puddle, watching the gas ignite, the flames swooshing toward the house. He turned around and jogged back toward his truck, climbed inside, started the motor, and drove away.

• • •

There was a dirt road that led into the hills. Keith knew the place well. He followed the road until he reached the highest point of the hills where he turned off his lights and motor and stopped to watch the house far below as it burned. At first, he was pleased, but when the fire trucks and police arrived at the scene, as they always did, he grew disappointed. They showed up with unusual speed this time, almost as if they were expecting a fire.

The family was rescued from the burning house and whisked away to safety. Nobody was hurt. The fire was extinguished. The house was not destroyed.

Keith had been defeated. His masterpiece destroyed. This was an outrage. He would get even. There were plenty of other houses to burn. And if they wanted to get down to the nitty-gritty, there were numerous buildings in town that were like fireworks just waiting for the fuse to be lit. He would show them.

Later, he thought. I'll show them later and I will enjoy every minute of it. He decided to go home, exchange the Ford truck for his

Harley Davidson motorcycle and then go and have a drink—after all burning down houses was hot and thirsty work—at the local watering hole. He sped through town and pulled up in front of the Oasis Cocktail lounge. Inside, he sat down and ordered a beer, relishing the vivid images of flames in his mind's eye.

• • •

"Can I buy you a drink?" the girl asked, catching Keith off guard. He turned and looked up at her. She stood next to him, a drink in her hand. Her hair was long and jet black, cut straight over her icy blue eyes. She was wearing a black leather jacket, red blouse, and a black miniskirt, her legs were smooth and curved, and her feet were clad in cherry red stiletto heeled shoes.

"Uh . . . sure," Keith said, surprised at his good fortune. "Please sit down," he said, pointing at the chair across the table.

"Thank you," she said, sitting down.

"I'll buy the drinks," Nick said, calling for the waitress. "What are you drinking?"

"Whatever you are," she replied.

He ordered two Budweiser beers. The drinks served, they looked at each other awkwardly.

"So, do you—" Keith started to say.

"Tell me something . . ." she interrupted, cutting him off in mid-sentence, ". . . do you like wild sex?"

"—come here often?" Keith looked at her, confused for a moment, and then shocked by her straightforwardness. "Well, uh . . . do I like wild sex? You sure don't waste any time, do you? What kind of man wouldn't like wild sex? I mean, unless he was a prude, or something."

"Forgive me for being quick," she said, sipping on her beer. "I'm usually not this way—I don't know what's come over me. There's just something about you that turns me on."

Keith gazed at her suspiciously. This was too good to be true. This sexy little vixen had all but thrown herself at him. Maybe she was trying to sell herself to him; or maybe she had a devious plan devised. What was her ulterior motive? Nowadays, foxy little ladies don't just walk up to a stranger and throw themselves at you. Or did they? Perhaps she just wanted a quick fling; a dive in the sack; a roll in the hay. Hey? But there were dangers to think about; a person could never be too cautious these days. What the hell, Keith thought. She looked good, and his libido was burning hot.

"You don't even know me," he said, swigging from the bottle of beer.

"As a matter of fact," she said, eyes beaming, "I do know you."

"You do?"

"Yes, I do. You're the singer for that band. What's it called?"

"Spasmodic Jerks," Keith said, proudly.

"That's right. I've seen you guys play before."

"You have?"

"A couple of times, actually," she said. "Once, a while back at a party down by the Riverside Park; and before that at the county fair. You guys are pretty good."

"Thanks," he said.

"Something about rock and roll singers just turns me on."

"I understand—I think."

"I was sitting over there at the bar, and I saw you come in. I recognized you after a while, and I said to myself, 'get over there and introduce yourself.' I knew I'd be a fool if I didn't. So . . . here I am."

"What's your name?" Keith asked.

"Andrea."

"Nice to meet you, Andrea."

"I dunno, to tell you the truth. I think my parents were stoned when they picked it out."

"I like it. It has a nice ring to it."

"Okay, now what is your name?" she asked.

"Keith," he replied.

"Nice to meet you, Keith," she said, extending her hand.

"Let's get some music going here," she said, glancing at the jukebox, then around at the other patrons in the bar. "These old farts in here keep playing that damn redneck music. I can't stand hillbilly music like that, can you?"

"You're a lady after my own heart."

Presently, the jukebox was pounding out a country dirge. They stood up and went to the jukebox. After pumping in five dollars and selecting songs, they went back to the table and ordered more drinks.

"I'm sorry if I seem to be kind of in a hurry," Andrea said.

"What? A hurry for what?" Keith said.

"But I'm serious about it," she said. She was silent for a moment, then looked at him and said, "How would you like a night you'll never forget?"

"You really don't waste any time, do you?"

"Life's too short to be shy," she said, finishing her drink. "A girls gotta take what she wants if she plans on getting anywhere in life. As the saying goes: a closed mouth doesn't get fed."

"What do you have in mind? I mean . . . what's your definition of 'wild'?"

"Oh, I don't know," she said with a devilish grin. "I just like anything dangerously exciting. Living on the edge. Let's do something really crazy and then fuck each other's brains out."

Keith was awestruck. He said, "You're serious, aren't you?"

"Serious as a heart attack."

"Let's get it on, then," Keith said, smiling.

Brian Adams came through the jukebox singing about how it cuts like a knife.

"Do you dance?" Andrea asked.

"Sure," Keith said. "I'm a singer. Why wouldn't I?"

She led him to the dance floor. There were a few other couples dancing there in front of the jukebox. Keith put his hands on Andrea's waist and pulled her close to him. She put her hands on his shoulders. They looked each other in the eyes; there was a promise there; a twinkling of lust and passion promising that tonight would be a night they would never forget.

The song ended and they went back to their table. Ted Nugent filled the air, gripping the jukebox speakers with a stranglehold.

They sat down. Andrea lit a cigarette, offered one to Keith.

"So, what did you have in mind?" Keith asked, puffing on the cigarette.

"I dunno," she said, drawing on the cigarette then blowing the smoke between her luscious, red lips. "I like fire," she said, flicking her lighter and gazing at the dancing flame. She ran her fingers through the flame. Her eyes twinkled like diamonds.

"Fire?" Nick gasped. This was strange. Did she know something that he didn't? Had she been following him? Or was it just a coincidence? Keith was a pyromaniac in the truest sense of the word; in fact, he had been responsible for scores of arson fires around town.

It was uncanny that she should mention fire.

"You like fire? What kind of fire?" Keith asked.

"There's only one kind of fire, babe. But I like it when it's wild-fire," she said. "It makes me feel so good to see flames. I like it hot."

"You don't mean—not . . . no," he said, shaking his head. "You couldn't mean—"

"Arson?" she quizzed, feigning naivety.

"Shh," Keith hissed, looking around. "Don't say that too loudly. Besides, that's not the proper word for it anyway. It's an art form. It's called pyromania." He stopped, suddenly suspicious of this strange girl. He examined her closely.

Guns and Roses came over the jukebox with a song about a sweet child.

"How do I know you're not trying to set me up?" Keith asked, watching her closely for any betrayal of her true intentions.

"Because I'm not, and you believe me. I know how it looks. But you don't have to worry. Relax. Just let me do all the work. To-night's on me. How's that? Why would I put myself in jeopardy if I was trying to set you up?"

"It's just too coincidental, is all."

"Listen," she said, "we don't have to do anything illegal; it was just an idea."

"No, I want to," Keith said, standing up. "Let's do this."

She stood up. They left the bar and went out into the warm summer night. They were alive with excitement.

Keith went over to his Harley Davidson motorcycle and climbed on. He jumped on the kick-starter, the motor starting with a roar, rumbling, and sputtering.

"Get on," he said, revving the motor.

Andrea climbed onto the motorcycle and held on tight.

They pulled away from the curb and went down the street with a rumble from the V-twin engine.

• • •

The ride on the motorcycle was invigorating. Wind whipped back their hair, tears welling in their eyes, adrenaline pumping through their veins as they cruised down the back road through the country. The vibration from the engine was causing a pleasant tingling sensation throughout Andrea's body. She held on to Keith around his waist, hands placed lightly on his crotch.

The headlight lit up the road, yellow lines zipping by in a blur. Keith was driving away from town, out into a sparsely populated area; and for this, Andrea was pleased. There were no houses out here; it was mostly trees and rolling hills and the river.

Keith made a turn, driving up into a secluded dirt road. He stopped the motorcycle, leaving the engine running, and leaned it over on the kickstand. He turned off the headlight.

"Wait here," he said, swinging off of the bike. "I'll be right back."

He disappeared into the darkness. After a minute had passed, he came back with something in his hands.

"What's that?" Andrea asked.

"Can't start a fire without gasoline . . . and a spark." He flicked his Bic lighter and a flame instantly appeared lighting up the darkness and exposing the red gas can.

He gave her the can. "What am I supposed to do with it?"

"Just hold on to it until we get where we're going."

He climbed back onto the motorcycle, put back the kickstand and twisted the throttle. As they reached the main road, he turned on the headlights. The motorcycle roared across the smooth concrete surface, past the sleeping houses and shops.

Keith and Andrea were excited and invigorated by the feel of the rumbling motorcycle beneath them, the rush of the cool night air across their faces and the thoughts of fire and naked flesh. The anticipation was almost too much to bear.

He turned the motorcycle down a desolate road where they passed an occasional house, vast expanses of empty fields, and groves of pine trees. A set of railroad tracks lay parallel to the road, the smell of creosote drifting from the ties beneath the rails. Turning again, to the right, and crossing over the railroad tracks, he made another quick turn to the left—shifting down—and then followed a dirt road that ran alongside the tracks. A plume of dust rose behind them like a dark, malignant cloud rising in front of the crescent moon. The dirt road grew bumpy and rough as they pulled up next to a building which was the first in a series of connected structures. They were square in shape and large. They appeared to be warehouses. The buildings were built on a high cement foundation, but they looked to be built out of mostly wood, which had grown dry and brittle over the years.

Keith made a U-turn and stopped, turning off the engine.

"This is it," he said, climbing off the bike. "What do you think?"

"It's beautiful," Andrea replied, gazing at the buildings in the moonlight.

"These old warehouses should go up like a bale of hay," he said, climbing up a wooden ladder and standing on a boardwalk. "Okay," he said, motioning to Andrea, "give me the can."

She lifted the gas can up to him.

"I'm going to go in," he said, turning toward an old, rickety door.

"What about me?" she asked.

"Just wait out here," he said. "I won't be long." He kicked the door in with the heel of his boot, paint flakes bursting from it, wood splintering as it tore loose from the hinges. "Keep watch," he said, then entered.

Andrea watched with a nervous smile. This was too good to be true.

Keith knew his way around, for he had been inside the building before when he was just a boy. The building was a storehouse for the city maintenance crew. There were all sorts of machinery, barrels of exotic and noxious smelling liquids, bundles of railroad ties and other highly combustible odds and ends. Now that he thought about it, he realized that he didn't even need the gasoline that he had brought along; but it had become such a habit to bring it along, that he didn't even think about it anymore. It was just an unconscious act. He dumped gasoline over the stack of wooden beams, the barrels, and a pile of boxes. The fumes stung his eyes and lungs. He splashed it on the walls, on the tractors and strange machines, saving just enough gas to make a trail out through the door. He poured it out as he backed through the doorway, letting it soak into the wooden boardwalk beneath him. He tossed the can back inside the building and then jumped down to the ground, landing hard on his boot heels.

"Ready for this?" he asked.

"Yes," she said.

Keith pulled a handkerchief from his pocket, flicked his Bic lighter and lit it on fire, holding it out at arm's length until it started to burn robustly in a ball of flame.

"It's show time," he announced with a grin. He tossed the flaming handkerchief onto the puddle of gas on the boardwalk and jumped back to get out of the way. Instantly the volatile liquid burst into flames, making a swooshing sound as the fire shot across the boardwalk and through the busted door.

"Come on!" Keith shouted, dashing toward the motorcycle. He jumped on it and started the engine. Andrea sprang onto the seat behind him, her heart beating rapidly in her chest, her stomach turning over nervously. He twisted the throttle, the back tire kicking up a rooster-tail of dirt and rocks as he shifted through the gears and raced down the road.

Behind them, the building exploded into flames with the sound of breaking glass and splintering boards.

Keith turned the motorcycle to the left and drove away from the inferno, taking a different route than when they had arrived. The road was primitive, nothing more than an old trail with two worn paths where an occasional truck or car had passed over it. He was driving fast; a little too fast, but Andrea was enjoying the thrilling ride. He maneuvered around sharp corners, leaning into them and working the clutch and throttle and brake; he jumped the bike over giant mounds, becoming air born and sailing across the sky line like Evil Knievel doing a dangerous, bone-breaking stunt, then landing smoothly; and upward, ever upward, as the road climbed higher and higher, weaving back and forth until they were at the top of a hill— several miles away from the burning building.

At the crest of the hill there was a clearing where they could view the entire town. He stopped the motorcycle and turned off the lights and engine. The lights of Paynesville stretched out before them like hundreds of twinkling stars reflected in a calm, still lake. There were cars moving along the highway; the rhythmic strobe of the airport spotlight—white and green—and the brilliant orange flames of the burning buildings, now appearing no bigger than a saltine box in the distance. The flames lit up the sky, smoke billowing upward.

"It's magnificent," Andrea crooned. "Spectacular . . ."

Keith remained silent, watching the fire. He was pleased with his handy work; he was an artist, and this was his masterpiece.

Suddenly, the whale of a siren pierced through the night, rising and falling like an air raid warning. Twirling lights flickered red and blue, as the first patrol cars cruised toward the blazing buildings, then fire engines roared toward the fire. The night was alive with the shrill sirens and blaring horns as the authorities raced toward the scene, growing ever closer, on the verge of destroying Keith's artwork. But then, they always did—he had grown accustomed to it, for it was all part of the game—and it only inspired him to strive for bigger and better things, defeating the fire fighters. That would be his ultimate achievement.

• • •

"Come here," Andrea said, wrapping her arms around Keith's waist and pulling him close to her. "And now a reward for a job well done," she said, moving her lips toward his.

He put his arms around her and leaned down to kiss her. He could see her features by the light of the moon; she was so sexy that he could not resist. There was a stir in his groin as their lips met, tongues probing each other's mouths, licking, exploring, tasting one another. She moaned softly as she reached down and unbuttoned his jeans, pulling down his briefs.

He let out a gasp of pleasure, closing his eyes and tilting his head back.

She licked her lips and then went down on her knees, sliding his jeans down and letting them fall to his ankles. She took him into her mouth, completely, then released him slowly, then went down again. He moaned, placing his hands behind her head, and pulling her toward him, deep, deeper, deepest. The pleasure was almost unbearable; the tingling sensation swirling in his loins, throughout his limbs and mind. His body was on fire with friction, ecstasy filling his veins. He could feel himself getting close to overflowing; she could feel that he was getting close to release. She stopped short and sat up.

"My turn," she said, rising to her feet. She licked her lips, glancing at him with sultry eyes. She straddled the motorcycle, placing her feet on the handlebars. She pulled up her skirt and bent her knees, spreading them apart and exposing herself.

"You bet," Keith replied, hopping toward her, keys jingling in his pants pockets. He lifted one of her legs over his shoulder, spreading her wide, and leaned down, running his tongue back and forth.

She squirmed and bucked her hips, grinding them and rising to meet his mouth. She grabbed handfuls of his hair and jerked his face into her.

He became frenzied with desire and excitement, and he could stand it no longer.

Kicking off one of his boots and stepping out of the pant legs, he climbed onto the motorcycle. Placing both of her legs on his shoulders, he moved toward her and pulled her closer—she grabbed his shaft and guided him in—as he slid into her tender, warmth, entering her was like being draped in satin and immersed in exotic oils. She coaxed him to a climax, each stroke urging satisfaction. He pounded fiercely into her, driving his shaft to the hilt, feeling the tip of his member probing deep within her.

She was moaning and crying out, with each lunge, raising her hips to meet his thrusts.

They were both getting close to exploding in climax, each stroke lifting them higher and higher. She clamped tightly around him like a hand in a glove, and he hammered away even harder than before. For a moment the world seemed to stand still; both of their bodies joined together as one, each individual body cell joining together with its mate, completely in tune with each other.

And then they burst together in orgasm; she let out a cry of pleasure, her body quivering and shaking; he felt his balls erupt inside her. The pleasure seemed to last forever.

• • •

After the festivities were through, they sat back and shared a cigarette.

"So, where do we go from here?" Keith asked.

"Oh, I don't know," she said. "What do you mean, exactly?"

"I mean, will I see you again after tonight?"

"Maybe," she said. "We can see each other again soon. You can come to my house and meet my family."

"Uh, okay," Keith said. "Is that a good idea . . . do you think?"

"Why wouldn't it be," she said. "You can come over tonight, if you like."

"Don't you think that might be rushing it a little?"

"We just burned down a warehouse and then made love, two perfect strangers . . . and you think coming to my house is rushing things?"

"I see your point," Keith said. "I guess it wouldn't hurt. I just think maybe—"

"Shh," Andrea said. "I understand. You want to take it slow. Don't worry. We don't have to rush. After all, we had plenty of fun for one night. I should be getting home, anyway. I'll tell you what . . . why don't you meet me somewhere tomorrow night?"

"Sure, okay," Keith said. He was beginning to feel a funny feeling (was it love?) in the pit of his stomach; perhaps he was just infatuated with her. He looked at her and thought that she was beautiful. "Where do you want to meet?"

"You can give me a ride and drop me off," she said. "And when you see where you drop me off, that is where you can meet me tomorrow."

"Great," Keith said. "That will be just great."

"Well?" she said, looking at him intently. "What are you waiting for? Let's get going."

"Oh, right," Keith said. He got on his motorcycle and started it with a mighty kick. The motorcycle roared to life, loud and proud, much like Keith was feeling now. He was invincible. "Get on," he shouted.

She climbed onto the back of the bike.

They pulled out and took off down the dirt road.

Andrea navigated from behind, giving him commands with her hands and sometime shouting into his ear. They drove across town and into the wooded section of hills that lined the northern side of Paynesville. Keith knew the area well. It was the rich district where doctors and lawyers resided—he had burnt a few houses out in this area. The path he was following led them past the Serenity Hill Cemetery and then up to a secluded driveway with a wrought iron fence gate. He couldn't see the house, but he was sure that it was magnificent.

She climbed off the bike and said, "This is where you can meet me tomorrow."

"You live *here*?" Keith asked.

"Yep," she said. She rummaged through her purse and brought out a pen and a piece of paper. "I am going to give you my phone number so that you can call me before you come out here again. I might be busy. You never know."

"Sure, okay," Keith said.

She scribbled a number on the paper and handed it to him.

"Thank you," he said. "When do you want me to come out here, tomorrow?"

"Just call me tomorrow evening, right around dusk," she said. "I'll be busy until then—"

"Doing what?" Keith said, realizing that he was being rude. "I mean, what do you do for a living?"

"I am a nurse," she said.

"Oh, I see," he said. "I'm sorry for being so nosy. Anyway, thank you for a wonderful night."

"Same to you too," she said. "Now you better get going. And do be careful driving back on this road this late at night."

"I am a professional," he said, beaming with a devilish grin.

"I'll say," she said, touching his chin softly with her fingertips. "You are wonderful. Now, go home. Call me tomorrow."

"I'll do that," Keith said. He realized that she wanted to watch him go, and not the other way around; he thought this was strange, and it wasn't until much later that the oddness of the whole thing sunk in—he looked at the wrought iron gate and saw that it was locked with a rusty chain and padlock. "What is that for?" he asked, pointing at the chain and lock.

"For safety reasons," she said. "Now just go home."

He wondered if the chain was to keep people out or in . . . and then he let the thought slip from his mind. He was getting tired, and he decided that it was a good time to go home.

"I'm going now," he said. "I'll call you."

"Swell," she said. She kissed him on the cheek.

"See you tomorrow," Keith said, as kicked the motorcycle to life and revved the engine, putting it in gear. He let out the clutch and took off down the road. He could see her in his rearview mirror as he sped down the road. She was standing and watching as he headed away into the distance around a corner and out of sight into the night.

• • •

Keith had been worried that he would never see Andrea again after their night of excitement. First, he called the number that she had left him, making sure that she was home. She said that she was busy, but that she would meet him later in the evening. She had picked the place: Serenity Hill Cemetery at 7:00 p.m. sharp. Keith was shocked at her choice of meeting places, but then after a while it kind of appealed to him—this meeting in a cemetery sounded kind of . . . dark, and mysterious and he liked that. She said to look for her car, a teal-green Honda Civic, parked outside the cemetery gate.

It was a little after seven o'clock, he was running late, as he drove his motorcycle between the gateposts of the cemetery. Now he was beginning to think that it was a bit strange that she wanted to meet in the graveyard. Night was coming; it was almost twilight as he cruised past the tombstones. Up ahead was the mausoleum . . . and parked in front of it was Andrea's car.

Keith parked behind the car. He stood looking at the mausoleum. It was a large, square building with a flight of cement stairs climbing up to a set of vast iron doors. There were two satyr-faced gargoyles perched at the sides of the door. The building had windows—which were not visible to Keith from where he presently stood, but he knew what they looked like—that were arched-framed and set with colorful stained glass. It looked foreboding, and for a moment he thought about getting back on his motorcycle and leaving.

And then she came through the doors, wearing a brilliant white gown, her hair flowing over her shoulders, lips red like roses, eyes twinkling and blue like sapphires. She looked stunning.

"Keith," she said with an angelic voice. "You're late."

"I'm sorry," he said, stammering. "You look lovely." He was entranced by her beauty. "I never expected you to look so—so unbelievably beautiful."

She giggled, stepping down the stairs and stopping halfway. She gazed at him with alluring eyes.

"Come here," she said, beckoning him with a delicate and creamy white hand, "there's something I want you to see."

Keith was focused on her bosom where her breasts were squeezed together in the form of dimpled cleavage. He was dazed, looking back to her eyes—his own eyes opening wide as if hypnotized by her. He followed her up the stairs and inside.

After passing through the towering doors, he was greeted by the smell of dry cobwebs and dust. The hallway lay before him with faces of marble on each side. There was a magnificent carpet on the floor with paisley patterns in red, gold, and aqua.

He stopped just through the doors. "What are we doing here?"

he asked.

"Come here and I'll show you," she said over her shoulder without stopping or looking back.

Still in a daze, Keith followed her; but he sensed that something was not quite right, as though this was a trap, and he was staggering willingly into the jaws of doom. Why was he trusting this woman whom he had only known for a matter of a day? He didn't know the answer to the questions his mind was asking. It was not a matter of trust, for he trusted no one, as much as it was a matter of longing: he needed her; wanted her; must have her. And for that he would be willing to do anything—even if it meant making love in the company of the dead; surely, they wouldn't mind, although they might be a bit envious or even jealous. She had woven a spell and left him writhing in her web; now she was reeling him in for the kill. He felt his groin stirring, his member growing hard, as he thought about making love to her, and if she wanted to bite, or be kinky, or even be a little bit macabre . . . then that was fine by him, too.

The main hallway spanned the entire length of the mausoleum, and every fifty feet, or so, there were chambers to the left and right, forming an intersection. These were small rooms where the tombs ran lengthwise, the coffins being placed within them sideways as opposed to the tombs in the main hallway that were placed in feet first. There was a stained-glass window in each of these chambers, and if the sun had been shining there would have been brilliant rays of colored light, but now they were only dull and lusterless.

Andrea turned and stepped into the first chamber on the right, slipping out of Keith's view. Desire was flowing throughout his frame, flooding his mind and body with anticipation. He turned into the chamber and stepped toward her. "What . . . uh . . . what are you going to show me?" Although he was in a trance, something inside screamed in disagreement about this whole situation. But her eyes . . . they were like vast chasms in the depths of the blue sea and he was falling into them from a great height, drowning in them, sinking down into the bottomless abyss.

"Come here, my love," she said, spreading her arms wide. "You do love me, don't you?"

"Yes . . ." He went to her and fell into her arms, embracing her and pulling her close. "I love you more than anything."

"Will you die for me?"

Now things were getting a little *too* intense. Was she out of her mind? "Yes—I will," Keith said, entranced. "Anything for you."

"Kiss me," she said, putting her delicate hands on his shoulders. "Take me, right here, right now."

Keith was much obliged. He put his lips to hers and closed his eyes, feeling an electric current vibrating throughout his body. It was a wonderful kiss, full of passion and fire, and as sweet as the nectar from some exotic fruit. It was a kiss to beat all kisses for he felt a stir in his groin then the ecstatic tingle of pleasure as he reached rapid orgasm, emptying his sac into his briefs. Now that was a kiss. But it was laced with poison. Her venomous lips were sickly sweet.

It was the kiss of death.

Keith felt something inside of him moving as though he were falling apart. She was sucking his breath out, suffocating him. He opened his eyes as something came loose in his chest with a sickening ripping of flesh, like the sound of cotton sheets being torn in half. Terror drained him to white. He tried to scream but she sucked the cry out of his throat and swallowed it whole.

Before his very eyes, she was changing, her face shriveling like an old apple core, her eyes little black marbles, her hair drying and turning brittle with streaks of gray. She was withering away into a hideous corpse. Her lips turned black and cracked like sun baked clay; he could feel her lips on his own like rough sandpaper. He tried to pull himself away, but she latched onto him with gnarled, bony hands that had turned into hooked talons, dead claw-like things. She was pushing her dried tongue between his lips, licking inside his mouth. She tasted like death, he thought, like something fowl and rotten. His heart was beating hard in his chest, each pulse heightening his terror. And then the lights began to dim, the world spinning beneath his feet like some wild carnival ride, his knees buckling as he swooned.

And then everything was gone.

Blackness.

He passed out of existence with a kiss of death as Andrea exploded into a cloud of white sparkling light and buzzing flies, laughing hideously as she vanished into thin air. Keith collapsed dead on the floor of the mausoleum. The marker on the face of the burial vault next to his dead body read: Andrea Brocton, Born Dec 10, 1884, Died April 13, 1919.

The Cursed Stone

It was late in the Autumn of 2017, almost Halloween, and the trees were covered with red, gold, and green leaves, some of them falling onto the road. It was getting dark, which was perfect, because the forest was spooky as hell in the dark. All of us were students at Indiana University in Bloomington and we had brought some freshmen with us to break them in with a good scary trip to a local cemetery at night. I had a surprise for them, but I would wait to tell them when we got out into the cemetery.

When we arrived at the gate to the cemetery, we quickly parked our cars and turned off all the headlights. The cemetery was closed after 11:00 p.m. and we still had about an hour before it was off limits. When everyone was gathered around the gate, I held a flashlight under my chin, illuminating my face in what I hoped was a spooky light in order to set the mood, and I told them the story about the legend of the cursed stone.

"Laura, did you bring your video camera?" I asked. Laura Miller was my girlfriend and companion to my constant college high jinks.

"Yes," she said. "Right here." She held up the camera to prove it. I looked at her for a moment and realized how much I loved her; she was beautiful.

"Good," I said. "Start filming now."

She pressed the record button and watched the scene through the LCD viewfinder.

"Alright, you guys," I said. "I don't know if you are all familiar with the legend of the cursed stone. For those of you who are not, let me tell you—"

"Hurry up Ray," Stephen Anderson said. "The cops are going to catch us before we even get started."

"Okay. Just be patient," I said. "It goes something like this:

"During the civil war there was a farmer who had a beautiful daughter, her name was Annie. He guarded her jealously. Anybody who tried to date her would get the old man's shotgun right up his ass. Nobody in town ever tried to court Annie because the farmer was so mean.

"Anyway, there was a black slave named Benjamin, who had escaped across the Mason-Dixon Line from Alabama. He traveled up through Tennessee and Kentucky until he reached Indiana. Now, Benjamin was hiding out and camped in the woods behind the farmer's property and he had to keep a low profile. He would sneak around at night and steal chickens so he could have something to eat. In the daytime he stayed concealed in the woods, hiding from passersby.

"Annie had found Benjamin one day while she was picking wildflowers. He was sitting up against a tree when she crossed his path. He started to run away from her, but she called to him and told him she wouldn't hurt him. They became friends immediately. After that, she would sneak out into the forest and bring him food and spend as much time with him as she could. Eventually she fell in love with him.

"Well, one thing led to another, and soon they were caught by the farmer. He was furious. He gathered up some of his buddies and they went out, captured the black slave, and hung him from an oak tree right on the spot. They beat him with sticks and axes and baseball bats. They covered him with gasoline and lit him on fire. The farmer made Annie watch the whole thing. She was hysterical, sobbing and weeping; face down on the ground because she didn't want to watch. She begged them to stop and the farmer slapped her across the face.

"After it was all over the farmer dragged Annie back to the house and locked her in her room where she stayed for months. He was disgusted and didn't want to look at her. The worst part about the whole thing was that Annie got pregnant. She didn't tell anybody, and she kept it a secret as long as she could, but eventually she started to show, her belly swelling like a ball of dough, and it became obvious that something was wrong.

"The farmer beat the truth out of her. 'How could you do that?' he screamed at her. He was going to disown her. A midwife came and delivered the baby, with strict instructions that the baby should not be born alive, should never take a single breath. The midwife was more than willing to follow these instructions and the baby was stillborn.

"The remains of the black slave and the stillborn child were buried in an unmarked grave right here near this very spot, in this cemetery. But not in the cemetery, because black slaves weren't allowed to be buried in a white man's cemetery, so they were just dumped in a hole in the woods outside of the cemetery and buried.

"Annie left her father's house and never looked back. She all but disappeared from existence. She was never heard from again. She is said to have fled to the woods where she lived off the wild, surviving off plants, mushrooms and berries, and she would visit the cemetery and sit on a stone and mourn the loss of her lover and child. Eventually she died and it is said that her ghost haunts this cemetery and that she visits the stone every night at midnight, guarding the graves. She is even said to dig up the baby and cradle it in her arms. If she sees you in the cemetery, she will chase you away. It is also said that anyone who sits on the stone will be cursed and die within a year."

I finished the story and looked around at my audience. They were all getting nervous by now.

"That's bullshit," Scott Garcia said. He was one of the freshmen with the most heart. "I don't believe it."

"Is it?" I asked. "We're going to find out, tonight. The test is to see who has enough balls to sit on the stone."

Laura was gripping me tight and clinging to my side.

"I don't think this is a good idea," she said. "Maybe we should just go now."

"Oh no," I said. "We are here and we're going through with it. Let's go."

I climbed over the gate, which was only a few feet high, and motioned for the others to follow. They were reluctant at first, but eventually they came up behind me.

The trail leading to the cemetery was about the length of three football fields. It was a dirt path surrounded by dense trees and thickets. I shone my flashlight ahead of me, scanning the path ahead of me. A black snake slithered across the trail, stopped, and looked at me, hissing, its black beady eyes shining in the light.

One of the girls screamed.

I stopped short, picked up a stick and chased the snake away.

"It's alright," I said. "They're harmless."

We continued down the trail.

There is a granite marker stone at the entrance to the cemetery. It reads: Sykes Cemetery, Est. 1800. It is creepy, to be sure. It doesn't mark a grave, it just greets visitors to tell them that they have arrived at the cemetery and are entering sacred ground.

The Sykes Cemetery is shrouded in mystery. Nobody knows much about it other than it has been around for a long time and it is spooky. It is an old pioneer cemetery with about a hundred graves. Some of the gravestones are so old that the writing has been obliterated by weather and the elements. There were civil war veterans buried there, and some modern stones as recent as 1996, one of which had an eerie epitaph: "Never at rest." There was a big problem with vandalism, too, and there were rumors that a satanic cult used the grounds to perform their rituals. There are strange plants that grow there, spiky looking things, that reminded me of cactus. The grass was always kept mowed, but nobody ever saw the caretaker, as far as I know.

There were large pine trees, which are not native to Indiana, and a gnarly old oak tree with stunted growths, warts, and distortions that had the weird appearance of a dog protruding from the limbs, and if you looked at it long enough you could see faces in the deformations in the trunk.

I shone my flashlight on some of the graves, scanned the parameter, and felt a shiver tingle along my spine. The air was thick and electric and hazy. I remembered that whenever people took pictures, they would catch orbs of blue and white light and vaporous phantom clouds. We were now well into the middle of the cemetery. I looked around for the stone, and there it was, far toward the back of the cemetery where the woods seemed dark and dense and forbidding. It was a large chunk of limestone that jutted from the ground like a giant tooth. I thought about how the legend claimed that if you sat on the stone you would die within a year. I suddenly wondered if I wanted to go through with this challenge; I didn't believe the myth, but the atmosphere was taking on a sinister quality and I was feeling a little tinge of fear, I must admit.

"Okay," I said, shining my flashlight on the stone. "There it is. Remember, the legend states that if you sit on that stone you will be cursed and die within a year."

"Fuck this shit man," Kevin Miller said. He was the freshman voted most likely to fail. He was a coward and failed at nearly everything that we dared him to do. "What are we even doing here in the first place?"

"That is the surprise I promised, right there," I said. "Each one of you must sit on that stone for a full minute. Prove that you are not scared of the legend."

"I ain't scared," Scott, the brave freshman, said. "I'll do it." He promptly walked to the stone and climbed onto it without hesitation, sitting down confidently.

We followed close behind him, shining our flashlights on him to illuminate the stone.

"This is stupid," Scott said. "It's just a rock, for Christ's sake. You all are a bunch of pussies."

I looked at my watch and marked the time. Laura filmed it all with her camera.

"Sixty full seconds starting now," I said, counting down the time.

"I'll sit here for five minutes," Scott said. "If it makes you happy."

Kevin, James Clark, and David Blommer were next. I could tell they were getting anxious. Kevin was at the back of the group, as if he could hide from his appointed time to sit on the stone.

"Times up," I said. "Scott, you've passed the test."

He got up from the rock and approached us.

"Give me a beer," he said. "That sucked. Just some stupid old rock in a cemetery. That wasn't scary at all."

"Kevin," I said. "You're up next."

"No way, man," Kevin said. "I ain't gonna do it. I know about that rock. I heard stories about things that have happened to people who've sat on it. I know about this place. Ain't no way."

"You know what happens if you don't do it, don't you?" Richard Biskup said. "You'll get twenty whacks with the 'Paddle of Love' if you don't do it." He was referring to the wooden paddle we kept back the frat house for disciplining freshmen. It was signed by many freshmen who had been administered a good whacking.

"Fine, I'd rather take the paddle," Kevin said. "I ain't sitting on that rock."

"What a fuckin' pussy," Marcus Hunter said. "I'm going to burn your ass with that paddle when we get back. And I'm going to enjoy it, immensely."

"Why don't *you* sit on the rock?" Kevin said. "Let's see if you guys got the balls to sit on it."

Marcus looked at me and Richard. "What do you think?"

"I'm game," I said. "It's just an old myth. Everyone in this cemetery is dead and that's it. No ghosts. No bogeymen. Just dead people. I'll sit on it."

"Jay, don't," Laura said. "You don't have to prove anything to anybody."

"I'm not scared of some old myth," I said. "I'll sit on the rock and drink a beer and you can take my picture. I'll try just about anything . . . once." I turned and looked at my frat brothers. "I'll do it, if you guys do it, too."

"I'm right behind you," Marcus said. "We can both sit there and drink a beer. Show these skinny freshmen how the 'big boys' do it."

Marcus and I climbed up on the rock and sat down. The rock was cold, and the texture was rough, like sandpaper. It felt like climbing onto the back of a prehistoric creature.

"Richard," I said. "Are you going to get up here, or what?"

He hesitated, shook his head, and said, "Nope. Not me. I don't believe it, but I ain't going to do it."

"What about you, Stephen?" I asked.

"No way in hell, man," Stephen said. "I don't really think it's a good idea. You guys can't pressure me like that. It ain't right"

"What the fuck are you talking about?" Marcus said. "Pressure? What the hell do you think we are doing to these freshmen? You are part of that, you know. Now get your ass over here and sit on the rock."

Stephen grudgingly dragged his feet as he approached the rock. "You guys are assholes, you know that, right?"

"Uh-huh," Marcus said.

Stephen sat down on the rock. Laura filmed the three of us sitting on the rock. We were all holding a beer and each of us had a different look on our faces; looks of fear, perplexity, and apprehension, all mixed together. It was a picture that should have marked a high point in our lives, but it turned out to be a picture of the beginning of the end. After a couple of minutes, we finished our beers and then climbed down off the rock.

"Okay," I said. "That wasn't so hard now, was it? You two other freshmen need to get over there and sit on the rock."

David and James were the last two to sit on the rock. They weren't too excited about it, but they got up there and tried not to be scared. We could see that they were scared, but they played it off, coolly, casually. Laura caught it all on camera.

Without warning, there came a crashing sound in the bushes. It sounded like something big was moving through the trees and bushes, coming directly toward us. It made me think of what a grizzly bear might sound like just before it came out of the bushes and attacked.

"What is that?" one of the girls asked.

"Everybody run," Kevin shouted. He turned and ran down the trail.

The noise in the bushes came closer, stopped, and then sounded like it was slowly creeping toward us.

"Let's get the fuck out of here," Stephen said. He broke into a sprint and was right on the heels of Kevin.

That was the end of that. Everybody took off running in a panic, the girls screaming hysterically, the guys stepping on each other as they tried to get ahead of everybody else. The thing in the bushes was pacing us. Whatever it was, it was running headlong through the woods beside us. I could have sworn that I heard it growling and breathing as it followed us.

"Hurry," I said. "It's following us."

"Go, go, go!" Marcus shouted. "Get in the cars. Hurry."

We made it to the cars in a pack, piling in on top of each other, slamming the doors shut and locking them.

"Hurry up, Steve," I said. "Get this thing started and let's go, now."

"I'm trying," Stephen said, fumbling with the keys. He started the car and turned on the headlights.

That was when we saw it, the thing that had been in the bushes. We didn't really see it, however, just its eyes. They were glowing red and orange like hot embers in the darkness. I remember thinking this is what the Devil's eyes must look like.

"Holy shit," Marcus said. "Look at that."

"I see it," I said.

"Fuck this," Stephen said. He put the car in gear, did a Rockford maneuver and spun the car around and stomped on the gas. "We're out of here."

The other two cars at our party were right behind us. I remember that I almost got whiplash from the high rate of speed. We must have broken several laws and world records on the drive home that night from the cemetery. When we got back to the house we went inside, still catching our breath, and sat down and went over the details of what had just happened. There were several different renditions of the tale during the next few days, but I know what happened that night. The others were fortunate enough to never find out what I know.

• • •

Laura gave me the SDRAM card from her camera a few days later. She didn't want to watch it; she had seen enough that night and didn't care to relive it. I agreed with her and I put the SDRAM card in a drawer and forgot about it, that is until everyone who sat on the stone began to die.

A month or so after the night in the cemetery, Marcus Hunter was killed in a motorcycle crash. He had met a car head-on and was killed instantly. Nobody really gave it much thought. We were sad, of course, and we mourned at his funeral, but nobody thought about the cursed stone. I didn't put it together until much later.

We were seniors and we graduated the next year. We handed the torch off to the juniors and let them take over the fraternity house. I moved back to my parents's house until I could figure out what I was going to do with my life. I had a bachelor's degree in the fine arts, but that wasn't going to get me a job anytime soon, so I went back to working construction with my father.

Laura and I broke up. She said that she had to move on with her life and that things could never be the same after that night. Why? I don't know. She never explained. She just said that it wasn't going to work out and that was that. I know that it had something to do with that night in the cemetery; something uncanny had come be-tween us, put a spell on us, made us unkind to each other. God, I miss her. I really loved her. I kick myself in the ass every time I think about it. One stupid night of hazing freshmen had separated me from the prettiest girl in the world.

The next summer, the brave freshman, Scott, drowned in Lake Monroe and it took the searchers a week to dredge his body up from the depths. There still wasn't an obvious connection with the cursed stone and his death. I remember reading about the drowning in the paper and then seeing it on the news and thinking, *damn, he was the one that I expected to go the distance, but there he is dead and bloated and gone.*

David Blommer was the next to go. He died in a very mundane way. He choked on a hamburger in the cafeteria. What a way to go. They tried the Heimlich maneuver on him, but the hamburger chunk was lodged snugly in his throat. They even tried an emergency tracheotomy, but it was useless. David died right there in the cafeteria in front of God and everybody. When I heard about it, I began to get a sick feeling in my stomach. That was when I started thinking that maybe the myth of the cursed stone might be true.

I called Richard first, because he was one of the ones who didn't sit on the stone. He must have known or was just smart enough to stay away from it.

"Hey, Jay," he said. "It's been a long time. How have you been?"

"I really don't know how I am doing, to tell the truth," I said. "I've been busy working with my dad. Isn't that the way it goes. I go to college just to come back and do the same thing I was doing before I started college."

"I hear you," Richard said. "I joined the Army. I ship out for Afghanistan in a week. Can you believe that?"

"What? Get out of here," I said. "Why in the hell would you do that?"

"My dad thinks it is a good career move," he said.

"Oh, I see," I said. "Your dad always was the drill sergeant type."

"I don't know how to say this," I said.

"What's on your mind, Jay?"

"You remember the night we went out to the Sykes Cemetery with those freshmen?"

"Yeah. Sure," he said. "That was a trip. Why?"

"Well, I think something weird is happening," I said.

"Don't tell me you believe that shit about the curse of the stone."

"Three of the people who sat on that stone that night are dead."

"What?"

"Marcus, Scott, and that fat kid David," I said. "They're all dead, and it hasn't been a whole year yet."

"That's just coincidence," Richard said. "I don't believe in that superstitious bullshit. Why do you think I didn't sit on that rock? I don't believe it, but I do think that people can convince themselves of weird shit, like that."

"I don't know" I said. "I got a funny feeling about it."

"Aw, shit," he said. "You worry too much. You need to go get laid and get your mind off all that morbid shit. Hear me?"

"I guess," I said. "Afghanistan? Are you crazy? Americans are getting killed every day over there."

"I ain't worried about it," Stephen said. "I'm going to kick some ass and take names. You watch. I'll be back next year and we can get together and have a beer, or something."

"I—Just be careful," I said. "Watch your ass."

"Yeah, you too."

"Okay. Stay in touch."

"I'll send you a post card."

"Cool."

"Take care, Jay."

And that was it. The conversation was over. I knew that would be the last time that I ever talked to him.

Richard shipped out to Afghanistan and was killed within the first thirty days of being there. I went to his funeral and cried until my eyes were as red as Atomic Fireballs—the red-hot candy jaw-breakers. He hadn't even sat on the stone, but he was dead, none-theless.

The final blow was when I tried to call Richard Biskup. I wanted to discuss the curse of the stone with him, see what he thought about it, but, as I suspected, he was already dead.

His mother answered the phone: "Hello?"

"Hello, may I speak to Richard?"

"Who is this?"

"This is Jay Collins," I said. "We went to college together."

"Yes," she said. "I remember you." There was a pause and then a sigh. "I'm sorry to tell you this, but Richard is dead."

I swallowed hard, my throat dry; I had been expecting that, but I wasn't ready to hear it.

"What happened?" I asked.

"I don't feel comfortable talking about it," she said. "It has only been a day since he died."

"Oh, I'm sorry," I said. "That's too bad."

She invited me to his funeral. I said that I would be honored to attend. I had been to a lot of funerals since the fateful night we visited the cemetery. Later I found out that Richard had committed suicide. He had put a shotgun in his mouth and used his toe to pull the trigger.

I was the only one left who had sat on the rock that night. Why had I been spared this long? I wondered. It had been exactly eleven months since that night, and I had only a month left, if the curse was true. It couldn't just be coincidence. An unimaginable, horrible dread filled my entire being and such a mood of melancholy racked my being that I felt like I might already be dead. There was only one thing left to do: watch the SDRAM card from Laura's camera.

I dug the SDRAM card out of the drawer and put it into my computer. The Windows Media Player popped up and I pressed play. There were some previous shots of Laura and her friends doing girly stuff and it broke my heart. I paused the video player and cried for a while. I missed her. How did it come to this? I wanted to call her and just talk for a while. I knew it would be useless. So, I dried my eyes and regained my composure and watched the videos on the SDRAM card until I came to the clip with our adventure to the Sykes Cemetery. It was horrible. I almost couldn't stand to watch it. The lighting was poor because all we had were flashlights and it was dark. It reminded me of that movie *The Blare Witch Project*. It was very amateurish. The events unfolded in the manner that I have outlined in this tale, except there were some extra features that we hadn't seen that night.

When Scott had climbed up on the rock, there was a hazy fog lingering over his head, all around him, swirling like gossamer threads. Behind him, barely visible in the darkness and fog, I could make out the vague silhouette of what looked like a woman with long white hair, red glowing eyes, dressed in a black gown, grinning a hideous grin. She was watching intently. Scott was puffed up and saying that he wasn't scared and then he got up from the stone and walked toward the camera.

Next, Marcus and I come into view, climbing up onto the stone. The woman was still standing there, grinning that hideous grin, watching as Richard joined us on the stone. Suddenly, the grinning lady in black vanished from view, and we were left in a picture-perfect clear shot. We were drinking beer and cutting up and whooping it up like the two self-absorbed college seniors that we were. We got up from the stone and walked back toward the camera.

Finally, the last two freshmen, David, and James, climbed up onto the stone. The strange fog appeared again, this time with three or four strange little glowing orbs circling around them. Something crossed quickly into view and vanished, so fast that it was blurred. I hit pause on the video player and rewound the video to the frame with the flying object. I stared at it for a long time until I realized that it was some kind of dog, looking much like a wolf, or hyena, and it was looking at the camera with eyes glowing a sinister, devilish red color, tongue hanging from its mouth, drooling and snarling. That was enough for me. I had seen all I wanted to see.

I hit the cancel button and closed the Windows Media Player. I ejected the SDRAM card and snapped it in half, taking it out on the back porch and tossing it into the barbecue grill. I squirted lighter fluid on it and lit it with a Bic lighter. The flames leaped up quickly, melting the blue SDRAM card into a smoldering, bubbling mass of black plastic. It was destroyed and there wasn't much else to do except wait. Wait for the end of a year and see if the curse would strike me.

• • •

I just finished writing this and I'm trying to decide what to do. I've got a month to go. I'm counting the days on my calendar. If I make it past a year, maybe the curse will be lifted. I don't know.

I finally called Laura and we are at least on speaking terms now. We see each other every now and then, but she just wants to be friends. I'm cool with that. I still love her dearly, and anything is better than nothing.

When I finish writing this, I am going to print it out and put the pages in a manila envelope and place it into a security box down at Wells Fargo Bank and give Laura the key. I will give her specific instructions to open it if I should come to an untimely demise. I will instruct her to deliver the manuscript to someone who will do what is necessary to make the public aware of the events that took place that night. I believe that the world needs to know about this tale. I believe that those who died need to be remembered and that the truth be known. It happened and I was there. If you are reading this then the curse was true, and I am already dead.

Scared Crow

An object struck the kitchen window just after sunrise one Friday morning on September 21, 2018. It hit with such force that it rattled the glass pane violently, startling Marshall Hunter and causing him to spill coffee on his white Van Heusen shirt.

"What the—" he said, startled.

Anita, his wife, heard the commotion in the kitchen and went to see what all the hubbub was about.

"What was that?" she asked, staring at the stain on Marshall's shirt.

"Something just hit the window," he said. He walked over to the window and examined the glass; it was cracked and riddled with lines like a spider's web. The glass crackled and popped as the cracks settled.

"What was it?" Anita asked.

"I'm going to take a look," he said. Marshall went outside, Anita followed close behind him, and they looked down into the damp grass where they spotted a big black crow lying in a ball of mussed feathers, flapping a wing in an attempt to fly away. One of its wings was bent back in an impossible angle, leading Marshall to believe that it was broken.

"It's a bird," he said. "Come over here and look at this—it's a crow."

"A crow?" she said, standing next to him. She looked at the mass of black feathers with a mixture of pity and slight disgust. "Is it dead?"

"I don't think so," Marshall said, nudging the bird with his toe.

It moved, flapping, and twisting as it struggled to fly away.

"Oh, thank Heaven," Anita said.

"But what are we going to do with it now?"

"I don't know."

"Get me a towel, or something, please," he said.

She went into the house and then came back out with a dishtowel.

"Thank you," he said, taking the towel, kneeling and gently swaddling the frightened, injured bird like a newborn baby. "Easy, big fella," he said, standing and carrying the fragile bundle toward the house. "We're going to get you fixed up and you'll be on your way in no time."

"I don't think I want it in the house, Marshall," Anita said, curling her lips in a disgusted grimace. "They carry germs and bugs."

The crow glared at her with cruel, beady, jet-colored eyes, as if offended by the statement.

Marshall took the bird inside despite Anita's protests. He placed the bird—still bundled neatly inside the towel—down onto the kitchen table.

"What are you doing?" she shrieked at the atrocity. "Not on the table. That's where we eat."

"Don't worry about it," he said. "They're cleaner than you think."

The bird opened its beak and snapped idly at the air.

"It's dirty," she said.

"It's injured, and in shock, and it needs our help."

"I'll call the vet—"

"Don't do that," he said, interrupting her. "They'll just put it to sleep, won't they?"

The bird emitted a hollow, contemptuous sound from deep within its throat.

"I don't think so—but . . ."

"No buts about it," Marshall said. "I know how to set a broken bone. We'll just fix him up ourselves. It'll take a while to heal, of course—"

"No. I'm not going to have that dirty bird staying in this house for that long. Absolutely not, no way, no how. We need to call the professionals. They'll know what to do."

Marshall gently stroked the bird's head, trying to calm it down.

The crow squirmed and wriggled, craning its neck as it tried to get loose from the confining towel. It cackled and cawed, snapping at Marshall's fingers until its beak locked onto his thumb.

"Ouch," he cried, jumping backward. "You little shit."

The crow slid loose from the towel and flapped its wings, as if to show that the wing was not broken after all. It immediately took flight and circled around the ceiling and then landed in a corner near the refrigerator. Marshall approached with hands outstretched, which caused the bird to tremble and shake and shrink away into the corner like a coward recoiling from an intimidating bully.

"Good. Its wing isn't broken after all," Anita said. "Now you can let it go and be rid of it."

The crow ducked and dodged away from Marshall's groping hands; looking for a quick escape, it darted between his legs and flew up and landed atop the lamp stand. Marshall tried to coax the bird down by talking gently to it as he slowly reached up with steady arms. The bird took flight again. After a long game of cat and mouse, he caught the crow. It snapped and pecked his fingers as he carried it through the door and outside into the night. He released the bird and watched as it flew around him, over Anita's head, and back into the house through the open door. Each successive capture and release resulted in the crow finding a way back inside.

"I don't think it wants to go," Marshall said.

"Too bad," Anita said.

Neither Marshall nor Anita noticed Billy as he came out of his bedroom. He had been watching, intently, and now stood with mouth agape and eyes bulging in wonder.

"Watcha doing?" he asked. "Where did that bird come from?"

"Just you never mind," Anita said. "Isn't it past your bedtime, mister?"

"It flew into the window, Billy," Marshall said. He was still trying to catch the elusive crow. "We thought it might be hurt, but it turns out that everything is fine."

"Cool," he said, enthusiastically. "Can we keep it?"

"No," Anita said, firmly. "Absolutely not."

"Your mother doesn't think it would be a very good idea to keep it inside the house—"

The crow took flight as Marshall was speaking and zigzagged

past the two adults, landing on Billy's shoulder, and perching there contentedly. It cawed with satisfaction and then nuzzled the boy's ear, nipping affectionately at his hair.

"It likes me," Billy said. "Can I keep him? *Please?*"

"No, Billy," Anita said, putting her hands on her hips. "And that's final. Don't ask me again."

The bird croaked dryly, making a profane sound, then began to groom itself from its perch on the boy's shoulder.

Marshall said, "I don't see any harm in keeping it . . . just for a while."

"Please, Mom," Billy said, looking at her with large, sad, pleading eyes. "Just for a little while?"

The crow cawed again, looking at her with blinking eyes like polished stones, as if it, too, was waiting for her answer. She hesitated, looked at Billy and the bird, at Marshall, and then back and forth again. "I guess you can keep him for a little while," she said, reluctantly. "I know I'm going to regret this. If there are any problems . . . it is out of here. And don't forget to wash your hands after you play with it. Okay?"

"Okay," he sang with glee. "Thanks mom. There won't be any problems. I promise. I'm going to take good care of him."

She smiled halfheartedly, unconvinced, for she had a premonition that there would, indeed, be problems in the future. She just felt it somewhere deep inside.

"I'm going to build him a perch in my room. I'll feed him . . . and put newspaper down on the floor for when he . . . poops. And I'll feed him every day and maybe even teach him some tricks." He took the bird down from his shoulder—it didn't resist—and carried it to this bedroom, ignoring whatever warnings or advice that his parents were giving him. He shut the door behind him.

The bird cooed as Billy set it down on his desk. The crow's jet-black feathers shimmered in the lamplight. The crow preened its feathers and then scratched behind its ear with a deft stroking motion from its claw.

"You and me are going to be best friends," Billy said to the crow. "I'm going to show you to all my friends—maybe even take you to school someday for show-and-tell. Don't you think that will be great? I bet you'll like it. I bet you're hungry, too. Are you hungry? You need a name, too. What would you like for a name? I sure do wish you could talk."

"I can," the crow replied, nonchalantly.

Billy was astounded; he looked at the bird with wide-eyed amazement. He was speechless. He gathered his wits together then said, "You *can* talk? Wow! I don't believe it."

The crow looked back at him, amused, but indifferent. "What did you expect? Why wouldn't I talk?"

"I don't know," Billy said. He couldn't believe what he was hearing.

"Well don't just stand there with your jaw hanging wide open . . . you might catch something in your mouth, like a fly. Although I like flies, and they are mighty tasty, when I can catch them."

"You really can talk," he cried. "Holy molly! How come you didn't say anything in the kitchen to my mom and dad?"

"Because most grownups—especially moms and dads—don't really understand or appreciate a wild bird's ability to talk. It tends to make them nervous and upset at times. But they sure think it's cute when a parrot talks—and parrots are not the smartest of birds, either."

"Oh, I see," Billy said, sitting down on his bed. "How come you flew into the window?"

"It was an accident, you see? I thought it was open. And to tell you the truth I was in a bit of a hurry and wasn't paying too much attention. My mind was somewhere else, you could say. I was trying to get away from that dreadful . . . terrible . . . *thing* out there in the garden."

"In the garden? What thing?" Billy quizzed. "What do you mean?"

"I don't want to talk about it," the crow said. "It is not fitting conversation for a young lad, such as yourself."

"What? I'm eight years old, you know . . ."

"Eight years old, indeed. But still very young, and I don't think you, or your parents, would like to know the secret—"

"Secret? Oh, I love secrets. I won't tell anybody, honest. Scout's honor." He saluted the bird, then put his hand over his heart. "Cross my heart, hope to die."

"You should be careful what you wish for, young man," the crow said. "You might get more than you bargain for . . . I'm afraid I can't tell you."

Billy pleaded again, offering food as a bribe. "I'll get you something to eat from the kitchen . . . wouldn't you like that?"

"Well, I am very hungry . . . but if I tell you this secret you must never tell your parents a word. You must promise me that. Okay?"

"Okay," Billy replied. "I promise. But why?"

"Because parents don't understand certain things . . . they call it 'make believe' and get angry at too much fantasy in opposition to reality."

"I won't tell."

"Very well, then . . . if you must know . . . I was trying to get away from that dreadful man-thing in the garden. I believe you—humans—call it a scarecrow . . ." The bird had a distant look in its eyes, a shiver rippling through its body as it remembered the image of the scarecrow.

"Scarecrow," Billy echoed. "You were afraid of it? They're not real. My dad just put it in the garden to keep the—"

"To keep the birds out of the garden," the crow finished, with absolute loathing and dread.

"I'm terribly sorry," Billy said. "But it isn't really alive. It's just a bunch of old work clothes stuffed with straw and newspaper."

"But it is put there to scare away the birds and that is all that matters. It is very frightening to us, you know. And it *is* alive. You do not see it moving because it is smarter than that. It waits until after dark, or when it knows nobody is watching, to come to life. Sometimes it catches a bird and . . . and . . ." The crow bowed its head, grief stricken by its own words. "It's absolutely awful . . . and you should know that I have lost quite a few of my family and friends to those evil watchers in the gardens."

"So that's why you flew into the window? The scarecrow was after you?"

"Yes. And it almost had me. If it hadn't been for your father coming outside when he did . . ." The crow swallowed hard, struggling as if a lump of something dry was lodged in its throat.

"That's awful," Billy said. "I had no idea. Is that why they call them scarecrows—scare . . . crow. Get it. Scared crow. That's you. You are a scared crow."

"I wish you would stop saying that," the crow said. "He might hear you talking about him."

Billy opened the curtains and peered out into the darkness. He could barely see the outline of the scarecrow in the garden by the light of the moon. It looked like a figure that had been crucified, arms held out wide, body straight and narrow, head stuffed and sagging with a straw-hat on top, all held together with wooden poles in the shape of a cross. It was exactly where it had always been, right in the middle of the garden; however, the longer he looked at it, the more he fancied that he could see it moving. He checked the lock on the window and swiftly shut the curtains.

"It is a true object of fear," the crow said, watching the boy intently. "Even you are afraid of it, and with good reason. I bet you didn't know that they like to hurt little boys and girls as well as birds."

"What? That's nonsense. I don't believe you."

"It's true. They like to eat birds, but they also like to smother the life out of little boys and girls, stuffing them full of straw in the middle of the night while their parents are sleeping."

Billy's eyes swelled to the size of baseballs. "Why on earth would they want to do that?"

"They are seeking revenge, I guess. They are angry at their creator—your dad, for instance—and they strike back by destroying that which the creator holds nearest and dearest and closest to his heart. In most cases that would be their children . . . and by stuffing them full of straw they are symbolically reenacting their own creation while getting revenge. I just think they enjoy it, to tell you the truth."

"I think you're crazy," Billy said. "And I don't want to hear anymore."

"I told you so," the crow said. "Please just don't ever make me have to go back out there with it. I was extremely frightened and that is why I flew into the window, because I was trying to get inside of the house. Why do you think birds usually *do* fly into windows. . . ?"

Billy was lost in deep thought, pondering on what the crow had been telling him, a bit spooked by the horror of it all. He was a statue carved from melancholy. "I don't know, but you're scaring me, and I wish you would stop."

"Most certainly," the crow said, flying over and landing on the bed next to the boy. "I will stop. But you should be aware of these things so that you will be prepared if anything should happen. I didn't mean to scare you. I guess that misery loves company, though. I'm sorry."

"It's alright," Billy said. "I just never knew these things."

"What about that food you were talking about? I'm hungry. Do you have any crackers? I know it sounds cliché, but I do love a good, saltine cracker with peanut butter on it."

"We've got lots of crackers and peanut butter," Billy answered. He was relieved by the change of subject. "Would you like some?"

"I would love some. What about fruit? Do you have any apples, oranges, or bananas? I especially like bananas, and nuts of any sort are especially fine. Something to drink, water, would be nice, too."

"Let me see what I can do," Billy said, getting up from the bed and starting toward the door. "Make yourself comfortable. I'll be right back."

"Excellent," the crow said, relaxing a little. "Thank you very much for your hospitality."

"You're very welcome," Billy said, and then he was gone. When he returned, he had an armload of food, a virtual smorgasbord that he laid out on the bed. The crow hopped over to the pile of food and quickly devoured bits of chopped ham, orange wedges, crackers and peanut butter, potato chips, and then washed it all down with a cool drink of water from a glass with ice-cubes bobbing and tinkling at the surface.

"You were hungry," Billy said.

Suddenly there came a gently tapping outside the window, startling both Billy and the crow. There was a scratching sound like fingernails across a blackboard and then another tattoo of drumming knuckles against the wall.

"What was that?" Billy said. His heart was galloping in his chest as fear crept and tingled up and down his spine, causing the hair on his back to stand on end.

"Oh no," the crow said. "He's coming for me. Please don't let him get me. I don't want to die. Quick . . . open the closet so I can hide."

"You're a big scare-dee-cat," Billy said, ignoring his own urge to panic in terror. "There is nothing out there. It is just our imaginations, or something. Maybe the wind."

"If you heard it . . . and I heard it . . . then how can it be imagination? You did hear that, didn't you?"

"Yes. I did."

"Well then, what was it?"

"I dunno. I'm going to find out, though." He went to his closet and brought out a Louisville Slugger baseball bat. "Whatever it is I'm going to hit it over the head with this." He patted the palm of his hand with the bat. The crow flew into the closet and concealed itself behind a box full of comic books, peeking out cautiously to watch the boy.

Slowly and stealthily, Billy crept to the window and swiftly yanked the curtains open, exposing the dark windowpane. He could see out into the night by the moonlight and for a moment he thought that the scarecrow was gone from its place on the makeshift crucifix; he looked closer and saw that it was still there, but it appeared as though it had moved a little to the left; it had been near the rows of corn before and now it was closer to where the beanpoles were posted. If he had not known any better, he would have said that it had certainly changed its position in the garden, but he thought that he did know better, and that his imagination was getting the best of him. It was a trick of light and shadow from the moon and trees that was distorting his perception, he thought.

A gust of wind blew through the treetops causing the branches to sway and wave back and forth.

"It was just the wind," Billy said, closing the curtains. "The . . . scarecrow is still in the garden. It is safe. You can come out now."

"That still doesn't explain that noise outside," the crow said. It reluctantly left its hiding spot. "It was him. I know it. He is out to get us. I should go so that you will not be in any danger."

"Nonsense," Billy said. "You can stay. I'm not afraid of an old scarecrow. I'll beat the stuffing out of it with this baseball bat."

"I'm scared," said the crow. "I don't know what to do. Wherever I go there is always one of those man-things around to sneak up and try to catch me. And they are so damn sneaky. They are silent and can stalk you like a cat, pouncing on you before you even know what hit you. Oh, dear. What shall I do?"

"The window is locked," Billy said. "And I have this bat . . . so I think we'll be alright. Let's just try to get some sleep, okay. And in the morning, everything will be alright."

"Perhaps you are right," the crow said. "But I don't know if I can sleep. Maybe I'll stay up and keep an eye out, kind of like a sentry keeping watch over the castle."

"Suit yourself," Billy said, pulling back the covers on his bed. "I'm going to get some shuteye." He crawled into bed and tucked himself in, saying, "Goodnight." After a moment, Billy sat up and looked at the crow. "What is your name, anyway? Do you even have one?" he asked.

"Yes, I have a name, but it doesn't really translate into your language. You can just call me Harbinger . . . that is probably the closest word you've got for my real name."

"*Harbinger?* That's a funny name," Billy said. "What does it mean?"

"It means to warn of events yet to come," the crow said. "I got the name because my family thought that I would be a great prophet someday—somebody who can foresee the future. But I don't really believe all that gibberish. Who knows the future? Not me."

"And your name is Billy," Harbinger said. "I couldn't help hearing your parents call you by that name."

"Yes, it is," Billy said. "Now can we get some sleep, Harbinger?"

"Very well," the Harbinger said, finding a comfortable spot at the foot of the bed to rest. "I'll not bother you anymore tonight. Goodnight, Billy."

"Goodnight, Harbinger," Billy said. The word felt funny on his lips; he repeated it several times before reaching over and turning off the lamp.

The room was swallowed instantly by darkness. Moonlight poured in through the cracks in the curtains. The sound of a ticking clock filled the room. Soon they were both soundly asleep and dreaming.

• • •

Anita was cooking bacon and eggs while Marshall read the Sunday edition newspaper when Billy came into the room. He was carrying the crow on his shoulder. The smell of breakfast was strong and delightful in the kitchen. He sat down at the table and poured himself a glass of orange juice.

"Don't sit at the table with that bird, Billy," Anita said. She flipped the eggs and then poked the spatula at the bacon. "They are very unclean. You need to wash your hands before you eat. Put that bird back in your room until you are finished with your breakfast."

"Mom . . ." Billy moaned. "Harbinger is not hurting anything."

"Aren't you overreacting a little, honey?" Marshall said, peering at her through reading glasses over the newspaper.

"I don't want that bird at the breakfast table. Do I make myself clear? We don't let dogs sit at the table . . . why should a bird be any different?"

Marshall was looking intently at Billy and the bird. "What did you just say? Harbinger? What is that?"

"Huh? What?" Billy said, allowing the bird to drink some of his orange juice. "Uh . . . that's his name . . . Harbinger."

"He has a name?" Marshall said, perplexed. "You already have a name for him? That's great." Marshall continued to peruse the pages of the newspaper again.

Anita grew pale when she saw the bird drinking from Billy's glass. "You quit that this instant," she said. "Give me that glass. Now I'll have to pour you a new one." She took the glass from Billy's hand; the crow squawked at her. "You be quiet . . . you dirty bird," she said.

"His name is Harbinger, Mom," Billy said. "He is really smart, and he can talk, too."

The crow squawked again, pecking sharply at Billy's ear.

"Hmph . . . Harbinger, smarbinger," she said, putting her hands on her hips. "It is just a dirty black bird, and nothing more."

"He can talk, too?" Marshall asked, bemused. "He's got a name *and* he can talk! Now that is interesting. I'm impressed. And what can he say, this bird named Harbinger?"

The bird clucked and cawed, looking intently at Billy with a forbidding stare.

"He can talk about all kinds of things, just as plane as you and me," Billy said, ignoring the crow's glare. He remembered his promise that he wouldn't say anything to his parents and thought that he should quit while he was still ahead. "It's nothing really. Just a silly, old bird . . ."

"Please, please tell me more," Marshall said, toying with his son's fantasy and imagination. He was grinning, obviously not believing that a crow could speak, but humoring Billy, nonetheless. "What does he talk about?"

"Don't encourage him," Anita said, putting plates of food on the table.

"I've heard that crows can talk," Marshall said, "but only if you split their tongues, or something like that. I'm just curious to know what a bird would say if it *could* talk."

"Nothing important," Billy said, cutting an egg with his fork and stuffing it into his mouth. "Just a bunch of gobbledygook."

"But he *does* talk?"

"These are good eggs," Billy said, attempting to change the subject. He pinched a piece of crust from his toast and fed it to the crow. It was an obvious digression from the topic of talking birds.

"Eat your breakfast, Marshall," Anita said. "Birds don't really talk. It's only through imitation of sounds they hear and then mimic that gives them the illusion of speech. I think that only parrots are blessed with this ability, anyway." She looked at the crow—which was beaming back at her piercingly—and said, "Sorry, bird, but that is what I've heard."

The crow shrieked back at her in disagreement.

"I think you hurt his feelings," Marshall said.

"You are having entirely *too* much fun with this, dear," she replied.

Billy finished his breakfast and asked if he could be excused. "I'm going to build him a perch today," he said, scooting his chair away from the table and rising. "I was wondering if I can take him to school with me tomorrow. . . ?"

"I don't know about that," Anita said. "Maybe you should wait and see if it is okay with your teacher."

"Mrs. Anderson won't care."

"Don't back talk your mother, Billy," Marshall said. "You need to get permission first. They have rules about animals in school."

"I know. I'll ask about it tomorrow—but what will I do with him in the meantime? I mean who will watch him while I am away?"

Anita and Marshall looked at each other, puzzled, and shrugged at the question.

"You can leave it with me," Anita said, "and I'll look after it . . . as long as it behaves, that is. Otherwise, its goose is cooked—and I mean it." She said this, eyeing the crow coldly; the crow flinched and recoiled away from her.

"Thanks mom. Don't be mean to him, though."

"I won't. I promise."

Marshall went to the crow, saying, "Pauly wants a cracker. Can

you say that? Pauly wants a cracker . . ." He stuck his finger out at
the bird; the crow promptly pecked the waggling finger. "Ah, ah,
ah," he said. "Don't bite the hand that feeds you."

"That's not going to work, Dad," Billy said. "He's not going to
talk if you make it into a big joke."

Marshall picked up a piece of toast and broke off a wedge. "Here
you go," he said, giving the morsel to the crow. "Can you say,
'hello'?"

"*Craaawwwk*," the crow screeched. It snatched the toast from
his hand and swallowed it with a gobble and gulp.

"I guess that means no," Marshall said.

"Dad? Do scarecrows really eat crows?" Billy asked, out of nowhere.

"What—scarecrows? No, they don't really eat crows. Where did
you come up with that idea?"

"I don't know . . . I was just wondering," he said. "Harbinger
told me that they eat crows and that they like to smother little"—
the crow pecked savagely at his ear, cawing loudly, and flapping its
wings—"kids in their sleep and stuff them with straw." He swatted
the pecking bird away from his ear as it whispered, "You promised."

Anita and Marshall both spoke at once: "What?" They were both
stunned by the statement and didn't know how to respond.

Marshall said, "That is utter hogwash. Scarecrows are not alive.
They do not eat crows. And they don't hurt children."

Anita said, "That's it—*that's it* . . . I've heard enough. That bird
has got to go. I'm calling animal control."

"You've just got an overactive imagination, is all," Marshall
said, mussing Billy's hair. "Your bird can't talk, but you imagine
that he can. And you've created some pretty fancy stories about him,
too. I suppose that a scarecrow wouldn't be very nice if it really was
alive—but it's not. I know, because I made him myself. I stuffed him
with straw and newspaper. He's just an inanimate object."

"What does 'inanimate' mean?" Billy asked.

"It means that he is not alive."

Anita was distraught. "I want that bird out of here today," she
said. "If it is causing you to imagine these things then it has to go."

"He really can talk," Billy said. He couldn't help feeling like he
had betrayed the crow by breaking his promise—because that is exactly what he had done—but he felt compelled to make his parents

believe that it was true and not just his imagination. Setting the bird down on the table, he stepped back like a magician doing a trick, saying, "Talk for them, Harbinger. At least say 'hello', or 'Pauly wants a cracker', or something so that they don't think I'm crazy."

The bird just cackled and hummed; it had a puckered expression and had decided to clam up and remain silent. It looked at Billy with an exasperated gleam in its eyes. If the crow ever had a notion to speak in front of the adults, the moment of Billy's betrayal was not going to be appropriate.

"Tell them about the scarecrow and all the other stuff you told me. Show them how smart you really are," Billy said. "I know you can do it, so show *them* that you can."

The bird didn't speak. It let out an assortment of profane coos, caws, and squawking sounds, but nary a word was spoken.

"Well, son," Marshall said, "maybe you should take him to school with you . . . it looks like he could use some formal training. I'll tell you what we're going to do . . . we're going to go out to the garage and build him a cage with some plywood and chicken wire so you can keep him in there when you're at school."

"Marshall," Anita said, still upset. "I'm not too happy with that bird."

"It's not the bird's fault."

"I'm sorry," Billy said. "I shouldn't have even said anything."

"Let's go build him a cage," Marshall said. "No worries, mate."

Billy picked up the crow and followed his father out the door and into the garage. They constructed a nifty cage that was wide and tall and very spacious with a piece of branching wood inside for a perch, some newspaper and straw on the bottom and a shelf for watering and feeding the crow. Two bowls were placed on the shelf, one with water and the other with nuts, grain and fruit. A small silver bell had been strung from the top of the cage and suspended with a piece of hemp twine. At first Marshall had suggested that they keep the cage outside, but Billy protested, saying that he wanted it in his bedroom because it was too cold outside, and the bird was afraid of the scarecrow. Marshall was perplexed by this statement, but he let the comment slip away and tried not to think about it too much. They moved the cage into Billy's bedroom, against Anita's protests, and placed the crow inside. The crow seemed unimpressed as it perched on the branch and toyed halfheartedly with the silver bell.

"I think he likes it," Marshall said.

The crow croaked out a snippet of sad, disagreeable chirps and tones.

"I dunno," Billy said. "I bet he likes his freedom more."

"You're probably right. But it'll have to do . . . and it'll keep your Mom pacified for a while. It will take some getting used to, I'm sure, but he'll probably be able to live with it . . . especially if he really *is* afraid of the . . . scarecrow." Marshall couldn't believe that he was entertaining the childish idea of an animated—living— scarecrow. He left the room without giving it much further thought and went outside to mow the lawn.

Billy spoke to the Harbinger in a calm and serene tone, sooth- ing the crow as it adjusted to the confinement of the cage. It didn't respond, instead it sat withdrawn and brooding, a distant look in its eyes. Although it regarded the cage vehemently, it made no attempt to escape. All that day and all that night the bird remained silent, perched on the branch like a statue. Billy tried to coax the crow into conversation, but it was of no use; and so, at the end of the day he turned out the lamp and went to bed, saying goodnight one last time and then nodding off to sleep.

He dreamed about being pursued by a hideous scarecrow through endless rows of corn. The more effort he exerted in eluding the beast the more he felt as though he was running against a gale force wind. His feet felt like they were stuck in a muddy muck, sucking him down like quicksand. The scarecrow was cackling like a fiend, ex- haling hot air that rolled down his neck like dragon's breath. The crow was circling overhead, telling him to run quickly . . . to run as fast as possible before it could catch him because it wanted to hurt him, to smother him and stuff him full of straw and it was only the length of an arm behind and gaining ground. That is when Billy tripped and fell. He hit the ground like a wrecking ball and rolled through the corn stalks. Coming to a sudden stop and lying on his back, he looked up and saw the scarecrow as it dived down toward him, grinning with a mouthful of razor sharp teeth, its eyes ablaze like fiery coals from the pits of hell, grinning and laughing and tilt- ing its head back in an awkward posture, its hands outstretched and clutching as it prepared to celebrate its glorious victory with a grand finale.

As the scarecrow was falling on top of him it changed, metamorphosing, and shifting shape like melting wax, forming into a more familiar, but even more hideous form: that of his uncle, The Honorable Preston C. Davis, Judge of the Superior Court. He was Anita's older brother. He was a large, corpulent man, who smelled of sweat and cigars and rye whiskey, and as he squished Billy into the ground his hands were groping at the boy's crotch, fondling, and fumbling with the button and zipper.

"It's going to be alright," Preston said. "You'll like it. Trust me. Sooner or later, it happens to everybody, and they like it."

"No, I don't want to," Billy pleaded. "Just get off me. You're squishing me. Don't touch me there."

"Come on, boy," Preston said, working the zipper down. His breath was rife with booze and tobacco and something else, something bad that smelled of death and decay. "I want to show you something."

Billy tried to squirm loose, but the weight of his uncle was too great. He could feel the groping hands working their way into his briefs and touching him there. Preston rubbed the iron hard stiffness of his own bulging member against the boy's thigh. He was pulling down his pants and trying to roll him over onto his stomach to gain access to his buttocks.

"Quit it! I'm going to tell Mom," Billy said.

"Shut up, punk," Preston said, putting a hand over his mouth. "You won't tell. And even if you do, no one will believe you because you are just a snot nosed brat. They will believe me. They will believe me because I am an outstanding member of the community. I am a judge, and everybody believes what I say. If you do tell, I'll kill you. Remember that. I will kill you and bury you in this cornfield. So, if you're smart you won't say a word. Just relax and enjoy it, because I'm going to enjoy it immensely."

Preston had pulled his pants down and was rubbing himself against Billy's bare skin, drooling and wheezing in his ear. "Easy, now," he said. "Don't tell on me. Just don't tell on me. Because I don't want to go to jail, and you don't want to die. So just don't tell on me. Easy does it. Just relax a little."

Billy awoke with a start, shouting out into the darkness, cold beads of sweat covered his skin. He was breathing hard, puffing, and wheezing as he clutched his pillow, thinking how he would never tell, for he was too ashamed and felt like it was all his fault.

The crow jumped up and flapped its wings, startled from the sudden outburst, then resumed its deathly still perch on the branch. It watched silently from its cage as the bedroom door opened, light pouring in from the hallway as Anita poked her head into the room.

"What's the matter, hon?" she said, entering the room.

"I had a bad dream," Billy said, lying back down.

The dream was unreal but reflected a real incident. Preston had indeed molested the boy, but Billy had told himself that he would never tell, not in a million years because he was too ashamed, and they probably wouldn't believe him anyhow, for the Judge did hold a high position in the community and people respected him; however, if Billy had told, he would have found that his mother would have believed him for the same thing had happened to her by the same man, and she had never told anybody, either, for the same reasons. But it would now be in vain, for Preston had recently met a gruesome and bloody end by the hand of an enraged parent whose children had accused The Judge of molestation and took matters into his own hands. The man—an unsung hero to most, a vigilante to others—walked up with a shotgun and blasted Preston with both barrels, splattering his head across the whitewashed walls.

"I'm okay, Mom," Billy lied.

"Are you sure?"

"Yes."

She went to the bed and sat down, messaging his temples. "You're sweating. It must have been a bad nightmare."

"It was. But I'm fine, now." He looked over and noticed that the closet door was hanging wide open and couldn't remember if it had been closed earlier. "Could you shut the closet, please."

"Okay, honey," she said, kissing him on his forehead. She rose from the bed and went to the closet. "All that nonsense talk about . . . well, never mind—"

"About what? The scarecrow?"

"Yes. That's just plain foolishness. There are no such things as living scarecrows, or bogeymen in the closet, or monsters under the bed." She peeked into the closet, looked around inside and said, "Nope. There's nothing in here." Then she peeked under the bed and outside through the window. "The coast is clear. There are no such things as monsters or bogeymen, honey. That's just something that people made up to scare other people, especially children. Why?

I do not know. The simple fact is that they just don't exist in the real world. If you have another bad dream, or you get scared, just remember that it isn't real, and it will go away. And I'm right down the hall if you need me, okay?"

He nodded.

The crow accidentally hit the silver bell causing it to lightly jingle.

Anita stiffened at the unexpected sound. She turned and looked at the cage. "You scared the daylights out of me," she said. Inwardly, she was thinking of how the bird was probably the main reason that Billy was having the bad dreams, and how she should find a way to be rid of the bird without hurting her son's feelings; she knew that he and the bird were already getting attached to each other and that the longer she waited the more impossible the separation process would become.

"I'm fine, Mom," Billy said, interrupting her thoughts. "You can go back to bed now."

"Do you want me to leave the door open?"

"No, that's okay, mom," he said. "I'll be alright."

"Well, goodnight then," she said, kissing him one more time before she left the room and closed the door behind her. She stood at the door, eavesdropping.

Neither Billy nor the crow said a word, for they both knew that she was listening, because they could see her feet and the shadow, she cast in the hallway light that streamed underneath the door. She stood there for quite some time—perhaps she was waiting to hear if the crow really could talk—and after a long period of silence, and when she heard Billy snoring, she finally left and went down the hallway to her bedroom.

She wanted to have a long talk with Marshall about the boy and the bird, but he was fast asleep when she entered the room, so she slid into bed beside him and, after mulling the subject over for a while—she came to the conclusion that she would either have Marshall get rid of the bird or call animal control—she drifted off into a deep sleep.

• • •

Marshall was in a hurry because he was late for work, and he was feeling a little bit angry about the conversation he had had with his wife early that morning. She had caught him right at the moment that he awoke and told him that the crow would have to go today; she wouldn't stand for her son being scared and fantasizing about monsters because of the suggestions and implications the bird provoked; and she just didn't like the mangy bird and would be glad to be rid of it once and for all. He had argued with her—for he felt a strange fondness for the crow—until they had both turned shades of crimson in the face, but she was firm and insisted on having it her way.

He had put the bird in a cardboard box and closed the lid—the crow looked at him with sad, bemused eyes—and carried it out to his BMW in the garage. Since he had to commute over thirty miles to work, the plan was to take the bird and release it near the ocean where it would be able to fly away into a patch of wilderness and make its way on its own. He wasn't really worried about the crow surviving, for everyone knew that a crow was a scavenger and probably liked the city better than the countryside, but it just seemed poetic to him to let it go near the sounding sea.

After driving for nearly half an hour, he pulled the car over onto the side of the road and took the box out of the car. He was a little saddened by the event, but time was of the essence and he would have to be on his way, so he opened the lid and shooed the bird out into the brisk morning air. The crow didn't move at first, but soon it gathered its wits and, looking back at Marshall with a betrayed glance, it took flight and caught the gentle, salty breeze blowing in from the water. In a matter of seconds, it was soaring high overhead and flapping away over the nearby trees. Marshall waved goodbye to the bird, feeling mildly foolish as cars passed by and the passengers stared at him as if he was crazy. The bird was gone and that was that; so he got into his car and drove to work.

• • •

When Billy came home from school, he saw the empty cage and went into a frenzy.

"Where is Harbinger?" he asked, nearly in tears. "What did you do with him?

"It was for your own good," Anita said. "I didn't think it was good for you to be pretending that you could talk with a bird."

Marshall was pulling into the driveway. Both Anita and Billy looked out through the window and watched as the electric garage door opened, swallowed the silver BMW, and then closed like a giant mouth.

"It's not fair," Billy pouted. "You said I could keep him. You lied." He opened the door and stormed outside past Marshall who was just about to open the door. Billy didn't say a word and stomped away around the house and out of sight.

"I take it he found out that the bird is gone?" Marshall said, putting down his briefcase.

"You need to go talk to him," Anita said.

"No . . . *you* need to go talk to him," Marshall said, crossly. "It was your idea to get rid of the bird, so now perhaps you should explain why."

"I did," she said, nearly in tears. "Don't talk to me that way. I can't make him understand why I did it. I tried to talk to him, but he won't listen."

Billy burst back through the door in an excited commotion startling his parents. To their surprise the crow was sitting happily on his shoulder. "Harbinger came back," Billy cried with joy. "He came back and was waiting for me outside in a tree. Isn't that great?"

Anita shook her head in disbelief; Marshall was surprised and astonished by the bird's uncanny navigational skills; it had remembered where the boy lived and flew back without any apparent effort at all.

"Well, I'll be a son-of-a-gun," Marshall said. "I wouldn't have believed it unless I saw it with my own two eyes."

"He came back," Billy said. "You should be happy for him. He's like part of the family now."

Marshall said, "Why don't you take Harbinger to your room, son. I need to have a word with your mother."

"Okay," Billy said. He promptly went to his room.

Marshall and Anita had a long talk. She was extremely upset and felt that because the boy was talking to a bird that perhaps he should get some counseling. Marshall didn't understand why she felt this way, but if it would make her happy, they would at least look into visiting a professional counselor.

• • •

The next day Billy was full of stories about faraway places and monsters and scarecrows and all kinds of things that he said that the bird had told him. This only served to strengthen Anita's resolve to get him to a trained professional and she wasted no time in finding a nearby psychologist in the yellow pages in the phone book. She talked at length with the man named Dr. Richardson, who was kindly and spoke in a soothing tone and listened to her dilemma and suggested that they pay him a visit later in the week, without the boy at first, so that they could get acquainted and discuss the facts in the situation. They left Billy and Harbinger at home and made a trip into the town to pay a visit to the good doctor.

Dr. Richardson suggested that they make Billy face the object of his fear—the scarecrow—by showing him that it was just a stuffed, hallow, lifeless creature. He said that perhaps they should leave his bedroom window open, the curtains wide, so that he would see that the scarecrow didn't really move and was stuck in the garden permanently. As to the bird and the conversations, Dr. Richardson thought this was perfectly healthy for an eight-year-old boy, and that the fantasy was natural. Lots of children carried on conversations with their pets and they should not worry about it, he told them. If the problem persisted afterward, they should bring Billy into his office and they could discuss other options.

They left the office and went home. Anita and Marshall were not too pleased with the idea of what they thought of as a mild form of psychological shock treatment, but if it would help to cure the boy of his senseless fears, then so be it.

Over the course of the next few days, Marshall took Billy down to the garden and showed him that the scarecrow was nothing but old clothes and stuffing. The crow would not go near the garden, in fact it flew away and landed high up on the tip of a pine tree and watched from a safe distance. They looked under Billy's bed at night, and in the closet, they made trips down into the basement and up into the attic in hopes of curing his overbearing, senseless fears. And then every morning before breakfast, they would visit the scarecrow in the garden.

"It's not a monster, Billy," Marshall said. "If you want me to, I'll take it down. Would you like that?"

"I don't know," Billy said. "I know I'm acting stupid, being afraid and all, but I really do believe that Harbinger is telling the truth. I swear I seen the scarecrow move the other night."

"That's just your mind playing tricks on you."

"Yeah, maybe your right."

"Dr. Richardson said that you're going to have to sleep with your window open for a few nights," Marshall said, putting his hand on Billy's shoulder. "Can you handle that?"

"I don't think so."

"Well, we're going to give it a try, okay?"

"Sure."

They went back to the house and went inside.

• • •

Anita and Marshall tucked Billy into bed and talked to him, trying to calm him down as he insisted on closing the window and curtains. Anita said that she thought the chilly night air would cause him to catch a cold so she thought it would be alright to leave the window shut, but they would have to keep it unlocked. The idea was to make him face his fears. The curtains were spread wide open, affording a perfect view out at the garden and the scarecrow.

They left the room, saying goodnight, then went to bed and slept soundly.

Billy sat wide awake and watched the dark, shadowy mass that was the scarecrow in the garden. He thought he saw it move and felt terror shoot through him like a jolt of electricity.

"He's going to come for us," Harbinger said from his cage. "He's going to get us. Why are they doing this to you?"

"I don't know," Billy said. "I'm scared."

Harbinger and Billy watched in fear as the scarecrow left the garden and walked toward the bedroom window.

"Mom! Dad!" he screamed. But there was no reply—Dr. Richardson had told them not to respond when the boy cried out on the first night. Billy froze with fear, unable to get out of his bed.

The scarecrow opened the window, ever so slowly and crawled inside. It went over to the boy and smothered him to death, stuffing him with straw. The crow flapped about, making lots of noise, sounding an alarm. It was too late for the crow, too, for the scarecrow reached inside the cage and grabbed it, squeezing its neck, and stifling the cry within its throat. The scarecrow gobbled the bird up with one large bite and then swallowed it whole. Afterward, the scarecrow crawled back out the window and went back to the garden.